Dear Reader,

Remember the "old days" of having babies? The mother-to-be got wheeled off to who *knew* where, while the poor father got to hang out in the waiting room—pacing, smoking cigars and generally not knowing a thing...until a nurse arrived showing him a pristine, all-wrapped-up little bundle of joy.

Well, things sure have changed! Now men aren't responsible just for getting women *to* the hospital— they're expected to hang out, watch and do their best to be as useful as possible.

And in this, Silhouette Books' latest Mother's Day collection, we see what happens when the hero and heroine of three very special stories get *to* the delivery room. In the skillful hands of Kasey Michaels, Kathleen Eagle and Emilie Richards, the exciting, delightful and very *un*expected happens.

Yes, parenthood can be amusing, exasperating and enthralling—and in *A Funny Thing Happened on the Way to the Delivery Room* it's also romantic. So enjoy!

The Editors
Silhouette Books

a funny thing

HAPPENED ON THE WAY TO THE

DELIVERY ROOM

KASEY KATHLEEN EMILIE
MICHAELS EAGLE RICHARDS

Silhouette Books

Published by Silhouette Books
America's Publisher of Contemporary Romance

SILHOUETTE BOOKS

ISBN 0-373-48341-4

Copyright © 1997 by Harlequin Books S.A.

The publisher acknowledges the copyright holders
of the individual works as follows:

PARENTS BY DESIGN
Copyright © 1997 by Kasey Michaels

DADDY'S GIRL
Copyright © 1997 by Kathleen Eagle

A STRANGER'S SON
Copyright © 1997 by Emilie Richards McGee

Printed in U.S.A.

CONTENTS

PARENTS BY DESIGN

Kasey Michaels

To Catherine Charles and Anna Seidick,
my mother and mom
And to all moms, everywhere

Prologue

"Somewhere in time..."

"**I** want a baby."

Chip Risley didn't even raise his chin from his chest. After all, his beloved Oakland Raiders were primed to blow a big lead in the third quarter, and he had little inclination to ponder the mumbled words of his best friend as they sat on opposite sides of the couch, their feet plopped on the coffee table, beer cans propped on their stomachs, fatalistically watching their team go down the tubes.

He winced, watching as the Philadelphia Eagles picked off an errant pass on their own twenty and returned it to the Raiders' forty-yard line. As a commercial touting the benefits of a career in the United States Armed Forces shot across the screen, blocking out the Raiders coach as he smashed his headset to the ground on the sidelines, Chip lifted the ice-cold can to his lips and took a sip of beer. "I'm sensing that I'm missing something here, Doug. You want a what?"

"A baby," Doug Marlow repeated, punching the channel changer, trying to catch up on other games while the one they watched was at commercial. With proper timing, some help from his satellite dish and a little finesse with the clicker, they could watch three games at once, and never miss a play. "I want a baby."

Chip chuckled, the slight extra padding he had begun carrying around his middle doing a small dance as he slouched against the sofa cushions. "A baby. Okay. That's a neat trick, if you can do it. Can I sell tickets?"

Doug missed a beat with the clicker, ending up with a screen full of Barbra Streisand posed on the bridge of a tugboat, singing her lungs out about how she didn't want "nobody" to rain on her parade. Just as Chip was drizzling all over his. "You know what I mean. I don't want to *have* a baby, for crying out loud. I just want one."

Chip looked at his friend for a long moment, seeming to be fighting what could only be an unholy grin. "I want a bright red, two-seater sports car with five on the floor," he said at last, "just like you've got. Now, babies I've already got. More than I need, actually. Here's an idea for you, sport. Want one? What the hell, Dougie boy—take two, they're small. Now, would you turn the damn station?"

Doug was quiet for a long time, long enough for Barbra to stop singing and get off that damn tugboat, before he hit the clicker again. Long enough for the Eagles to score a touchdown and recover the fumbled kickoff on the Raiders' five-yard line.

At last, after Chip had lost his reputed cool in the face of his team's adversity and had ripped his Raiders hat into two unequal parts, Doug gave Chip a healthy slap on the back just as his friend was draining the last of his beer, and announced, "You're on! I'll take them!"

Chapter One

Monday—Day One

It was seven o'clock, and Liz Somerville had not spent a lovely day.

She'd been making her way home for the past twelve hours after being in New York for the past week on business for her firm. Fog, a last-minute glitch with her connection in Detroit, a piece of lost luggage, a rare, two-minute Las Vegas downpour just as she stepped out of the terminal at McCarran International Airport—not to mention dropping her car keys in a puddle after walking the parking lot for ten minutes until she located her car—all had combined to set her jaw in a teeth-clenched spasm.

Not that her jaw hadn't been tightly clamped for most of the day. She had set it firmly, determinedly shut after that horrible interlude in the hotel bathroom the moment her head had left the pillow that morning. She had redoubled her efforts after the second unpleasant session in the minuscule rest room on the plane, when her lunch had come back for an encore presentation.

And yet now, when she had thought she would

never want to eat again, she knew she would kill—or at the very least, maim badly—for a hot fudge sundae with two scoops of chocolate ice cream, and a small mountain of whipped cream on top.

Candie Risley had explained all of the intricacies and lunacies of early pregnancy to Liz a week earlier, but Liz had been disbelieving, and totally unprepared for both the waves of nausea that had racked her these past days in New York and the ridiculously irrational cravings that seemed to follow each vow never to so much as *look* at food again.

Maybe once she was home, and settled, and had a good night's sleep in her own bed—tucked up spoon-fashion with Doug—she would regain her former good health and cast-iron stomach.

She certainly hoped so. Because tomorrow she and Doug would begin painting the condo, and she had never been a great fan of the smell of fresh paint. And the following Monday, the first day of the second week of her long-overdue vacation, was also going to be the first day of her baby-sitting stint with seven-month-old twins, Charlie and Chelsea.

Once she broke the news to Doug, that was.

Liz's stomach did another small half-gainer at the thought, and she lost her craving for ice cream as the compact car's air-conditioning kicked in and sent a shiver down her already damp spine.

How *was* she going to tell Doug what she had

done? How she had volunteered herself—and him? She certainly wasn't going to tell him *why* she had done it, that was for sure!

It had all seemed so simple, and so wonderfully logical, when she had broached her idea to Candie before her trip to New York.

"The stick turned blue," she had told Candie glumly as the two of them sat in Candie's cluttered living room, folding their way through a small mountain of baby clothes. "The brand I used yesterday turned pink. Unless I want to try for some new, psychedelic color, or a game of *X*'s and *O*'s or whatever in heck the others do, I think the verdict is in. I'm definitely pregnant."

"Ya-*hooie!*" Candie had flung a snap-front undershirt in the air like a West Point cadet tossing his hat in the air at graduation and hugged her friend. "This is wonderful news. Wonderful!" Then she rescued the undershirt from the floor, sat back against the cushions of the couch, lowered her eyes, and added quietly, "Unless you're bummed about it, of course. What does Doug say?"

"He says Chip looks like five miles of bad road every morning when he comes to work," Liz had told her. "He says he can't imagine what it's like to juggle two babies and a job and not have gone out to dinner or a show in seven months. He says you and Chip have to buy a minivan just to hold car seats and playpens and diaper bags, when he could remember Chip buying his cars by checking first to see if his golf clubs fit in the trunk.'' Liz had folded the same undershirt three times, and it still looked as if she had wadded it into a ball. "I think Doug sees babies as one *huge* impediment to his life-style.''

Candie, a short, pleasantly plump redhead with bright blue eyes and a neon smile that could light all of the Vegas Strip, had loaded a stack of tiny garments into the wash basket at her feet, then picked up a small blue plush teddy bear and hugged it to her chest. "I see," she said, sighing. Then she scowled. "No! Damn it, I *don't* see! You and Doug have been dating for three years, and living together for two of them. You've traveled to Europe together, to Mexico—had yourselves a high old time. Well, now it's time you settled down, made it legal. And, yes, damn it, it's time you had yourselves a couple of babies. Did he really think he could play the game without showing the bruises?''

"My pregnancy is a *bruise*, Candie?" Liz had asked, feeling close to tears, also a new experience for her, as she *never* cried. "Well, that's encouraging.''

Pushing the remainder of the unfolded clothes out of her way, Candie had scooted across the couch and put her arms around Liz. "Look, honey, I know I'm not saying this at all right. And you're probably seeing everything all cock-eyed, anyway.

Pregnancy will do that to you. At least, it did it to me. How else do you think we ended up with a lilac-colored nursery? Surely you and Doug have discussed children? Marriage?''

Liz had nodded, sniffling into Candie's comforting, motherly shoulder. "Sure we did. In the beginning. But then the days seemed to turn into months, and now years...and I don't think he's even said he loves me. Not for a while, anyway, and only in bed. We're just...*comfortable* together, I guess, and pretty much on the fast track career-wise. He's had three promotions in the last year...and my career is really taking off, so that I'm traveling a lot...and, oh, Candie—we're more of an old married couple than *real* old married couples!''

"Do you love Doug?"

Liz had groaned. "Desperately."

"Does Doug love you?"

"Yes, I think so. No—I know so. It's just that he doesn't *say* so anymore, you know?"

"I know. I sometimes have to hit Chip over the head before he remembers to tell me he loves me. We want the *words*, and men just think we want the *actions*. It's like—okay, I said it once this month—isn't that enough? And now the big question, honey. Do *you* want this baby?"

Liz's full bottom lip had begun to quiver. "Do I want this baby? More than my life, Candie. More than I could ever believe I'd want anything."

Liz had suddenly found herself sitting alone on the couch, watching as Candie paced back and forth across the carpeting, careful not to bump her shins on the matching baby walkers. "All right, then. You love Doug, Doug loves you—although he doesn't say so. You're pregnant. You want this baby. You want *Doug* to want this baby. Do I have all of this right, so far?"

"I know it's considered a piddling little thing in this day and age, but I'd sort of also like to be *married* before the baby is born," Liz had supplied, sitting forward, watching in awed amazement as she swore she could see the gears turning in her friend's head. "Factor that into your brainstorming, if you please. That, and the fact that I don't want to think I've trapped Doug into marriage in some way, because I haven't—honestly! It's just that we were celebrating his most recent promotion last month. We went to see Michael Crawford in that great *EFX* show at the MGM Grand, and came home singing some of the songs about magic and mystery and dreams and a world where rules don't apply...and...and things... Well, things sort of got out of hand, if you know what I mean."

Candie had stopped pacing to thump her hands onto her hips and look at Liz owlishly. "I'm the mother of twins, honey. Trust me in this—you don't have to explain basic biology to me. However, don't toy with me, woman. I haven't seen

that show yet, if you remember. As a matter of
fact, other than the grocery store, I haven't been
much of anywhere for what seems like a lifetime.
Though I have to admit, even a solo trip to buy
formula has a certain charm to it now. God, how
far we can fall!''

"Sorry," Liz had choked out, laughing at her
friend.

"All right, back to business," Candie had continued, pacing once more. "The way I see it, all
Doug knows about babies is that they keep you up
nights and make you buy minivans. There's a lot
more than that to parenthood, of course, but Chip
probably thinks he's too macho or something to
tell Doug about how it feels to have one of those
two terrors in there smile at you like you're some
sort of godlike figure, or how your heart swells
when you tiptoe into the nursery to see them sound
asleep, their little rumps stuck up in the air. Why,
I've seen Chip reduced to tears when either Charlie
or Chelsea holds out their arms to him and says
'Da-da!'''

Liz had joined Candie in her pacing, carefully
shortening her usual long-legged strides to match
those of her friend. "You're right! Doug has never
really *been* with babies. He was an only child, like
me, and probably doesn't understand the first thing
about what it's like to have a baby in the house.
If only he could see more of Charlie and Chelsea,
but they're already in bed whenever we come to

visit, so all he sees is the mess in here, the toys everywhere, all the paraphernalia the babies need. Oops—sorry, Candie!''

"No need to apologize," Candie had said, bending over to pick up a rattle shaped like a barbell. "Now that they're mobile, the twins can wreck a room with all the finesse of the Goths sacking Rome—only faster. And, with twins, you've got twice the mess, without doubling up on the necessary stamina. I tell you, Liz, I think I'd give up my lusting after Pierce Brosnan for just the chance of a few days alone with Chip. I'd sleep like the dead for two days, and then maybe we could get to know each other again. I mean, the taste of dried rice cereal on my neck is beginning to be a turn-on to the poor guy. But—to get back to your problems—''

"That's it!" Liz could remember having said, an idea popping into her head with such sudden brilliance that she was surprised to look up and see that no light bulb had appeared there, like in the Sunday comic strips. "Candie—that's it! You and Chip need a break, and Doug needs to see that babies can be wonderful. We could kill two birds with one stone!"

Candie had frowned, shaking her head so that her carroty curls bounced around her cheeks. "You've lost me. I used to be pretty quick, but five hours of sleep a night can kind of dull the edges, you understand. Run that past me again, okay?''

Liz had made a beeline for the kitchen, and the coffeepot resting on the warmer. "I can still have decaffeinated, right? Or maybe not. You have any milk? Stupid question. Of course you've got milk.''

"*Formula*, Liz. The twins will be on formula for at least another month or so, even if I have added rice cereal to their diet to keep them from howling at three in the morning. For months, the two of them thought we were running an all-night diner. You really aren't up on all this, are you? But, to answer your question, there's bound to be a quart of milk in there somewhere.''

Liz opened the refrigerator, talking even as she stuck her head inside, sifting through a jumble of baby bottles until she found what she was looking for, and still talking so quickly she nearly stumbled over her words. "You and Chip get a vacation— a well-deserved second honeymoon—and Doug and I get to know what it's really like to have a baby in the house. I can watch Doug, see his reactions, wait for him to fall head over heels in love with Chelsea and Charlie, and then, when Doug is reduced to drooling over the idea of having a baby of our own, I'll tell him about my pregnancy. Surprise him, if you know what I mean.''

She withdrew her head and shoulders from the refrigerator, the cool carton of milk pressed against her warm forehead, and looked at Candie, feeling her chin begin to wobble again. "It'll work, right? Please, Candie, tell me it'll work!"

Whether it had been the brilliance of Liz's plan, or Candie's burning desire to revisit the Pennsylvania Pocono Mountains and the honeymoon hotel that catered to lovers by way of heart-shaped beds and bathtubs in the shape of champagne glasses, Liz probably would never know, but Candie had jumped at Liz's offer to take the twins for a week.

Which, probably, Liz thought now, would have been a good time to let Doug in on at least the "Guess what—the twins are going to stay with us!" part of her plan.

But she hadn't. She had merely gone home to the two-bedroom apartment they shared, pretended everything was the same as it had been before the one stick had turned pink and the other stick had turned blue, and told him she had to go to New York the following week.

Now, with that week and a Sunday reserved for sight-seeing but spent moaning in her hotel room behind her, she was on her way back to the apartment to say "Surprise!" and let him know that, after the painting was done and the condo looked all fresh and spiffy, little Charlie and Chelsea were coming to stay with them, and would remain their houseguests for their second week together—the week Doug already had made noises about spending in a leisurely tour through the California Wine Country.

And now, just to add to the fun, the morning sickness Candie had warned her about—and Liz had laughed off as an old wives' tale—had come at her with a vengeance and shown signs of becoming "all-day" sickness. Just the *thought* of the smell of paint was enough to make her feel queasy. Plus, her breasts were unaccountably sore and tender to the touch. And she felt about as sexy and desirable as a wet sack. In fact, if the love of her life wanted to welcome her home from New York with anything more than a quick kiss on the cheek, she just might beat him senseless with her carry-on luggage—considering the fact that her other suitcase was probably even now winging its way to Zanzibar or some equally distant place.

Liz pulled into her reserved parking space, deciding to prudently leave her carry-on in the trunk until the morning. She took a deep breath, then dragged her reluctant self to the front door of the building that housed their condo, wondering if it was too late to rattle off a few quick prayers for heavenly guidance—at least rummage through her weary brain for a great opening line that had nothing to do with the words "Clear the way—I'm going to be sick!"

I wonder where she is?

Doug had asked himself that question three

hours earlier, almost at the same moment the door had closed on the widely grinning face of Chip Risley and the wistful, slightly moist smile of Candie Risley as they left their little darlings behind and went off to start their long flight to the Poconos and all the lovely cool air and turning leaves of Pennsylvania in October.

His question had shifted to *Where the hell is she?* when Charlie had presented him with a "gift" in his diaper. An hour later, when Chelsea had grabbed hold of his bottom lip with her strong little hands and tried to pull that lip up and over his forehead, he had stopped asking—and begun silently *begging* for Liz to come home.

Just as he was about to call the airline for the third time, to make sure Liz's plane hadn't been hijacked to Outer Mongolia, he heard her key in the door. He ran to greet her as a shipwrecked sailor forced to tread water for three hours would greet his rescuers. Yet his happiness was surpassed by his determination that she not call out, "Hi, honey, I'm home!" in anything more than a whisper. Because the C-C's had finally gone to sleep in their matching Portacribs that he and Chip had set up in the spare bedroom. And if anyone woke the babies before he could shove a peanut-butter-and-jelly sandwich down his throat, he might... Well, he just might cry.

He whipped the door open so quickly that Liz, who still had her hand on the key, nearly fell into the apartment. "You're home," he whispered rather unnecessarily, then did his drowning-man-reaching-for-a-straw imitation, clasping her close, grateful for his rescue. His face half covered by her blond, rather-damp hair, he raised his eyes to the ceiling and whispered fervently, "Oh, thank you, God! She's home!"

Liz pulled half-out of his embrace, looking at him as if he had lost at least a tiny part of his mind. "Didn't my office call you to say the plane would be delayed?" she asked, then nearly straight-armed him and walked over to sit on the couch when he tried to press her body against his once more. She tucked her chin-length hair behind her ears, showing the clean, sculpted lines of her beautiful face and exposing the unusual dark circles beneath her tired-looking green eyes and looked up at him. "Oh, Doug, I should have called you myself. I'm so sorry if you were worried."

"Worried? *Me?*" Doug said quickly, walking toward the kitchen and hoping that her gaze followed along and did not immediately take in the sight of the blue teddy bear that still sat, smiling, on his black leather recliner in the far corner. He thought he'd safely hidden everything. How had he missed that damn bear? "Don't be silly. I just know you don't like flying in storms, and there were red screens nearly all over the Weather Channel from Utah to New York. You look exhausted. Was it a bumpy ride?"

"Bumpy? Um—yes. Yes, it was! Either that, or I've picked up some sort of stomach virus. I've been sick as a dog, actually. Would you mind if we didn't go out for dinner?"

Would he mind if they stayed home, and didn't go out? Ha! There was a God, and He was smiling down on Doug at that very moment! "Mind? Don't be ridiculous. As a matter of fact, I was just about to make myself a sandwich. Peanut butter and jelly. The chunky kind of peanut butter, with lots of bits of peanut in it. You want one? Or maybe you'd want peanut butter and marshmallow? I know it's your favorite, Liz. Liz?"

But he was talking to the air, because Liz had already jumped up from the couch, a hand pressed to her mouth, and was running toward the bathroom, slamming the door behind her.

Which woke up Charlie, or Chelsea—who woke up Chelsea, or Charlie. It didn't much matter who had awakened first anyway, because, within seconds, both of them were screaming at the top of their lungs and Doug was running toward the spare bedroom, already knowing he was a dead man.

"Come on, guys, cut me a break," he told them, picking up Charlie first, then trying to pry Chelsea's fingers off the crib railing so that he could lift her, as well. "Got a grip like a bulldog, don't you, honey?" he asked as Chelsea transferred her clutching hands to his shirt, then his black hair, which he wore fashionably long—although a crew cut was beginning to sound good to him.

"Now, listen up, okay? Here's the plan. If you two promise to shut up and look angelic and appealing, maybe she won't throw the three of us out of here."

"Doug?" Liz asked from the doorway to the spare bedroom, her voice rather weak and shaky. "What are the twins doing here? They're not supposed to—"

Doug cut her off. "I know, I know, they're not supposed to be here. But Chip got this last-minute call to speak to some symposium in Philadelphia— funny how you just got back from the East Coast and now Chip is there, huh—and, well, Candie was looking so sad that she couldn't go with him the way she used to, and I knew we both had a two-week vacation and hadn't planned to do anything except paint the condo this week, and...and... Well, I don't know, Liz, it just *happened*, okay?" He winced, doing his best to hide behind the twins. "You mad?"

"Symposium?" Liz repeated, taking Chelsea from him as the infant held out her arms to her. She kissed the child's cheek and then snuggled her close against her own body. Chelsea immediately dug both fists into Liz's hair. "But I thought— *Ouch!*"

"I know, I know," Doug interrupted quickly, believing if he could just keep talking, he might get out of this mess with his body in one piece. "You wanted to paint the place. *I* wanted to paint the place," he continued, wincing as he realized that Liz might eventually swallow some of his story, but she would never believe he actually *wanted* to paint ceilings and woodwork and those damn skinny slats of wood in the windows.

"The painting can wait, I suppose," Liz told him as she tentatively probed inside the leg opening of Chelsea's diaper, then winced. "She's wet clear through, poor baby. Charlie probably is, too. Look, explanations can wait, okay? I've got to hunt up clean diapers. Do you know where Candie put them?"

"There're four huge boxes of them over there, beside the bed. Oh—and Candie said she left you some kind of instructions tucked into Chelsea's diaper bag. I'll take Charlie into the living room for now, and you can call me when you want him."

A thin line appeared between Liz's eyebrows, warning him that she was about to say something he wasn't going to like. "When *I* want him? What's the matter, Doug? Do you think you're genetically disqualified from changing a wet diaper?"

He grinned, remembering their few, very few, conversations about the division of labor between the males and females of the species. He didn't much care for those conversations, for they almost all ended with him picking up yet another "chore" in the condo. The last one was changing the sheets on their king-size bed—and he would still like to find the guy who invented contour sheets that were always a half-size smaller than the mattress and give him a pop on the nose! "We'll negotiate later, Liz, okay? I'm sure we'll be able to come to some agreement."

"You bet we will, Sherlock," he heard her mutter under her breath as she stooped to extract a diaper from the already open plastic pouch. The moment her back was turned, Doug—clutching Charlie to him like a shield—got the heck out of the room, worrying that he might just have handled the first "Guess what—we've got the twins!" encounter with less than his usual panache.

Liz found Candie's note as she was rummaging through the pink diaper bag on the hunt for baby powder and wipes. She put the thick, sealed brown envelope to one side—idly wondering if Candie had attempted to write her own version of *War and Peace,* the package was that full—and cooed and kissed Chelsea through their first shared diaper change.

"Now, that wasn't all that bad, was it, darling?" she asked the infant, who answered by trying to pull off Liz's right ear. Quickly finding a small terry-cloth squeeze toy in the Portacrib, Liz gratefully reclaimed her ear in exchange for the toy and Chelsea subsided happily in the Portacrib. "That oughta give me at least five minutes to read your mommy's opus," she told the child. "And she'd darn well better have left me some clue to what the heck is going on," she continued as she sat on the edge of the bed and slid a fingernail under the envelope flap.

First to fall out of the envelope were five closely typed pages—Candie had once been Chip's executive secretary—detailing any problems that might come up with the twins, and several possible hair-raising emergency scenarios Liz hadn't considered. There were separate lists of Charlie's and Chelsea's likes and dislikes, their favorite toys, their sleeping habits, even their "pooping" habits, as Candie termed it.

This last cataloging of information gave Liz her first real smile in hours because, if the schedule was correct, Charlie had given Doug a "gift" about two hours ago. "Boy, do I hope she's right!" she mumbled, then frowned as she saw that, if Chelsea was prompt with her own daily "gift," there would be another diaper change within the hour.

She barely skimmed the pages—each done up on Candie's home computer, each page titled, each subject broken down into outline form—then picked up the smaller white envelope marked "For Liz's eyes *only*."

Liz turned the envelope over several times before opening it, strangely reluctant to read its contents, then gave in to curiosity. "'Dear Liz,'" she began, reading out loud, then read on silently, moving her lips as each new sentence drove her further into stunned speechlessness.

I know you must be shocked spitless, Liz, but personally, I think this is wonderful! Couldn't have worked out better, actually.

Guess I'll tell you what happened, huh, so you can laugh along with Chip and me. It was this way—Chip and Doug were watching the football game together last Monday night, with you already in New York, when Doug all of a sudden blurted out that *he* wanted a baby! Honest to God! Is that *cosmic,* or what?

Liz began to chuckle, for reading Candie's note was the same as listening to her speak. She just rambled along, going here and there as the whim took her, and taking her own very singular path to the point. But her chuckle died when she reread the words "Doug all of a sudden blurted out that *he* wanted a baby!" Pressing a hand to her once-again-queasy stomach, Liz read the rest of the letter.

Now, I hadn't told you, because you were in New York, but Chip couldn't get time off from the office so close to the end of the month, so we'd we'd already decided to give you the twins the first week of your vacation instead of the second—but Chip *did* know all about our plans. When Doug started waxing poetic about having a baby, Chip jumped at the chance to say, "You can have one of mine. Take two, they're small." He told me that line four or five times, Liz—all the time expecting me to laugh as if it was the funniest joke ever told. Honestly! Men!

Anyway, with you in New York, and Chip already on the phone to Pennsylvania, getting us reservations—and me selfishly not wanting to tell you what Doug said because I really, *really,* do need this time away from the babies—I realized that you and Doug were kinda like that old fable about the girl selling her hair to buy her love a watch fob, while the guy goes and hocks his watch to buy his girlfriend a comb. Well, not really. But it's something like that, right?

The thing is, Liz—I think it was a pretty dirty trick Doug planned to pull on you. Throwing the C-C's at you without warning, then expecting you to go all squishy and momlike over them and agree to have his baby. Then I thought—hey, that's what Liz was planning! But it seemed so much kinder and gentler when *we* were doing the planning and *Doug* was the dupe. Either way, I knew I wasn't going to be cheated out of this second honeymoon because the two of you could hear your biological clocks ticking. So I'm selfish. I admit it!

So now what are you going to do? Tell him you know what he's hoping for? Tell him you were planning to do the same thing? Tell him right away that you're pregnant?

I hope not, Liz. I really, *really* hope not. Personally, having given this a lot of thought these past few days, I hope you leave the guy out there to twist in the breeze for a while. Watch him trying to convince you of the joys of motherhood. Stand back and giggle as he goes climbing through hoops, saying it's okay with him if he only gets a couple of hours' sleep a night. Let him try to diaper a crawling child, let him wear a little rice cereal on his eyebrows while trying to smile and pretend he's just loving it. He's talking the talk, as Chip says. Now let him try to walk the walk. *Then* let him in on the joke.

Say, about Friday at three? When we'll be coming home to pick up the twins and rescue them from their part in this sitcom?

You can do this, Liz. You can get that guy on his knees, crawling, begging you to have his child so that he can stop pretending that everything to do with childrearing is just one big bowl of cherries—because it's not. He has to learn to take the bad with the good, you know?

And besides, he still hasn't learned to say he loves you except when the spirit moves him, remember? He owes you big time for that one, like Chip does me. Strike a blow for womankind, Liz—hang this guy out to dry for the week. When he says he loves you and you're not both in bed when he says it, well, *then* you can tell him the truth.

Well, have a great week. We're not going to phone. Chip says this is to be a real second honeymoon, but you have our number at the hotel if you get desperate.

For my sake, darling, *don't* get desperate!

Liz folded the letter and replaced it into the envelope, then quickly tucked it in her pocket as Doug and Charlie reentered the room. She looked at Doug, smiling guiltily, and maybe a little misty-eyed, knowing he wanted a child as much as she did. And he looked so sweet, holding the baby high against his chest. So...so...*fatherly.*

She almost told him the truth.

Almost.

And then she heard Candie's voice in her head, just as if her friend were sitting beside her, whispering in her ear: "Strike a blow for womankind, Liz—hang this guy out to dry for the week."

"Your turn, bucko," she said, gesturing to the stack of diapers, knowing she would pay real cash dollars to watch him struggle with the tapes on the disposable diapers.

"I know. And us guys were missing our women," Doug said, laying Charlie on the plastic pad Liz had already placed on the bed and beginning to unsnap the child's cotton overalls in preparation for changing his diaper. As he worked—and he did rather well after realizing he couldn't leave the squirming Charlie for the millisecond it would take him to grab a diaper, so Liz helped him out by supplying one for him—he eyed her rather nervously, saying, "You're not mad about this, are you, hon? Chip and Candie really did need a break from the C-C's. But I guess I should have asked you first, huh?"

"It might have been nice," Liz agreed, trying not to wince, for she had planned to do to him what he had just done to her. "But we'll muddle through. We can paint next week, if you like. Or not," she ended weakly, feeling her stomach begin to rise in revolt over her suggestion.

"No, I think we should definitely paint next week," Doug told her as he lifted the dirty diaper clear of Charlie's plump bottom, then quickly placed a small washcloth over the baby's lower body. "He got me this afternoon when I wasn't expecting it," he explained. "Laughed his evil little heart out while he was at it, too. Just thought I'd warn you."

"Warning taken," Liz said, smiling at the

thought of Doug trying to duck as Charlie performed like one of the water-spraying statues in the park. "Are you sure about the painting? I thought you wanted to drive to California. We might need a vacation by then."

"True enough, but I had a day off last week and took a drive outside town, looking at a couple of the developments going up near Chip's house. Some damn nice homes, Liz, and well within our price range, even if we were only considering my new salary as vice-president. You've been saying that you wish we had another room you could devote just to your computer stuff. I know you hate traveling so much, and I think the idea of going out on your own is a good one. Graphic artists can easily freelance, work out of their home offices. Right?"

Liz had been biting the inside of her cheek while Doug spoke, deliberately keeping her eyes on Charlie, who was taking umbrage at having a new diaper put on him while he tried to play with his bare toes. "You want to buy a house? Mister Let's-not-bite-off-more-than-we-can-chew? You're kidding, right?"

She had moved in with Doug, giving up her apartment, as he already had bought the condo five years previously and, although she contributed her share of the monthly payments, she still considered it to be *his* condo, and not really her home. Now he was talking about buying a house.

And he wanted a baby. Candie said that Chip had told her so. A house. A baby. Did the word *wife* never enter this man's vocabulary? Obviously not.

Doug's expression became shuttered, and he picked up Charlie, giving the baby's dimpled hand a quick kiss. "You're tired, hon. We'll pick up on this another time, okay? Now, if I've got Candie's schedule right, we play for about an hour, then it's bath time, which Candie swears wears them out, then bottle and rice-cereal time, and then—around nine—it's bedtime. I like that part. You *are* ready for a little bedtime, aren't you, Liz? It's been a long week."

Oh, yeah. Candie was right. The guy deserved to swing in the breeze for a while. A *long* while. Liz didn't answer Doug, but only smiled through gritted teeth as she picked up Chelsea and followed him into the living room, where they would have "playtime."

And, if she had anything to say about the matter, it would be the *only* "playtime" Doug Marlow would see for a good week!

Chapter Two

Tuesday—You mean it's not Friday yet?

Doug sat at the bar in the kitchen, his legs wrapped around the base of the stool to keep him from sliding off in his weariness, and his head resting in his hands to keep him upright if he slipped into unconsciousness.

It was 6:00 a.m., and he hadn't slept in over an hour. He couldn't remember the last time he'd been awake, if ever, before the morning newspaper was delivered, and he had already decided that dawn wasn't all the poets had cracked it up to be.

To be fair, Candie *had* warned in her note, which had looked more like a legal brief, that the C-C's had, in the past week, learned how to stand in their cribs. Unfortunately, she had added in small print, they hadn't learned as yet how to get back *down* again.

At the time, while he was skimming all of Candie's instructions, that pertinent point hadn't really penetrated Doug's brain. But at midnight, the meaning had become much clearer. It had become crystal clear at 2:00 a.m., and embedded in the deepest recesses of his brain at 5:00 a.m. Each time, one of the twins had woken, stood, and then wailed when he or she couldn't sit back down again. Which had woken the other twin. Who had stood. And hadn't been able to get back down. Then had howled.

And Liz hadn't stirred. Not once. Well, maybe the third time, when she had rolled over, pulled the pillows out from under him and placed them over her own head, then muttered something that sounded a lot like "Fix that, why don't you, Bright-Idea Man?" before going back to sleep.

Doug was pretty sure he hated her.

The teakettle began to whistle and Doug jumped up, quickly rescuing the stool before it toppled over, making a sound like a cannon shot in the quiet condo, and raced to remove the kettle from the heat before its harsh peal could wake the twins.

He poured himself a cup of hot water over the tea bag he'd found in the closet—he, who never drank tea—then ladled in three teaspoonfuls of sugar to give him energy, and stumbled out onto the balcony that faced the ring of dark, mud-brown mountains in the distance. It was so quiet now. Peaceful, even. And while the peace lasted, he wasn't going to do anything to disturb it.

He lowered his long frame into the nearest chair and propped his bare feet on the wooden railing, resting the teacup on his bare chest until the heat penetrated his skin, proving to him that he was *not* dead, he could still feel. He was dead tired, though.

And with three more nights to go before Chip, his good buddy, came home and rescued him.

Because it was already crystal clear that Liz wasn't going to wade in with any sort of nocturnal help. "As plans go, bucko, this one looks to be a wash," he told himself, then took a sip of tea, the hot liquid burning his tongue. "On the other hand, the only way to go is up."

The thought was not comforting.

Liz lifted her head a millimeter from the mattress, testing her stomach's response to this shift in her body's position, and looked at the clock on the night table. A quarter after six. She dropped her head back onto the mattress, groaning. Her stomach hadn't liked the movement any more now than it had during the night, in those horrible minutes between hearing the twins first begin to stir and the moment Doug left the bed. Each time he did, he shook the mattress with his movements—the shifting becoming more and more violent with each new awakening—until she thought she would have to make a dash for the bathroom.

But she had made it through the night, guilty conscience and all.

Now she had to make it through the morning. And when just the thought of becoming vertical scared the daylights out of her!

Still lying on her stomach, she slipped her arm over the side of the bed and began a quick search under the bed for the soda crackers she had hidden there last night when Doug was watching the ten o'clock news. The chambermaid at the Marriott Marquis in New York had brought her crackers on Sunday, swearing that downing two or three of the dry, tasteless things before getting out of bed had saved her during her own four pregnancies.

So far, Liz had decided that the chambermaid had been pulling a cruel trick on her, filling her not only with soda crackers but false hope, as well. The crackers sure weren't working.

But she would give them another shot. After all, what did she have to lose?

"Three soda crackers," she mumbled around her first tentative bite, then rolled onto her side, propping up her head with one hand as she doggedly chewed and swallowed that cracker and two more.

Doug must think I'm unnatural, Liz thought, as, still lying on her side, she tentatively slipped her bare feet over the edge of the mattress and aimed them toward the floor. He had to be thinking: How could she have heard those little darlings crying and not gone to them immediately? Did she have no motherly instincts? No pity on *him?*

As she gingerly levered herself into a sitting position, her head began to swim and her stomach began to roil, and she decided that she didn't give a good damn *what* Doug thought of her!

And then she ran into the bathroom and

slammed the door behind her with a loud bang. A few seconds later, penetrating her deep misery, came the sound of two babies, crying.

Both twins had, thankfully, learned how to hold their own bottles, so that Doug could lay them back in their Portacribs after changing them and dressing them in small matching outfits he'd unearthed from their mountain of luggage.

He'd done well, he thought. Talking to Chelsea while he dressed Charlie, mugging faces at Charlie to keep him happy in his Portacrib when it was his sister's turn to lie on the plastic mat on the bed, heating the bottles while holding Chelsea—deftly avoiding her desire to rip off his nose—and keeping an eagle eye on Charlie, who was crawling around the carpet, looking for microscopic threads to plop in his mouth.

He'd heard the shower running while he was heating the bottles and took a quick look at the clock, to find that it was nearly seven-thirty. Some people could sleep in, he'd supposed meanly, his lips curling into a sneer. Giving in to a dark side he had previously been unaware he possessed, he had then turned on the hot water in the kitchen sink, hoping Liz froze in the bathroom.

After all, she deserved to get a little of her own back after the way she had left him to manage all by himself last night. Doug was sure Chip had told him that he and Candie took turns getting up at night with the twins. That had to be the way parents handled these things. Didn't Liz know the rules? Maybe he should buy her some kind of mommy manual.

No matter what, so far his idea had been a big washout. Sure, Liz had seemed to enjoy the twins last night, especially during bath time, which had been more like a group visit to the tub than an exercise meant to cleanse two small bodies. By the time the twins had finished splashing, all four of them had been wet, the carpeted bathroom floor had been soaked, and he'd felt as if he'd just completed a five-kilometer run on his knees.

But Liz had been undaunted, spreading towels on the bedroom floor, then oiling and powdering each twin, rubbing sweet-smelling lotion into their every little crease and dimple, then slipping them into their pajamas, holding on to them tightly, grinning and saying they both felt so good, smelled so good.

Yes. Bath time hadn't been a complete disaster.

The rice cereal had been another matter. Charlie liked his thin, almost runny, but Chelsea liked hers thick, almost chewable, and she had fussed and pushed at the spoon of soupy cereal until Liz had, in desperation, referred to Candie's printed instructions and figured out the source of the problem. By that time, Chelsea had needed another visit to the tub, and a lot of the joy of sweet-smelling baby had gone out of the evening.

And then there had been the pillow. Doug frowned as he waded into the pile of soiled clothes lying on the bedroom floor, automatically picking up pajamas and small undershirts and stuffing them into the hamper Candie had brought with her when she dropped the kids off and took off like an escaping bank robber.

Yes, it was Liz's pillow that had really told the story of how badly his hastily constructed plan was playing out. Doug had bought the thing himself last year during their vacation to Mexico, thinking it was a great joke. And it had been funny, at the time.

But not now.

The pillow, a small, needlepoint affair, dark green with tan letters, spelled out "Tonight" on one side and "Not Tonight" on the other.

He and Liz had laughed about the pillow, then consigned it to the closet.

Until last night.

He had gone into the bathroom to shower once the twins were settled, and come out with a towel wrapped around his waist, expecting to see Liz already in bed, waiting for him, only to find that damned pillow lying in the center of the bedspread, just beneath the bed pillows.

And it was showing the side that said: "Not Tonight."

He'd opened the door to the living room and peeked out, to see Liz curled on the couch, a book in her lap. He had briefly considered sneaking up behind her, bending to kiss her nape, hoping to talk her out of her bad mood—or whatever the heck had gotten into her.

But he'd decided against it, and had crawled into the king-size bed alone, as he had been alone for the past week, only taking time to throw the pillow across the room, where it landed on top of the pile of his own laundry that he had somehow not quite gotten around to dragging to the laundry room.

Now it looked like his clothes would never be washed—not if he and Liz were going to have both washer and dryer going full tilt all day long, to keep the twins in fresh clothing.

Kids were a whole industry unto themselves, Doug had decided somewhere between watching Chip drag walkers, high chairs, Portacribs, jump seats, stroller, car seats and a myriad of other stuff into the condo that had once seemed roomy but now had all the elbowroom of a phone booth. Between the furniture they needed, and the toys, and the clothes, and the diapers, and the cartons of formula, and the bottle liners, and the bedding—well, buying stock in some baby company didn't seem like a bad idea.

Buying a house also wasn't a bad idea. A big house. Big enough for a baby and his parents. Because babies grew up. And needed bikes, and skateboards, and Rollerblades. And basketball hoops—for which a person needed a driveway.

And golf clubs. His kid would like golf, Doug was sure of that. And they would need at least a two-car garage. Space for the sports car and room for a minivan. Because a minivan was beginning to look more like a necessity than a symbol. Hell, his sports car didn't even have a back seat for a child's car seat.

So he would trade in the sports car on a safe, solid, four-door sedan. No big deal.

No big deal? No big deal! Doug stopped in the process of turning a small undershirt right-side out, dumbfounded by his own thoughts. Give up his sports car? What—was he nuts?

He unconsciously began rubbing the undershirt against his stubbly cheek, as he had yet to have time to shave even though it was nearly eight o'clock. And the smell of baby lotion, of baby, of sleep and a warm body, got all tangled up in his nostrils, and in his heart, and he shook his head, laughing at himself. "You're beyond help, Dougie boy," he muttered, stuffing the undershirt into the hamper and turning to pick up Charlie, who had finished his bottle and let out a loud burp. "Way beyond help," he added with a look toward the wall that separated the spare bedroom and master bedroom.

Chelsea took that moment to haul herself to her feet, holding on to the rail of the Portacrib with one hand as she winged her empty bottle through the air so that it clipped Doug on the shin.

"Guys," Doug said, going down on his knees beside Chelsea's Portacrib. "We've got to have a talk. Do you know what *adorable* means? Because if we're to have a snowball's chance in hel— scratch that—if we're to have any luck at all this week, you're going to have to be adorable. Work on it, okay?"

Chelsea reached over the Portacrib railing and grabbed on to Doug's nose with a death grip. "All right, all right," he said reasonably. "I guess we'll just have to wing it. And maybe cut those nails. Okay, dumpling?"

The twins were perfect darlings, both of them. They didn't cry for their absent mommy and daddy, for one thing, because Liz and Doug had been a part of their lives from the beginning. They amused themselves fairly well for up to twenty minutes or so at a time, and they still took long afternoon naps.

Which meant that the first full day of baby-sitting was humming along fairly well, for which Liz was more than grateful. She was still very nervous around the babies without having Candie there as a sort of backup while she changed diapers, made formula and generally cared for these two precious, precocious bundles.

And Doug was being wonderful. Helpful. Cute as the devil as he lay on the floor and let Chelsea pull his hair. Caring and concerned as he kissed

Charlie's boo-boo when the little guy tried to stand, using one of the living-room chairs as a support, and went tumbling sideways against the edge of the coffee table. And blessedly relieved when the twins went down for their nap and he could stretch out on the couch for some sleep himself.

Which gave Liz plenty of privacy when the phone rang while she was straightening the master bedroom. She picked it up to find that Candie was on the other end.

"I know I promised Chip I wouldn't call, Liz, but I miss my babies *so* much," Candie said quickly, after explaining that Chip had gone to the desk to beg another pillow for their heart-shaped bed and could be back at any moment. "Well, no, actually I probably won't miss them for at least another twenty-four hours, but I thought a good mother should say that. It's already six o'clock here, and Chip is going to take me to some nearby inn for dinner and dancing. Dancing, Liz! I haven't danced with anyone but the C-C's—to the strains of some 'Sesame Street' song, no less—since they were born. I tell you, Liz, I could get very used to this. So—how's it going? Did you tell Doug? Please tell me you didn't tell Doug."

Liz sat down on the edge of the still unmade bed. "No, I didn't tell him. I should have, but I didn't, and I can't tell you how guilty I feel about it. Oh, Candie, he's being so *good!* Better than me, to tell the truth. I didn't know anyone's stomach could do so many flips. How long does this last, anyway? I don't remember you being so ill every day."

"That's because you weren't around early in the morning, when I was beating Chip senseless to get past him and into the bathroom. Don't you have a doctor's appointment yet? You really should go see the doctor, you know."

"I'm going tomorrow morning," Liz explained, frowning. "If I can leave Doug alone with the twins. I'll have to tell him it's my yearly checkup and that it would be impossible for me to reschedule without having to wait another three months. He's feeling so guilty about siccing the twins on me without notice that he probably won't complain.

"By the way, is Chelsea teething, Candie? She keeps trying to bite me. And Doug. And Charlie. And the arm of the couch. And the coffee table, at least until Doug shoved it into a closet. But that's another story."

"Oh, dear," Candie said, giggling. "I did notice that she was beginning to drool all over everything. She's more advanced than Charlie in so many ways, although he's closer to walking than she is. Walking! They're only seven months old, for crying out loud. I think I'm going to have to tie bricks to their ankles, or else I don't know how I'm going to handle it when they're both mobile. Let her suck on an ice pop, Liz. That's what my mother told

me in her last letter. And you might want to use
the plastic bib for that. And don't let her bite it or
she could choke. Just sort of tease her gums with
it, you know? Oh, boy, I think I hear Chip downstairs. We have two floors, Liz, because the champagne-glass bathtub is so tall. Can you believe it?
I'll call again—bye!''

Liz heard the click in her earpiece, then the
sound of the dial tone. She sat there, holding the
receiver like a lifeline, wishing Candie back on the
phone.

''Who was that?'' Doug asked, stretching his
long body out prone across the mattress behind her
and snaking one arm around her waist from behind.

''Who was that?'' Liz repeated dumbly, then
hung up the phone. ''Oh, you mean on the phone?
Um, that was the receptionist in Dr. Wilbert's office. She was reminding me of my appointment
tomorrow morning at ten. It's my yearly, and I
have to go, Doug. I had to fight to get it during
my vacation so that I wouldn't have to miss work.
I'm sorry.''

His arm only tightened around her waist. ''No
problem. I can handle things here. Shouldn't be
more than one or two minor emergencies while
you're gone. Come here, hon, and let's take a nap.
Well, maybe not a nap. But I'm sure we can find
something to occupy us while the twins are asleep.
I promised them a walk in the park later, if they
sleep for at least two hours.''

"Not now, Doug," Liz said distractedly, wondering where she could buy chokeless ice pops. "Maybe tonight, okay?"

He rolled over onto his back, crossing his hands behind his head. "Maybe tonight? You mean the damned pillow goes back in the closet? It's nice to know I've been forgiven."

She turned to look at him, adoringly, she supposed, because she really did adore this man. "I've never really been angry with you. Not really. I think it was sweet to give Chip and Candie a second honeymoon. You were sweet for offering to keep the twins and I'm only sorry that I—um—that I didn't think of it first. I'm also sorry that my stomach is still on the blink, although I am starting to feel better, honestly. It must have been something I ate on the plane."

"Probably. Hey—what's this?" he asked, sitting up and running his hands over the mattress. "Crumbs? You've been eating in bed, Liz?"

She panicked, abruptly changing the subject. "My suitcase was delivered while you were busy with Charlie. I've got to unpack while the twins are sleeping," she told him, quickly rising from the bed as he wiped cracker crumbs onto the floor. "Will you please carry my luggage in here for me?"

His look was more than simply inquiring, as if he was trying to pierce her skull with his eyes and read her mind. "Is something going on, Liz?

Something I should know about? Who is Dr. Wilbert? I thought this was some general medical checkup your office required. That *is* it, right? Just a routine yearly physical?''

Her lips were numb, so that she had to speak through clenched teeth, snapping out her words. "Yep, that's it. Yearly physical. Either that, or I'm dying from some mysterious illness and just haven't gotten around to telling you."

"A little touchy, aren't you, Liz? It's probably because you're still on New York time. I should have thought of that." Doug jackknifed into a sitting position, then pushed a hand through his hair. "I'm sorry for overreacting, hon. But you said yourself that your stomach is playing games with you. I'll back off now and let you get over your jet lag."

"I'd appreciate that," Liz told him, turning away so that Doug couldn't see the tears that had come, unbidden and definitely unwanted, to sting at her eyes.

Blinking rapidly a time or two, she turned back and looked down at what could only be one very confused man. They hardly ever fought, and he probably hadn't the least clue as to why they seemed to be fighting now.

He had already lain back down on the bed, his hands crossed behind his head, his eyes closed. The poor guy had been up taking care of the twins most of the night and was obviously exhausted.

And yet she had to ask him the question that gnawed at her. She didn't know why. She just had to. *Now.*

"Doug? Do you love me?"

His eyes remained shut. "You know the answer to that, Liz," he said, then yawned.

Her bottom lip began to tremble. "No. No, I don't, Doug. I know your 'Of course, I do' answer. But that's just it, Doug. It's always an answer to my question. You never *volunteer,* you know?"

Now his eyes did open, and he sat up once more. "There was some dumb quiz in a magazine on the plane, wasn't there? One of those 'He only really loves me if' articles you and Candie are always driving Chip and me crazy over? What is it, Liz? You want a second honeymoon, too?"

She wanted to kill him. "We haven't had a *first* honeymoon, Doug. Remember?"

His grin was sheepish, and once again he was eminently adorable. All right, so she wouldn't *kill* him.

"No. No, we haven't, have we?" he said, rising from the bed and coming over to put his arms around her. "Do you want a first one, Liz? Because I'm sure it could be arranged."

She burrowed against his chest. "Is this a proposal?" she asked, feeling all misty again.

"Why not?" he asked, and she felt the rumble of his voice against her cheek. "We've been living together for two years. We might as well make it legal. Lord knows, we can't go more than three feet in any direction here in Vegas without tripping over a wedding chapel.''

She stiffened in his arms, unable to find the humor in his words, as she might have a month or so ago, before her hormones had begun playing on their up-and-down seesaw. How could the newly appointed vice-president of the largest investment bank in the southeastern states be so incredibly *blockheaded?*

"Oh, just forget it!'' she exclaimed, pushing herself free and heading for the living room and then the front door, slamming both doors behind her.

Which woke the twins.

Doug was totally lost. The woman who had returned last night had certainly *looked* like the same Liz Somerville he had kissed goodbye a week ago. But there had been a personality transplant somewhere between Las Vegas and New York, and he barely recognized the moody, weepy, mercurial woman who was at this very moment sitting in a darkened living room at almost midnight, a fussing Charlie on her lap, listening to the compact disc of the *EFX* show that was playing over and over on his stereo.

He'd made at least three different excuses to come into the living room, and had been variously glared at, ignored, or rudely told to "go away'' before he had given up any notion of being helpful and gone to take his second shower of the day. Chelsea's thick-as-glue version of rice cereal, as he had quickly learned, was a real bitch to get out of hair.

He came out of the bathroom to see that Liz had moved from the couch at least once, because the damned pillow was back, silently screaming "Not Tonight!" at him from the bed.

Well, that was okay, because he wasn't much in the mood, anyway. Not when it would feel as if he was making love to a stranger. A stranger who could knock him off his feet with her smile one moment, then slice him off at the knees with a few well-chosen words the next.

"Something's going on, damn it," he said out loud as he threw the pillow across the room. "But what? What?"

He pulled off the towel he had wrapped around his waist and climbed into a loose-fitting pair of knit shorts, the sort of thing that had served as pajamas for him since he had been in his teens. Sitting down on Liz's side of the bed, he stared at nothing, still trying to figure out what in hell was going on, and then looked at the telephone on the night table.

And the telephone book that sat beside it.

"What in hell was his name? Silbert? No. Some kind of a nut? Filbert? No, that couldn't be it. *Wilbert.* That's it—Wilbert!" he mumbled as he flipped through the Yellow Pages, hunting for Physicians.

And there it was: "Wilbert, Michael A., M.D. Board certified in obstetrics, gynecology, prenatal care and delivery."

Wilbert, Michael A., did some other stuff, too, but Doug didn't do more than skim words like "ultrasounds" and "menopause." He was too busy zooming in on the words "prenatal care and delivery."

Oh, yeah.

Now it was beginning to make sense.

The mood swings.

The upset stomach that had seemed to go away after breakfast, then had reappeared at dinnertime.

The "Not Tonight" pillow.

The crumbs in the bed.

Doug went down on all fours and reached under the bed, quickly finding the box of soda crackers. Chip had told him about those. How Candie had lain prone on the bed each morning as he fed her crackers.

Chip!

Chip knew! He had to have known! That was why he had kept smiling and smirking and, just the day before he and Candie had flown off to Pennsylvania, had dropped a folder extolling the merits of one of the latest minivans on Doug's desk. He had known because Liz told Candie everything and Candie told Chip everything.

Liz was pregnant!

Doug pushed the box back under the bed and stood, not knowing what to do next.

He wanted to shout. Scream. Jump up and down like an idiot. He actually started toward the door to the living room, eager to pick up Liz and smother her with kisses, before he controlled himself.

He was just guessing, right? No. She was pregnant. With child. Having his baby. *His baby!* He dropped his head into his hands before his skull exploded, grinning wildly, then shook his head, trying to contain himself. He and Liz. Having a baby!

His smile vanished.

And she was keeping it a secret from him.

Why?

He searched out Candie's homemade "Care and Feeding of the Twins" manual and thumbed through it until he found the telephone number of the resort in the Poconos. He actually made a grab for the phone before he realized that it had to be nearly three in the morning in Pennsylvania.

So? Doug's selfish side silently asked his better nature. *Your point? The guy knew Liz thought she was pregnant and didn't tell you, remember? Probably knew it the day of the Raiders-Eagles game. But he just kept his mouth shut and tricked you into offering to keep his kids for five days while he went off on a second honeymoon with his wife.*

And you thought he was your friend? Ha! Call him at three in the morning. Call him any damn time you please. The guy doesn't deserve any consideration!

"I can't do that," he muttered aloud, walking into the bathroom to get a drink of water. "If Chip knows that I know, he'll tell Candie that I know, and then Candie will phone Liz and tell her that I know. Liz may have been hard to read these last couple of days, but I know enough to know that she wants to be the one who tells me I'm going to be a father."

He looked at his reflection in the mirror over the sink, grinning once again. "I'm going to be a father! *Me!*" he told himself. "Liz is probably just waiting for some sort of official confirmation from this Wilbert guy, and then she's going to tell me."

His smile faded and his stomach knotted as he left the bathroom without his drink of water and looked toward the closed door to the living room. "Isn't she?"

He opened the door a crack, peering around it into the darkened living room. Liz was still on the couch, Charlie snuggled against her, soundly asleep, the soundtrack from the EFX show still audible in the background. The song Michael Crawford sang about "counting up to twenty" was playing.

Doug remembered the song, a sort of anthem of mingled concern and hope, telling of the struggles of living in the twentieth century, but holding out the promise that if mankind could make it to twenty, surely a caring mankind could find a way to make it to twenty-one. And the way to do that, according to the words of the song, was for the peoples of the world to put their faith in their children.

Doug tiptoed into the room, coming around the couch to look down at Liz and Charlie. She was holding on to him tightly, rubbing his little back with the palm of her hand.

And she was crying. Softly. Silently. Huge, shiny tears rolling down her cheeks, dripping off her chin.

She looked up at him and smiled a watery smile. Obviously her emotions were running at high tide again, and he would have to tread carefully or they would both drown in them.

Doug bent down and held out his arms, taking the sleeping child from her. Charlie instantly re-formed his warm, sleeping body against Doug's neck and chest as he stood and carried the infant to bed before coming back into the living room and sitting down beside Liz, pulling her against his shoulder. "It's all right, darling," he crooned softly. "It's all right."

"The world is so scary, Doug," she mumbled against his shirt. "And children are so helpless, so little."

"But it's like the song says, Liz," he told her,

pulling her fully onto his lap. "We have to be here for them, to guide them, to help them learn to count to twenty so that it's easier for them to count to twenty-one. The world has been around a long time, Liz, and we all keep stumbling through it the best we know how."

"I know." Liz sniffled, then laughed quietly. "I'm a jerk, aren't I? A stupid, soggy jerk."

He dropped a kiss on her forehead, suddenly aware of exactly how female Liz was, how soft, how fragile. How strong, how vulnerable. "You're not a stupid jerk. A little soggy, maybe, but that's all. And maybe a little tired?"

She nodded, as if the effort of speech was somehow beyond her. Then she raised her head. "But I have to tell you something, Doug. Something I should have told you before I went to New York. It's, well, it's sort of about the twins. You see—"

"Shh! I think I hear one of those twins starting to stir." He didn't know why, but he felt that this wasn't the time for Liz to tell him about the baby. He wanted her to go to the doctor first, satisfy herself that she was all right, that the baby was all right. Then she would tell him, just as she had probably planned.

He waited for another moment, then said, "No. I was wrong. All's still quiet on the home front." He stood, taking Liz with him, and held her high against his chest as he walked over to the stereo and motioned for her to push the button turning off the power, before carrying her into the bedroom.

She was already dressed in a soft cotton sleeveless nightgown, so it was a simple matter to deposit her on the already turned-down bed and lift her legs onto the mattress.

He went around to the other side of the bed and slipped under the sheets, moving over until he was directly behind her, gingerly, nervously slipping his hand around her waist, fighting the urge to spread his fingers wide over her still-flat belly. "No more talking tonight, Liz," he said, pressing his lips against the side of her neck.

He could feel her body relaxing against him as he put his knees behind hers and they curled up together, spoon-fashion, in the dark, the moon shining down on them through the twin skylights above the bed, the lazily rotating fan creating a gentle breeze that stirred the air.

"I love you, Doug," she whispered sleepily.

"Me, too," Doug responded, then winced as he mentally kicked himself, knowing he still hadn't gotten the hang of being the first to say the words. He would have to work on that. Just as he would have to work on how he was going to explain how he had used the C-C's to try to trick her into wanting the baby he hadn't known she was already carrying.

But he would wait until it looked like she was in a really, *really* good mood. After all, he wanted to live long enough to be a father.

Chapter Three

Wednesday—Toddling Ahead in Time

Liz woke early, turning over and snuggling into Doug's sleep-lazy embrace, nuzzling her nose against his chest and smelling...baby powder! Her eyes opened wide as she remembered the previous evening, remembered that the twins were in the next room, remembered her secret, remembered her deceit.

Remembered her queasy stomach.

Except that she was feeling pretty good. Marvelously well, as a matter of fact. Unbelieving of her good luck, she raised her head a fraction and waited for the nausea to assail her.

Nothing. Well, maybe a little hunger. Which certainly was different.

As a matter of fact, it was astounding. She wanted bacon. She wanted eggs, scrambled as only Doug could do them.

But she wasn't as hungry as she was feeling amorous.

She and Doug hadn't been together since the night before her trip to New York, and lovemaking had always been one of their favorite "wake-me-ups" in the morning. Their passion then was always quick, fervent and quite satisfying.

So thinking, she ran her hand across the soft curls on his bare chest, then trailed her fingers lower, to his waist. She lifted her head and took a gentle nip at his left earlobe, then teased it with the tip of her tongue. "Any or all of you want to rise and shine now?" she whispered into his ear, her hand sliding beneath the waistband of his knit shorts.

The next thing she knew she was most happily lying on her back, and Doug was kissing her. Madly. Passionately. Sliding his leg between hers, beginning to lever himself on top of her—when suddenly he moved away, as if her body were hot, and might burn him.

"Doug?"

"What?" he gasped out, his chest rising and falling rapidly, as if he had just run a long race.

"What?" she repeated, feeling deserted, and definitely on edge. "What do you mean, *what?* Stop me if I'm wrong, here, but I thought we were about to make mad, passionate, impromptu love. I know it has been a while, but I'm pretty sure I remember the preliminaries."

He pushed the back of his head into the pillows, raising his chin toward the ceiling. "I know, I know. But I shouldn't have…um… That is, I weigh a lot more than…um… I think I hear the twins starting to wake up. Yep—that was the kids singing, all right. It's best to get to them before they can get really warmed up. Be back in a sec!"

He was out of the bed and out of the room so fast that Liz saw him as more a blur than anything else, especially since her eyes had already filled with tears. He didn't love her. He cared more about Charlie and Chelsea than he did about her. And she had worried he wouldn't like babies? Ha! He liked them a whole fat lot better than he liked *her*.

She sat up in bed and pinned a smile on her face as Doug reentered the room, a sleep-rosy twin tucked against either hip. "Good morning, you sweet things," she said, reaching out to take Chelsea from Doug while studiously avoiding his eyes. "Did you have a lovely sleep?"

"I can't believe they only woke up twice last night," Doug said, joining her on the bed. "And both times it was only Chelsea who cried. Charlie was too busy hanging on to the rail and shooting her raspberries because he's figured out how to get back down now. I spent about an hour showing him how, you know. Last night, while you were trying to settle Chelsea and her sore gums. It's a riot, Liz. He starts aiming his rump toward the mattress, hanging on to the railing for dear life as he bends his knees and goes lower, and lower. Then he finally lets go and—plop!—he's down. The way they imitate each other, I figure Chelsea will have mastered Charlie's trick by bedtime tonight and we'll get our first real night's sleep."

Liz stared at Doug in openmouthed amazement. She hadn't even heard Chelsea during the night. But he had. And he'd gone in to the twins, taken care of them, and even seemed happy about it. "You're wonderful, Doug. A born father." Her bottom lip began to quiver and her eyes filled. "And I'm an unnatural woman. I didn't even hear this poor little darling cry!"

Chelsea reached up and took two handfuls of Liz's hair. "Da-da-da," she cooed with each violent tug. "Da-da-*da!*"

"You were wiped out, Liz," Doug assured her as he began opening little snaps and removing Charlie's two-piece cotton pajamas. "Jet lag, remember? So, how are you feeling this morning? I was thinking about some bacon and eggs after we get these little monsters dressed and fed. If you're up to it, of course."

Liz wiped at her eyes with a corner of Chelsea's nightgown hem, hoping Doug would think her tears had come as a result of having her hair pulled. "Up to it?" she repeated, looking at him curiously, cautiously. What was he saying? What was he *not* saying? "And just what do you mean by that?"

Doug stood, heading for the spare bedroom, where he would doubtless change Charlie, dress him, then teach the kid how to speak in full sentences—and maybe start him on long division. "I didn't mean anything by it, Liz. It's just that your stomach had been bothering you, remember?"

"Oh, yes. Yes, you're right," she said hastily, scrambling to pick up Chelsea and follow after Doug. "Wow, looks like whatever it was, it's gone. How about that? And would you look at the time? The twins really slept late. It's nearly seven-thirty. I've got to get moving if I want to shower and dress and get downtown in time for my appointment."

"Absolutely," Doug said brightly as he tossed her the pack of baby wipes. "Wouldn't want to miss your appointment with Dr. Filbert."

She looked at him, watching as he deftly slipped a clean diaper beneath Charlie. He was getting good at this baby stuff, she thought. Really, really good. "Wilbert," she corrected, wondering why Doug suddenly sounded so nervous. As if he was trying to be casual about something deadly serious.

"Whatever," Doug agreed, as if it made no difference to him, then picked up Charlie again. "Come on, sport. It's feeding time at the zoo."

Liz bent over Chelsea, holding on to the child's fat toes, and told her, "Men! Can't live with them, can't live with them. But you'll find that out soon enough, won't you, my little love?" And then she blew bubbles against the infant's fat belly while Chelsea giggled.

The pink stick was nice. The blue, nicer. But Liz had realized only a half hour earlier, there was nothing nicer, more *definite* than having a doctor say, "Yes, indeed, Liz, you're going to have a baby. Congratulations!"

She was back in her car now, the passenger seat covered with the half-dozen pamphlets and soft-bound books Dr. Wilbert's nurse had provided, a prescription for prenatal vitamins tucked in her purse.

And a smile so wide splitting her face that she was sure other drivers were looking at her and wondering if she had been drinking.

She *felt* as if she had been drinking. Tongue-tingling, bubble-tickling champagne. She felt light, and airy, and the world looked bright and clean and new and slightly larger than life.

She was having a baby. Doug's baby.

And then she frowned, coming slowly back to earth as she sat at the traffic light. Dr. Wilbert had told her he wanted to schedule an ultrasound in four weeks. It was no big deal, he had promised, but her uterus had seemed just a little too full, too expanded, for her to be only as far along in the pregnancy as she had told him.

"It happens sometimes," he had told her reassuringly. "You may have been pregnant for some time and just not realized it. Either that or—"

"Or what?" Liz had prompted as his voice had trailed off, pressing her hands protectively against her stomach. "Could something be wrong?"

His smile had reassured her. "No, Liz, definitely nothing wrong. And I'm probably way off base here, as it's so early. It's just that you're adamant about the date of your last menstrual period. But I won't be able to get a more definitive due date on you, and rule out multiples, until the first ultrasound. Maybe not even then.''

"Multiples? What are multiples?" Liz had pressed him, more confused than ever.

"That's what we now call more than one baby, Liz. Multiples. Now, go on home and celebrate your pregnancy, and don't give this another thought. I'm betting that you're just further along than you think. I'll see you in four weeks.''

Multiples. That meant twins. Like Charlie and Chelsea. Liz shook her head, then put her foot to the gas pedal as the driver behind her leaned on the horn, signaling that the traffic light had turned green as she had sat lost in a happy daze.

Her own mother had been a twin. Doug's paternal uncles were twins. So it *was* possible, if things like this did, indeed, run in families.

Wouldn't that be a hoot? Twins! Chip would probably tease her and Doug about trying to keep up with the Joneses—or the Risleys. And Doug would certainly have to kiss his red sports car goodbye, she thought, beginning to giggle.

Twins! Wait until she told Doug! He would be over the moon!

Maybe even happy enough to forgive her for hiding her pregnancy and planning to foist Charlie and Chelsea on him to see how he held up in the "daddy" department.

Just as he had sprung the C-C's on *her* to see how she would do in the "mommy" department.

If only they'd both known what the other had been planning. If only either one of them had the courage to break down and tell the truth before the confusion and the secrets bogged them down any further in this conspiracy of half-truths and hidden agendas.

Well, she would just have to wait until Chip and Candie came back and took their babies home, and then she would sit Doug down and make him listen while she confessed about her duplicity. Then, being the wonderful, loving person that she was, she would listen to *his* confession and magnanimously they would both forgive each other.

Then she would tell him about the baby.

But she wouldn't say anything about "multiples" until they both went to Dr. Wilbert's in four weeks and the ultrasound told them more.

After all, no matter how much Doug might want a child, it was probably best not to scare the guy.

Chip answered the phone on the second ring.

Doug had waited until Liz had left for the doctor's office. He had then waited an hour more because Chelsea, within mere seconds of Liz's departure, had pulled the nipple completely off her juice bottle, dousing herself with apple juice from head to foot—which had necessitated an impromptu bath for both twins, as Doug had figured that the tub was the only safe place to keep an eye on Charlie.

Then he'd had to put both twins in a single play-pen while he washed out Chelsea's, removing all the toys and washing those, as well.

By the time he had finished these domestic chores—ones he had performed quite well, he thought—he had pulled a frosted bottle of light beer out of the refrigerator, then collapsed on the couch, balancing the phone on his lap as he placed the call to Pennsylvania.

"Chip? That you? It's not an emergency. We just have to talk. Chip?"

There was a pause on the other end of the line, then Chip said, "So sorry. No English. No English. You have nice day, goodbye."

"Charles Alexander Risley, don't you dare hang up on me!" Doug bellowed into the phone, so that he quickly had to grin and pull a face at Chelsea, who had stuck out her lower lip as if ready to let loose with a mighty wail at being frightened.

There was resignation in the sigh Doug heard coming toward him all the way from the Poconos before Chip said, "You want us to come home, right? What did the dual demons do—upchuck into your VCR?"

Doug laughed. "Nothing quite that bad, Chip, although I hate to tell you what these kids can do with an ice pop. Look, I need this conversation to be between just the two of us. Is Candie there?''

"No, she went down to the main building for a massage. Dougie, if I haven't thanked you yet, let me thank you now. I had almost forgotten how sexy that wife of mine is. We're having the time of our lives, and she's gotten down to only mentioning the C-C's once or twice an hour. And, man, is this woman hot for my body! I'm exhausted, I tell you. I'll come back to Vegas a shell of my former self, so that you won't even recognize me, or the smile on my face. Now—what's up?''

"I'm glad you're having a good time, Chip," Doug said, smiling into the phone. Then he sobered. "Chip—is Liz pregnant? She is, isn't she?"

There was a sudden noise on the line, like static—or like Chip wrinkling a piece of paper next to the mouthpiece. "Doug? Damn, what a lousy connection. Doug? Did you say something? I can't hear you, man. How about you call back later, okay? Bye!''

"Hang up that phone, Chip, and I'll teach Charlie how to spit!" Doug growled into the receiver. "And this is between you and me, you understand—unless you want Candie to know about that time during our sophomore year of college when you talked me into spending spring break in Mexico. Does the name Lupe ring any bells, Chip, old buddy? Lupe, and that bottle of tequila and a certain all-night party?''

The "static" stopped. "I didn't even know Candie then," Chip grumbled.

"And that matters? I don't think so," Doug said, smiling, knowing he had won. "Liz didn't talk to me three days when she found out I had once *thought* about having the name Melissa tattooed on my backside."

"Point taken," Chip responded, sighing once more. "God, to be that young and dumb again. No, scratch that. I don't ever want to be that dumb again. So, how did you find out? From the way you asked, I've already guessed Liz hasn't told you."

"It was a couple of things. Crackers under the bed, Liz hugging the commode every morning. And she's gone to see some doctor named Wilbert this morning. I looked him up in the phone book and he's an obstetrician." Now it was Doug's turn to sigh. "Well, that nails it. She told Candie, and Candie told you. Liz is definitely pregnant."

"And you're what? Surprised? Thrilled? Grinning like a bear? Ready to look at that house that's for sale down the street from ours in the subdivision? Or have the C-C's put you totally off parenthood, and you've called to say goodbye before you board that plane to Bali?"

"What I *am*, Chip, is wondering why you didn't tell me Liz thought she was pregnant. I mean, you could have stopped me at any time before I moved the twins in here for five days to see if Liz got all soft and mommylike and started talking about the two of us having a baby of our own. Or did you only keep your mouth shut because you saw a chance to get Candie to yourself for a while?''

"I won't say I wasn't thinking about a couple of days and nights without the kids in the next room. I'd be lying if I said differently. But that wasn't all of it. Honest. And I take it you haven't told Liz why you took the twins?"

Doug frowned at the phone, even as he stood, walked over to Charlie's playpen and began picking up all the toys the little guy had tossed out onto the carpet. "How could you know that? The absence of a nuclear cloud over New Mexico being the lead story on the nightly news? No, I haven't told her yet."

"Oh, okay. But did she tell you— Never mind."

Doug handed Charlie a plastic rattle shaped like a barbell and the baby immediately tried to insert half of it into his mouth. Looks like Chelsea isn't the only one about to produce a tooth, he thought, mentally counting up the number of ice pops left in the freezer. "Never mind? Oh, no, Chip. You know something. What's going on? Spill it!"

There was another silence, then Chip began to talk. "I'll make this quick, because Candie could be back at any moment and she already told me to heat up the champagne-glass tub and drag out the bath bubbles. Okay, here goes. Doug, you remember how you said that you wanted a baby and I told you to take two, because they were small?"

"Yes," Doug said, relaxing against the cushions on the couch.

"Well, I may be brilliant and all, but I didn't come up with that idea straight off the top of my head. Liz did. About four days earlier, when she asked if she could borrow the twins to watch how you reacted around babies. Only you were going to get them the second week of your vacation, not the first. So, did Liz look surprised to see the twins when she got home? Surprised—but not too mad, seeing as it was her idea in the first place, right? And I'll wager you even money that Candie left Liz a note, saying that you had the same idea as she did, so Liz knows *exactly* what's going on, even if she hasn't let you off the hook yet. She's acting all mad that you landed her with the twins, isn't she? That's what Candie would have told her to do."

Doug sat forward so quickly that his beer bottle tipped over onto the floor. *"What?"*

"Yep. Surprise, Dougie. You're a good thinker, but not as original as you thought. The way Candie tells it, Liz was pretty sure she was pregnant but wasn't as sure about how you'd react. She didn't want to trap you into marriage—Candie's words, Dougie, not mine—and she wanted to have you fall so in love with the C-C's that you'd ask her if the two of you could start thinking about having one of your own. Then, I guess, after you did the get-down-on-one-knee thing and all, she'd tell you about the baby. I think Liz thought it would be romantic. God knows, Candie swooned all over the place, telling me about it. Women—who can figure them out? Not us, obviously. Right, Doug? Dougie, boy—you still there?''

Oh, Doug was "still there," all right. He was here, there, everywhere, his mind doing a sprightly jig all over the place, picking up bits and pieces and putting them all together into one big *mess!* "I don't believe it," he muttered into the receiver as he ran a hand through his hair. "I don't by damn believe it!"

"Believe it, buddy-boy. You each came up with the same idea. Definitely made for each other, you and Liz. And now I've gotta go. Candie will be back any minute now, and I can't find that damn bubble stuff she bought. Well, see you Friday, Doug. And I promise—my lips are sealed and Candie won't know a thing. You two can feel free to muddle through this one on your own. At least now you have an even playing field, sort of.''

Doug didn't know how long he stared at the phone after Chip had hung up before Chelsea started chirping and he came back to his surroundings, having been lost in a maze of "I did," "she did," "she didn't," then "*I* didn't." He looked at his watch, seeing that it was time for the twins' noon bottles.

And Liz still wasn't home. Which was probably a good thing. Because it was going to take him some time to figure out just exactly who was at fault here, and how much blame each thought they were carrying around, and just *how* he was going to get Liz to tell him the truth about her pregnancy.

Only then, after they had straightened out this seeming lack of confidence in each other, this certain want of openness in their long-term relationship, would he do that get-down-on-one-knee thing he should have done a long time ago—or so his mother had kept telling him these past two years on his biweekly calls home to Phoenix.

Doug had been looking at her strangely all afternoon. As if she had grown an extra head that morning. Or she had a piece of spinach stuck between her front teeth and he couldn't quite figure out how to tell her. Or—and this was most disconcerting of all—as if she were about to *explode* at any moment, like some party balloon.

No matter what his reason, Liz was beginning to tire of those looks, those strange requests that maybe, just maybe, she might want to consider taking a nap—and did she want some ice cream? There was a new carton of chocolate/chocolate-chip in the freezer. Her favorite. Was she sure she didn't want some?

In other words, Liz was beginning to think that Doug had been inhaling too many diaper-pail fumes, or was suffering from some sort of twinitis, or...*or,* he knew she was pregnant!

In which case, she would simply have to kill Chip Risley.

"Any phone calls today?" she asked idly as they sat down to a late supper, sitting on opposite ends of the living-room couch for a casual meal, for Charlie had occupied them both for most of the afternoon, having taken a spill in his playpen and split open his bottom lip. He'd cried for nearly twenty minutes, the poor kid, until Liz had finally convinced him he would really like the feel of an ice pop against his swollen lip.

"Phone calls?" Doug repeated, talking around the just-delivered pepperoni pizza he seemed to be doing his best to devour in a single bite—for he had somehow missed out on lunch. He looked adorably flummoxed, and she suddenly wanted to choke him, because he hardly ever fibbed. But when he did, he always tried to be adorable about it. "Um, let me think. No. Nope, not a one. Oh— some guy trying to sell us new windows, if you can believe it. But that's all. Why? Are you expecting a call?"

Oh, yeah. Chip had called. And Chip had spilled the beans to Doug like some blabbermouthed gossip columnist. Couldn't she even be allowed to tell Doug herself? After all, she was going to have a baby. *They* were going to have a baby. She and

Doug. *Not* Chip Risley, for crying out loud! Wasn't this supposed to be *personal?*

And, if Chip had told Doug about the baby, he had probably also told him how she had planned to take the twins next week, to do to him exactly what he was already doing to her—trying to make her fall in love with parenthood.

So, if Doug knew—and he damn well did!—then why wasn't he saying anything? Why wasn't he confessing to his own plans, and letting her off the hook? After all, she was pregnant. Didn't she deserve to be coddled, and humored—and let off the hook? It wasn't as if she was the only one who was keeping a secret.

Liz was suddenly so angry, so unexpectedly hurt, that she had to take a deep breath and count to ten before she could speak.

Then she lifted a piece of pepperoni from the slice of pizza in front of her and began to nibble on it, a plan already formulating in her mind. A plan that would turn Doug inside out and scramble his brains. A bit of revenge he richly deserved, no matter how much she loved him! "No. I wasn't expecting a call. Although I really must say that I'm surprised that Candie and Chip haven't phoned to check on the twins."

Doug chewed on this, literally and figuratively, for about ten seconds, then shot her a silly, embarrassed, patently false grin. "Well, damn, that's right, Liz. Candie *did* call. Misses the terrible twosome something terrible, I think were the words she used. Guess it must have slipped my mind.''

Liar, liar, pants on fire! Liz hid an evil smile behind a discreet cough. Okay. Now she knew what she was going to do. She was going to make Doug's life a living hell for the next two days, and she didn't care if they were both guilty of trying to trick the other one. Because he sure was acting more guilty than she, and she rather enjoyed seeing the great Doug Marlow, vice-president and all-around competent executive, laid low by a tangle of fibs.

"The terrible twosome, huh? They must really feel as if they'd made a lucky escape this week, don't you think? And," she added, looking down at the pizza so that Doug couldn't see her eyes, "I imagine I can't blame them."

Doug went rock still, a forkful of the tossed salad Liz had made halfway to his lips. "You can't blame them?"

"Could anybody?" Liz continued, picking up an empty baby bottle that had somehow gotten stuck between the couch cushions earlier and eyeing it as if it were filled with snakes rather than some rapidly congealing formula. "Charlie and Chelsea are real sweethearts, but they certainly take a lot of care."

Still holding the baby bottle, she swung her arm wide, indicating the clutter all around them. "I mean, just look at this living room, Doug. Wall-to-wall baby stuff! I'll give you five dollars if you can find the television remote control—and I don't think I've had a moment to so much as look at the headlines on that stack of newspapers you haven't had time to take out to the recycling bins.''

Doug looked at the room. "Well, yeah, we *have* been a little overrun—''

"And have you noticed Candie's figure? She still has at least twenty pounds to lose. But she says she can't seem to diet because every time the twins are sleeping or playing in the playpens, she makes a beeline to the refrigerator, eating to keep up her strength. I don't know, Doug. There's a lot to think about, you know?''

"Candie and Chip are happy," Doug said, looking as if he might pout at any moment.

"Oh, they're ecstatic! I agree. And I adore the twins. But there's more to consider than just how cute and cuddly they are," Liz persisted. "There're college funds, and braces, and their first driver's licenses—can you envision Charlie behind the wheel of a car? And what about a parent's own career?''

She picked up her plate and walked into the kitchen, unable to continue to look Doug in the eye and still keep a straight face. Poor darling. He was really suffering. But not enough to break down and tell her what he knew—which was why she wasn't about to let him off the hook. Not yet. "Yes," she said, sighing theatrically, "there's certainly a lot to think about. It's a good thing you said the C-C's could stay here this week, Doug. A very good thing.''

"Yeah. Right," Doug grumbled, following her with his own plate, which still held two uneaten pieces of pizza. "I'm just brilliant, I am. A regular Einstein."

Chapter Four

Thursday—Somewhere to the Left of Infinity

Doug woke up to find that he was hugging the "Tonight Not Tonight" pillow to his chest—with the "wrong" side facing him! A moment later the damn thing went flying across the room, helped on its way by a few choice words he uttered under his breath.

He collapsed against the mattress again after checking and finding that Liz wasn't lying next to him, listening as he heard her voice in the kitchen as she talked to Chelsea, who was singing for her breakfast.

How funny, he thought to himself. He could now tell which twin was crying, without ever going into their room. How had he been able to do that?

Chelsea had called him "Da" yesterday in the midst of trying to remove his left eyebrow from his skull. Da-Da. She had also called Charlie Da-Da, and her toy teddy bear, and the weatherman on Channel Seven—but it had made Doug feel all warm and sort of *squishy* inside anyway.

Doug closed his eyes, a smile playing around his lips, and said the words inside his head, testing them, measuring them. Da-Da. Daddy. Dad. They added up to a lifetime of parenting...

"Da-Da! Da-Da!"

"Daddy! Throw me the ball!"

"Dad? Can I borrow the car?"

"Hi, Pop! We brought your grandson to see you!"

Grandson? Doug sat up with a jerk, running his hands through his hair. "Slow down, Gramps," he told himself aloud, shaking his head. "First you've got to get Liz to admit she's pregnant."

His words hung there, suspended above him in the air, and he listened to them again and again, the voice of his conscience starting to sound like a broken record. *Get Liz to admit she's pregnant? That's first? Oh, I don't think so, bucko!*

"Yeah, you're right. I don't think so, either," he muttered, throwing back the sheet and walking into the bathroom, clad only in his sweat shorts. Quickly stripping, he turned on the shower and stood under the needle-like spray, soaking his weary head.

First, Doug's inner voice told him as he lathered his body, continuing this two-way conversation with himself, *you're going to have to do some real talking, buddy-boy. Some really, really good talking! Starting with "I love you, Liz. Will you marry me?"*

"Yeah, right. Just ask her. Miss 'Not Tonight.' And what if she says no?" he asked himself as he stepped beneath the spray of water once more. "Dumb question, Doug," he grumbled. "I can't even consider that she'd say no. Because she loves me. She does, damn it," he reiterated, trying to convince his conscience—or himself.

Okay, his conscience jabbed at him, clearly not impressed. *So you're irresistible, a real legend in your own mind. And the woman loves you, although heaven only knows why, seeing as how you aren't exactly the King of Romance. But, as long as we're doing what-ifs here—what if Dr. Wilbert told her she isn't having a baby after all? Have you considered that one? And, while you're doing all this deep thinking, have you considered that maybe, deep down inside, Liz doesn't want to have kids? That, even though she thought she was pregnant, and thought she wanted to have a baby, now that she has found out she's not, she's feeling pretty lucky? Especially with the C-C's bunking here, showing her just how totally involving a baby can be? Liz has got this great career going, remember. You want a baby, sure, but nobody's asking you to put your career on hold. Nobody's asking you to throw up. Or carry a bowling ball around everywhere you go for nine months. Or go through labor and delivery.*

"Not pregnant?" Doug shook his head, dismissing that thought, as well. "No, she's pregnant. The crackers, the races to the bathroom in the morning—the mood swings, for crying out loud. Oh, she's pregnant, all right.''

She's something else, Dougie-boy, his conscience—always quicker on the uptake than he expected—whispered in his ear. *She's one smart lady. If Chip talked to you, what makes you think Candie didn't talk to her? Huh? Think about that one for a couple of minutes while you stand here trying to drown yourself. If you know that she wanted the twins here, and she knows that you wanted the twins here, and if you both know that she's pregnant, and Liz is acting all mushy around the C-C's even while she's saying babies are too much work—well, aren't you beginning to smell a rat?*

"She's on to me!" Doug exclaimed, never before realizing what a great echo chamber his tiled shower made, so that he lowered his voice as he continued his conversation with himself. "That has to be it! The chocolate/chocolate-chip ice cream probably gave me away. I knew it was overkill, but I couldn't seem to help myself. And now she *knows.* She knows everything. And she knows *I* know everything, and that's why she's giving me all this junk about babies being too much trouble. Because she's mad as hell at me and wants to watch while I jump through a couple of hoops!"

He let his breath out in a rush. "Which also means that we've both descended to kindergarten level and neither one of us knows squat about what in hell we're going to do next.''

You could murder Chip, for starters. Without his big mouth, you could still be hiding only one secret, instead of three. Your plan, Liz's plan, and Liz's pregnancy. Yes, you might consider murdering Chip. Because now that Liz knows you know about the baby, how are you going to convince her that you want to marry her solely because you love her? Her, *Doug. Not a pregnant Liz. Just Liz. The woman who just happens to be carrying your child.*

''I've got to convince her that I love her,'' Doug agreed, slamming his hand against the chrome dial, shutting off the shower. ''I've got to go back to the beginning, to the way we were when we first moved in together—show her how special she is to me, how I can't live without her. God, I don't even say the words anymore! No wonder she borrowed the twins. No wonder she hasn't told me about our baby. She really didn't know how I'd handle it. Poor Liz. My poor, darling Liz. I've got to convince her of my love, convince her to marry me.''

He rested his forehead against the cool tile. ''Now, how in hell do I do any of that with Charlie and Chelsea in the house?''

His conscience, his oh-so-smart inner voice, was suddenly conspicuous by its silence....

''You want to go *where?*''

Doug's smile was dazzling. ''Treasure Island, to

watch the Buccaneer Bay Pirate Battle,'' he repeated, as if she hadn't really heard him the first
time. Which she had. She just hadn't believed him
the first time. ''I thought the twins would get a
kick out of the outdoor show. Booming cannon,
lots of explosions—you know. First show is at
four, after the kids wake up from their naps. Come
on, Liz, it'll be fun. And then we can all get ice
cream.''

''Fun.'' She looked at him owlishly, noticing
that he was wearing the T-shirt she'd bought him
the last time they had gone to the Treasure Island
Casino. The whole front of the shirt featured row
after row of the words ''plunder, plunder, plunder,
pillage, gamble, plunder, plunder, plunder,'' written in typewriterlike print.

She reached out and touched his shirt. ''You're
an idiot. You do know that, don't you?''

''Yeah, but you love me,'' he countered, bending to nuzzle the side of her throat. ''Remember
the first time we saw the show? You insisted we
get there an hour early so that we could get restaurant seats right next to the window overlooking
the lagoon. And then you started rooting for the
pirates even before the British ship was in sight.''

''Well, the pirate captain was cute. Sorta looked
like Antonio Banderas, actually.'' Liz smiled, remembering the night, and her first sight of the artificial lagoon complete with wave machine that

had been constructed outside the building. The entire front of the Treasure Island Casino had been fashioned by a master of set design, so that it looked like an old sailing village; with small houses lining the cliffs, and interesting, if fake, artifacts everywhere a person looked.

Earlier in the evening, before dinner, they'd walked along the wooden pathways that bordered the man-made lagoon, commenting on the wonderful detail of the decorations—right down to the real-looking mussels clinging to the real-looking pier supports, even though everything had been molded out of concrete. The artist in her had been dazzled by the originality, the technician in her astounded by the masterful execution of such a difficult design.

The pirate ship was "moored" in the lagoon, as if in its home port, and the British man-of-war actually sailed into the lagoon, hidden out of sight in a side area until the pirate lookout "spotted" it coming into port.

From that moment on, belief was gladly suspended, and the crowd of spectators eagerly entered into the fantasy, watching as the pirate captain rallied his men. There had been explosions enough for any Fourth of July extravaganza, and several graceful swan-dives into the lagoon by sailors "blown" into the water by cannon fire.

And the pirates had won—actually sinking the British man-of-war—and Liz had stood and applauded along with the rest of those gathered to watch the epic sea battle that took place several times a day.

"It was really something, wasn't it?" she said now. "Only in America can we be so splendidly, wonderfully, outrageously tacky. Oh, all right, Doug, it does sound like fun. Let's do it! Help me pack up both diaper bags."

And he had helped her as they made what Doug laughingly called a "troop movement." Two of nearly everything the twins owned had to be toted along with them, including bottles, diapers, wipes, a change of clothing, bibs, car seats—and the huge two-in-one stroller it took Doug twenty minutes to squeeze into the trunk of Liz's car.

But at last they were on their way, Charlie and Chelsea looking out the side windows in the back seat, gibbering and jabbering back and forth as if speaking a language only the two of them understood, apparently delighted to be getting out of the condo for a while.

It had been a long time since Liz had driven down Las Vegas Boulevard toward town, rarely traveling north of McCarran Airport unless she used Highway 15, and she was soon occupied with looking at the new construction that lined both sides of the roadway known the world over as the Strip.

"I see the New York New York is coming along nicely," she said, peering out the window at the casino-hotel under construction, built to look like a slice of the real New York City skyline. "Oh, and the Monte Carlo is going to be gorgeous!" she exclaimed a few minutes later, turning around in her seat to get a better view of the immense stucco structure.

She was getting in the mood for some fun, which surprised and pleased her. "After the show, do you think we could drive down the Strip to the Stratosphere? I've got to get another look at that roller coaster now that it's open to the public—not that I'd ever go on it. No way is anyone going to get me on a roller coaster that's one hundred stories above the ground!"

"Maybe you could try the Space Shot instead, since it's open, too? You know, that upside-down bungee jump that's on the needle of the building?"

"Yeah, right," Liz said, rolling her eyes. "Right before I take up skydiving and after I master lion-taming. I mean, I wouldn't bungee-jump even if I weren't—"

He sliced her a look as she quickly closed her mouth, wondering if it were really possible to swallow one's own foot. My, but the man looked pleased with himself!

"If you weren't what?" he asked, entirely too interested in what she would say next.

But she wasn't about to throw up her hands and confess: "Yes! Yes! I *am* pregnant, you idiot—just like Chip told you I was!" Oh, no. Not in this lifetime! "If I weren't so afraid of heights, of course. But it certainly is a good gimmick, that roller coaster. What do you suppose they'll think up next?"

Doug's smile slipped, but he covered himself nicely, taking them back into the realm of safe, everyday conversation. "Who knows, Liz, but it's bound to be good. You know how it's been lately—another year, another couple of casinos," he said, putting on the turn signal and making the left into the Treasure Island parking area. "And we still haven't been inside the Luxor."

"Silly, isn't it? That we live here, and still haven't seen all of the new casinos."

"Maybe not. I remember my mother telling me that when Dad came courting her, he took her to the top of the Empire State Building. She'd lived in Brooklyn all her life, and had never been there. I have an idea, Liz. We'll have to start going to dinner at a different casino every week for a while. We can start on Fremont Street, at the Golden Nugget. I remember how much you like their hot fudge sundaes."

Liz eased back against the car seat, smiling, willing to forgive him because he was back to "playing fair," which was one of the many things she loved about him. He really was one of the good guys. "That would be nice, and a welcome change from take-out, I'll admit. But we've both been so busy, Doug, especially—"

"I know, hon," he said, cutting off her apology—and she had been about to utter an apology, because it was mostly her work hours that had been creeping closer to sixty a week. "Sort of like ships passing in the night, aren't we? But that's going to change. It's time we got our feet unstuck from the fast track and enjoyed life a little more. Right?"

Liz took in a deep breath and let it out slowly, feeling something deep inside her begin to relax, uncoil. Bless the man. He was trying *so* hard. And, she thought, grinning, she was enjoying his trying *so* much! "Right," she said earnestly, then unbuckled her seat belt as Doug pulled up at the valet entrance and prepared to get Chelsea out of her car seat. "Starting tonight!"

It wasn't until the twins were safely buckled into their stroller that Liz remembered that she was still angry with Doug, and had meant to confound him with her hints that maybe, just maybe, she wasn't the happy camper she had pretended to be when she first realized that Charlie and Chelsea were to be a part of their lives for five days.

No. She had forgotten all about that plan, and the one that was meant to hint that she wasn't too crazy about being a mommy just yet.

And she kept forgetting it while she watched Doug as he wheeled the stroller along the wooden walkway surrounding the lagoon, pointing out the intricacies of the make-believe pirate village...

And while that nice older couple stopped to coo

at the babies, saying that it was easy to see that the twins certainly did favor their handsome, proudly smiling father...

And while the show went on and, each of them holding a twin, they had laughed and shouted along with the others in the audience as the stra-tegically-placed mist machines had sprayed water over their heads, keeping the air cool and fragrant in the midst of the dry Las Vegas heat...

And while the twins napped like little angels in their stroller as she and Doug sat on benches and licked at rapidly melting ice-cream cones...

And even while they were carrying two cranky babies back into the condo at twilight, and after Charlie and Chelsea had played through their baths, and giggled through their evening meal of rice cereal and formula...

And most definitely while they had closed the door to the spare bedroom on those same two sleepy little miracles and walked, arm in arm, to their own bedroom...

And then she remembered. Remembered that she was angry. Or at least she *should* be angry. Shouldn't she? Well, maybe not. At least not for the next hour or so.

"Which are you, Liz," Doug asked as he gently pushed her down onto the side of the bed, "tired, or hungry? Do you want to get into bed while I make you some toast or something?"

Liz felt herself melting under Doug's suddenly

warm gaze, heated by the sound of his voice, all but liquefied by the sight of his long straight legs beneath his khaki shorts. She quickly took refuge in smoothing down the front of her blouse. "Those twins! My blouse is still damp from their bathwater."

And then, just as she realized that she was blushing, she also realized that she wanted Doug. Really, really wanted him. Right here. Right now. Wow, but the mood swings of pregnancy were coming fast and furious tonight—and she decided she would like to hold onto this particular one for a while. Oh, yeah.

Liz began unbuttoning her blouse, knowing Doug was watching as her new peach-blush lace bra was exposed. She might not be very, very pregnant, but already there had been subtle changes in her body. Her new, expanded bra size being one of them, so that she had done a little shopping while she was in New York. And Doug couldn't seem to take his eyes off her.

She liked that. She really, really liked that. Hell, after the week she'd had, from morning sickness to mood swings, to this ridiculous charade they were both caught up in, she *needed* that!

Liz decided to be coy, because female coyness seemed to be called for, and she was feeling especially feminine at the moment. "You asked me a question, didn't you? Oh, yes—I think I would like some toast."

"You would?" He sounded disappointed, and her spirit soared.

She shot him a come-hither smile as she looked up at him. "Yes, toast definitely would be nice," she said, pulling the shirt off her shoulders, sliding the material down her arms until she was free of it. "With warm, melting butter all over it," she added, seeing the sparkle of interest in Doug's green eyes beginning to flare into flame.

How wonderful it was to be desired by the man she loved. How comforting to know that, after three years, she could still unsettle him, interest him, *tease* him, with just the sight of her body.

"With butter, melting butter," he mumbled distractedly as she stood, unzipping her shorts and allowing them to drop to the carpet so that she could step out of them. She had bought the peach-blush bra on a whim, and that whim had grown to include purchasing the peach-blush lace, French-cut panties that had also been on sale at Bloomingdale's. As whims went, this one now seemed to have bordered on brilliant inspiration.

"Uh-hmm, butter," she said, deliberately turning her back on him as she pulled down the bedspread and reached for the short nightgown she had stuffed under the pillow. She slid her hands behind her back to unclasp the bra. She was driving him crazy, and enjoying every moment of his journey. "And maybe a nice cup of decaffeinated tea? Yes. Tea would be perfect. With lemon."

"Huh?" Doug said, and she could tell that this was a man whose main concern in life, at this moment in time, had little to do with toast or tea. Oh, he was hungry, all right, but this particular appetite wouldn't be satisfied in the kitchen.

"Doug?" she questioned him, turning to face him as she slowly slid her fingertips under the front straps of her opened bra and slid it from her arms. "You look like you're under some sort of strain. Are you all right?"

He leaned past her, picked up her nightgown and held it out to her, keeping it just out of her reach. "Very funny. Do you really want this, Liz? Do you really want toast and tea? Or am I the only one dying here?"

She employed the tip of her tongue to moisten her suddenly dry lips. Maybe she was pushing him just a little too hard. Besides, if he didn't touch her, and touch her very, very soon, she just might explode. "I—I suppose I could, um, *wait* a while for..."

His hands were on her shoulders, drawing her closer. She could feel a tingling sensation in her newly heavy, exquisitely sensitive breasts, and could barely suppress the need to feel her breasts crushed up against Doug's strong chest, cupped in Doug's gentle hands.

"We shouldn't make love in the morning, Liz," he whispered, his voice husky. "You're even more lovely in the evening. And there's so much more time. A whole night stretching ahead of us, so that we can take things more slowly. Enjoy each other more.''

Liz couldn't swallow. Her mouth was as parched as the desert that stretched out beyond the limits of Las Vegas. She couldn't remember the last time Doug had actually tried to seduce her with mere words. Their lovemaking had become almost routine and, as he had said, mostly a hurried morning affair, before they both went off to their jobs.

She felt his hands sliding down her arms, then skimming her waist, his thumbs running along the thin elastic of her panties, teasing her as they trailed across her belly, along the base of her spine. Her knees turned to jelly and she had no choice but to collapse against him.

His hands slipped inside her waistband, cupping her buttocks.

A low moan escaped her lips, and she didn't care that he heard her. Didn't care at all. Had she really been considering employing the ''Not Tonight'' pillow again tonight to punish him for not telling her that he knew what she had to tell him? Had she been out of her mind?

She kept her hands at her sides, not trusting that she had enough strength to raise them to his shoulders, or even to pull that silly T-shirt free of his shorts and slip them beneath the fabric to touch his firmly muscled upper body. ''Doug, I—''

''Shh,'' he whispered into her ear as he moved

forward, holding her close, gently lowering her onto the bed. "Just let me love you, Liz. Just let me love you."

Pushing the bedspread out of the way, he lowered himself beside her, gathering her close. He kissed her again and again and again, his hands stroking the length of her back, soothing her even as he aroused her with his gentleness.

He kissed her forehead, her hair, her closed eyes, the tip of her nose. He nuzzled at her throat, ran the tip of his tongue around her ear, whispering nearly unintelligible love words against her skin.

He took his time, as if he were mapping her, learning every inch of her for the first time, and was suitably awed by the experience.

He didn't tease her. He was loving her. Worshiping her body.

And driving her out of her mind!

When his mouth finally covered her breast, sweetly suckling at her nipple, Liz couldn't hold back the soft moan that escaped her lips. She grabbed at his head with both hands, pushing him against her, feeling the taut line of desire that sliced through her, setting up a nearly unbearable tension between her legs.

"Touch me, Doug," she pleaded, pushing his hands lower when they stubbornly stayed at her waist, his fingertips sketching small, feather-light circles over her slightly rounded stomach as if memorizing this new dimension to her body. "If you love me, Doug—touch me!"

Her breath left her in a long, heartfelt sigh as he slid a hand between her legs, finding her, opening her, beginning to stroke her as she raised herself to him, gave herself to him.

"Do you like this, Liz?" he asked, his voice coming to her from the great distance that divided her body and her mind. "I like this. I like this very much. So warm, so ready."

"Yes," she gritted out from between clenched teeth, amazed at the urgency she felt to have him with her, in her, a part of her. "Please, Doug. Yes!"

And then she was gone, flying away, her body singing its own sweet song as he held her close, strumming her with his fingers, making sweet music on her sensitive, thrumming flesh. He was giving her pleasure, only pleasure, and he kept giving, and giving, and giving.

As she held him, as she nearly sobbed in her release, her pleasure, reaching up to him, he levered himself on top of her, then hesitated.

"Doug?" she asked, feeling his hesitation. "Please, Doug. I won't break. I need you, darling. I need to hold you. I love you so much!"

"And I love you, Liz," he whispered into her ear as his body met hers face-to-face, chest to breast, thigh to thigh. She opened to him, then slid her arms around his back, pulling him closer,

closer, until he had no choice but to give in to the age-old rhythms, the basic union that he had just made so extraordinarily sweet and passionate at the same time.

An expression of need, yes. But an even truer expression of love.

Later—much, much later—they sat together in the living room, feeding each other toast and sipping from their cups of tea, talking over the day as Doug unpacked the bags he had carried home from the casino.

"When did you buy these?" Liz asked, giggling over the pirate scarves and swords Doug dumped in her lap.

"While you were changing Chelsea in the rest room," he told her, grinning as she shook her head over his silliness. "I thought the twins would look cute in them. And they match their little shirts, don't you think?"

Liz did her best to keep a straight face. "Oh, yes, indeed. Although I doubt Charlie will be using that cutlass for a while if Candie has anything to say about it. Honestly, Doug, you're a marketer's dream. What else is in that bag?"

"I'm not sure. I just sort of grabbed, you know? Charlie's a great kid, but I never noticed that he has six hands—at least not until I was trying to push that damn stroller around the displays inside the gift shop. Feel lucky, Liz. We almost came home with a hot-pink plastic back scratcher.''

Liz fell back against the couch cushions, laughing at Doug's amazed expression. "You're going to be a wonderful daddy, darling," she said, then sobered, busying herself in replacing all the twins' booty in the plastic bag. "Someday, that is. If you ever decide to... That is, if the day ever comes when you... Oh, the devil with it!''

She dropped the bag onto the coffee table and turned on the couch, taking Doug's hands in hers. ''There's something I have to tell you—''

There was a stomach-turning dull *thump* in the next room, followed by a loud, ear-piercing scream, and Doug and Liz were both on their feet and running toward the twins' bedroom, to find that Charlie—such a bright, intelligent, *adventuresome* child—had awakened and discovered how to get out of his Portacrib.

Unfortunately, he had made a bad landing, jamming himself between the Portacrib and the dresser, and Liz watched, horrified, as Doug threw on the light, then lifted the Portacrib and all but tossed it across the room in order to get to Charlie.

Chelsea, awakening immediately, was already screaming as loudly as her brother, and Liz went to her and picked her up, cuddling her close as they both watched Doug run his hands along Charlie's body, checking him for broken bones.

"I think he's okay, except for this cut on his

ear," Doug said, taking the handkerchief Liz handed him and holding it to the side of Charlie's head, where there was a lot more blood than Liz felt comfortable looking at—not that seeing any injury on the little darling would be "all right" with her.

Charlie was still screaming, proving that he certainly was alert, and Liz took some comfort in that, but not much. "Did you get a look at it? Do you think he'll need stitches? Oh, God, I hope he doesn't need stitches."

Doug pulled the handkerchief away from Charlie's head, looked, and winced. "Stitches, Liz. One, maybe two. Poor kid! I had enough of them growing up to recognize the signs. Chip left us a written authorization-to-treat, just in case the C-C's needed a doctor."

Liz was already pulling out the thick sheaf of papers Candie had left for her. "Got it!" she said, starting for the door. "You're okay in your shorts, if you can slip into your sneakers, but I'll have to get dressed. I'll only be a minute."

He followed her out of the room, the little boy no longer crying, but trying to pull the handkerchief away from his head. "Are you sure you want to go along?" he asked her. "Charlie has to be in his car seat, anyway."

Liz had already laid Chelsea on the bed and was climbing back into the clothes she had worn to the casino. "And who's going to hold the handkerchief to his head? No, Doug. Chelsea and I are going.''

Liz couldn't believe how calm she was, buttoning her blouse, filling a diaper bag with two bottles of formula from the refrigerator—just in case the twins decided they were hungry—gathering together disposable diapers, pacifiers, baby wipes, and a can of soda for Doug.

They were out the door within five minutes, Doug saying ruefully, ''Ah, parenthood. I wonder how our parents survived it!''

Chapter Five

Friday—The Twelfth of Never

*Ah, parenthood. I wonder how our parents sur-
vived it!* Doug winced as he remembered his words
of the previous evening. Had they sounded as if he
had looked fatherhood in the face and not liked
what he had seen?

Not that Liz seemed to have heard him. Oh, no.
Liz had been too occupied in performing one small
miracle after another, beginning with her cool-
headed handling of the trip to the hospital, and
continuing with her mastery of the medical staff at
the emergency room of the local hospital.

She'd asked for, and gotten, a plastic surgeon to
care for Charlie after the physician on call had concluded that the baby did indeed need three stitches
on the outside of his little pink ear. She had produced the paper allowing treatment, then plunked
herself down on the bed, holding Charlie close, and
saying that she would continue to hold him as he
was given a shot to numb his skin, and while the
stitches were put in place.

She hadn't flinched. She hadn't winced. She
hadn't cried and run for "cover," asking Doug to

stay with Charlie. She'd just taken over, the mother lion protecting her cub, and the little guy had certainly been the better for it, holding tightly to her, his pacifier dangling out of the corner of his mouth as the doctor worked.

It had been only later—much later, around two in the morning when they had returned to the condo and both twins were back in bed and sound asleep, that Liz had begun to shake.

"That poor baby!" she had exclaimed, her hands trembling as she'd pushed them through her hair, pulling it away from her face, so that Doug could see tears glistening in her eyes. "He was *so* scared!"

"No, he wasn't," Doug had told her sincerely, sitting down beside her and slinging an arm around her shoulders, pulling her close. "He knew you were there. You were wonderful, Liz."

She sighed, then laid her head against his chest. "No. *You* were wonderful. It was all I could do to sit in the back seat between the twins, holding that clean towel to Charlie's head. I couldn't have driven the car, I was shaking too badly. You know, the twins are so cute, so lovable, that sometimes I forget what a responsibility they are. Babies aren't all pink-and-blue booties and sweet-smelling kisses, are they?"

"No, they're not," he'd assured her as she'd covered her mouth with both hands, hiding a most prodigious yawn. "And, when they come in bunches, like Charlie and Chelsea, they're even more responsibility. But they're also twice the joy, twice the love."

"Uh-hmm," Liz had murmured, snuggling closer, her whole body going limp, as if she had been running on all cylinders—which she had—and now had run out of gas. "Lots of love. Lots…lots of…"

Doug chuckled as he remembered how she had fallen asleep against him, just like one of the twins—awake and talking one moment, dead to the world the next. He had slipped his arms around her back, beneath her knees, and had carried her into bed, tucking the covers around her as she turned, sighed, and burrowed into the pillows.

But now it was morning. And he was hearing his words, and her words, and wondering if Charlie's little accident had once again put a crimp into his—and Liz's—"best laid plans."

Maybe he wouldn't have been so worried if Liz had awakened this morning full of vim and vigor, ready to tackle a new day, smiling and still caught in some vaguely remembered afterglow of what, he had to admit to himself, had been some of the most mind-blowing lovemaking the two of them had ever shared.

Instead, she had sat up when Charlie woke crying—and immediately raced headlong into the bathroom, where she had proceeded to be very, very sick.

"Reaction to Charlie's accident setting in," she had told him sheepishly when she'd finally joined him in the kitchen, as he held Charlie for his bottle and Chelsea lay in the playpen, being a very good baby and holding her own bottle. "I guess my stomach just registered its own vote on being hauled to the emergency room after midnight."

So now it was ten in the morning, and he was walking up and down the block, pushing the C-C's in their stroller, wondering yet again if Liz was *ever* going to tell him that she was pregnant.

"She's probably trying to forget it," he told the world at large, if the world at large cared to listen in to his dispirited grumblings. "She came so close last night—damn *close!* And then *wham!* we're off to the hospital. Well, I've had it. The minute Chip and Candie collect these kids this afternoon, Liz and I are sitting down for a long talk, and I'm going to tell her I know everything. It's the only way. I mean, if we wait much longer, the baby will be able to tell me himself!"

He stopped walking at the corner, preparing to turn around, when he realized that, if he was going to tell Liz what he knew—and what she already knew—he'd better be prepared to dazzle her with some pretty neat footwork meant to carry them over the rough spots. But how? What could he do?

Whatever he decided upon, it would have to be dazzling, yes. But also romantic. And sweet. And adorable. No. Charlie and Chelsea were adorable. He would have to settle for sweet and romantic.

But what?

"Of course! I have my charge card. Why not? Have plastic, will travel!" he exclaimed a moment later, turning the twin-size stroller on a dime, like a kid on a bicycle doing "wheelies," and headed back to the condo at a near run. "You want to go bye-bye in the car? Oh, yeah, kiddies. We're going for a ride. All the way back to the Strip. All the lights, all the noise, all the people telling you how cute you are. You'd like that, wouldn't you?"

Chelsea began to giggle as Doug jogged down the sidewalk, heading for Liz's car, thankful he still had her keys in his pocket, and he decided to take that giggle as a yes.

"Hi, Candie and Chip! Sit down, tell me all about your trip!"

Liz shook her head, deciding she sounded too cheerful.

"Candie! Chip! My goodness, was your plane early? We weren't expecting you so soon! The kids are napping. Why don't you go somewhere and come back later?"

No. That wouldn't work, either.

"Hi! Candie and Chip! Don't you look rested! Come in, sit down—and did I tell you that Doug and the twins are missing?"

Liz collapsed on the couch, dropping her head

in her hands. "Oh, God," she groaned, wondering if she could kill Doug and plead temporary insanity.

The laughably homely cuckoo clock Doug had brought back from his trip to Geneva last summer chirped out the hour of three, and Liz groaned again. What was she going to do?

Chip and Candie would be knocking on their door in less than an hour, and Doug had kidnapped the twins. It was bad enough that Charlie was wearing a big white bandage over his right ear, but to have to tell Candie that she had somehow *misplaced* two seven-month-old children? Oh, yeah. That made the bandage a mere trifle, definitely.

Liz leaped to her feet, unable to remain still. "All right, all right, you're panicking here. You went to take a shower and when you came out you were all alone. No big deal. You know Doug has the twins. You know the stroller is gone. You know your car is gone. Simple deduction here, Liz—Doug and the twins are in your car...heading for...heading for... *You don't know where they're heading!*"

She shoved a hand through her hair, trying to calm herself. "Don't lose your cool, woman. Doug has the babies. They're safe enough. If he remembers to strap them into their stroller, because Charlie is still trying to climb out of everything, and Chelsea always follows where Charlie leads. Climbing—at his age! Why did Candie have to give birth to a physically brilliant child prodigy? And there's so much else to worry about! What if Doug feeds them something silly, like a blueberry ice, so that they meet their mother, their lips and tongues all blue, looking as if they've got some terrible tropical disease or something? Oh, how could he be so *inconsiderate!*"

Stomping into the spare bedroom, Liz picked up a diaper bag and began loading it with baby things. Rattles. A box of wipes. The infant rectal thermometer she'd been so glad she hadn't had to use. A bottle of fragrant baby oil.

At least she would have everything organized and ready for Candie and Chip to pack up in their minivan and take back to their lovely house. Who knew? Maybe if she just kept throwing playpens and Portacribs and high chairs at them, they might not even notice that there were no two matching car seats—or twins to strap into them.

Just as she was reaching under the small sofa bed they'd shoved into the corner of the room to accommodate the Portacribs, trying to rescue an errant toy, the doorbell rang.

Liz froze in place, her heart leaping into her throat. "Oh, God," she said again, because He obviously had been busy elsewhere when she'd appealed to Him earlier. "Now, what do I do?"

Fake it, she heard from deep inside her head, and she suddenly began to laugh. "Fake it? That couldn't have been a Heavenly Helpful Hint," she told herself, shaking her head as she scrambled to her feet and headed back into the living room as the doorbell rang a second time.

She took a deep breath and opened the door.

"Elizabeth Somerville?" a young man in a tan uniform said from somewhere behind a very large bouquet of red roses.

"Um..." Liz stared at the roses, trying to find her voice. "Um—yes, *yes,* I'm Elizabeth Somerville. Are those for *me?*"

"Well," the young man began, stepping into the living room, "I only brought this one with me, just to make sure I had the right place before I unloaded the rest." He stopped in the middle of the living-room area, looked around, then placed the vase on the coffee table. "Twins, huh? My sister's sister-in-law has twins. Really can kill a room. I'll be right back."

"O-kay," Liz agreed absently, already searching the bouquet for a card, but there wasn't any. Maybe in the next batch? The next batch! There were more? She put a hand to her mouth, stifling a giggle that was threatening to escape. "Douglas Marlow, you're an idiot! And I love you, love you, love you!"

A huge Boston fern arrived next. The roses went on top of the television, the fern next to one of the playpens.

Which meant that the potted palm ended up on the kitchen bar, and the miniature orange tree was balanced precariously on the tray of one of the high chairs. The living room was rapidly turning into a jungle of beautiful plants, just like those she'd always wanted but never had bought for herself. And Doug had remembered that she had wanted plants. And that she adored red roses.

He was a wonderful man. Just wonderful. Even if he had kidnapped the twins.

Last to be brought into the condo was a small florist's box containing a delicate wrist corsage of creamy white tea roses with bits of baby's breath mixed in, the whole package tied with lovely golden ribbon.

"The note's in the box," the young man said, then refused a tip as he backed out the door, telling her that the "nut" who had ordered all of this had already taken care of it. "You'd better say yes, or my boss says the guy will probably stop payment on the check," he told her just before he closed the door—and only moments before Liz, nervous beyond belief, ripped opened the small white envelope.

Inside was only a small card that read: "As the song says, Liz, 'Our time is now, our journey is just beginning.'"

No. That's not quite right. It's "The time is now, your journey is just beginning." Isn't it? Liz frowned for a moment, then raced to the stereo, sliding in the compact disc with the music from the *EFX* show at the MGM Grand. She sat down, cross-legged, on the carpet in front of the stereo, listening to Michael Crawford as he played the role of the EFX! Master, urging her to give in to fantasy and enter a world where "magic and mystery turn to reality."

"Oh, you big dope!" she said, sniffling, blinking back tears as she listened to the first song from the show, the one that had become her personal favorite. The song spoke of love being forever, a love that would last for all time, a love that waited "somewhere in time."

And in the second song on the compact disc, Michael Crawford sang what Doug had so adorably misquoted: "The time is now, your journey is just beginning...."

His journey. Her journey. Their journey together.

The doorbell rang again.

"Delivery for Ms. Elizabeth Somerville," a young man in a blue uniform said as she opened the door once more.

Liz just nodded dumbly and accepted the thick white envelope, shutting the door on the young man without saying a word, already ripping open the envelope, feeling like a young girl on Christmas morning.

A pair of first-class, round-trip airline tickets to Hawaii, and a brochure on a luxury hotel spilled out into her hand. *Hawaii?* Liz had always wanted to go to Hawaii! She opened a folded white sheet, saw the letterhead of a local travel agency and read the itinerary: leaving McCarran airport Saturday morning...returning the following Saturday.

"Oh, you wonderful, *adorable* man!" she exclaimed, spinning around in a circle. "Who ever said you couldn't be romantic?"

This time, when the doorbell rang, Liz didn't even think about the possibility that Candie and Chip might be standing on the other side of the door, chomping at the bit to see their babies.

"Ms. Elizabeth Somerville?" asked a fashionably dressed young woman doing her best to hold on to a large white plastic garment bag, another white shopping bag at her feet. "Your wardrobe for this evening. And a note you're to open first," she ended, passing an envelope to Liz, who had gone beyond stunned, beyond pleased, and all the way to giggling insensibility. She had never had so much fun in her life!

After the woman had left, Liz laid the garment bag on the couch and read the note which was, as she had suspected, from Doug. "No peeking, darling! Just be ready when Candie comes to the condo at six, and she'll help you. Hey—are we having fun yet?"

When Candie comes to the condo at six?

Liz eyed the garment bag as if it might be filled with live snakes, then went into the kitchen to make herself a cup of tea. Tea seemed like a tame choice, considering the state of her nerves, but she was an expectant mommy now, and her choices were limited.

The phone rang and Liz nearly jumped out of her skin.

"Hi, Liz!" Chip Risley all but chirped into her ear. "Funny thing happened at the airport. Doug and the babies were waiting there to meet us. So we took the C-C's home with us, in case you were worried—which you shouldn't be, because Doug is a natural dad in case you haven't noticed, and he sure does hope you have—and they're taking their naps in their own cribs, and darn happy about it, Candie says. Love what you've done to Charlie's ear, by the way. He looks all boy now, you know? Doug says he was a real champ through the whole thing. So, anyway, Candie will be at the condo around six, or sooner if I can't hold her back. See you later. Bye!"

Liz stood there holding the receiver, having said nothing after her first tentative "Hello?"

In the background, breaking through the haze of her excitement and confusion, Michael Crawford was singing the words: "Magic and mystery turn to reality...."

And Liz giggled. Again.

Candie arrived at five-thirty, looking refreshed from her trip, beautiful in her pale pink suit, and as if she was about to burst with happiness. "You've got your makeup on already? Good!" she declared, after giving Liz a big hug and kiss. "Have you guessed what's happening?"

Liz nodded. "I have a fairly good idea, but I still don't believe it."

"Believe it, Liz. The man is crazy! Met us at the airport, the twins in tow—God, how I missed those two hellions!—and all but dragged us along with him, all the time making calls on your car phone. Flowers, plane tickets—" She hesitated, then ended sheepishly, "And other stuff." She walked through the living room, which was fairly back to normal except for all the folded baby equipment Liz had stacked against the far wall, and opened the door to the master bedroom. "Is the gown in here? Isn't it *gorgeous?* You did peek, didn't you?"

Liz felt her stomach do a small flip. "Gown? I had thought a dress...or a suit. But a gown? And *no,* of course I didn't peek, Candie!"

Her friend shook her head. "Such willpower, Liz. If I had half the willpower you do, I'd fit back into my pretwins clothes by now. Ah, here it is. Take off that bathrobe, Liz, and let's get you dressed. The limo will be here soon."

"Limo?" Liz parroted as she mechanically stripped out of her blue satin bathrobe, revealing the skimpy white lingerie she had somehow decided might be "appropriate" for the definitely exciting evening Doug had planned for them. "Will I need our suitcases? I may be dim, but I figured

I should pack for Doug and myself. Hawaii, Candie! Can you believe it?''

And then, as Candie unzipped the garment bag, and pulled out a tea-length wedding gown of softest silk, the bodice overlaid in lace and pearls, Liz didn't say anything at all. She just sat down on the edge of the bed, and cried.

"I knew you'd do that," Candie said, putting down the gown and coming to sit beside Liz, pulling her into her arms and rocking her, as she would have one of the twins. "Should I show you the veil and shoes now, or will that just increase the waterworks? You know, Doug is a brilliant, brilliant man. No explanations, no confessions—just marry the girl, and let everything else work itself out later. He'll probably own that bank he works at someday. Oh, that's it, honey, you just have a good cry. For ten minutes. It's your hormones. They're all over the place right now. Then we'll have to fix your makeup and get you dressed. Time's a-wasting, you know."

Doug was wearing out the sidewalk outside 200 South Third Street, looking at his watch one moment, walking to the curb and peering down the street the next.

"Maybe she decided to elope with the flower-shop guy," Chip said as he watched from his vantage point, leaning up against the wall of the building where everyone from eloping lumberjacks to multimarried movie stars had come to get their "no hassle, thirty-five dollars and you've got it" marriage license. "Or she figured out she really doesn't love you, after three years of knowing you. God knows, she'd have her reasons, if you're always so thin-skinned. I mean, you nearly took my head off the last time you asked if I still have the wedding rings in my pocket."

"You could shut up any time, Chip, you know," Doug all but growled at his best friend. He hadn't been this nervous since...since— Hell, he'd *never* been this nervous!

It had all seemed so reasonable while he was in that "Let's just *do* this!" whirl of planning and buying and arranging. But now, with Liz being damn near fifteen minutes late...? Well, reality was beginning to set in.

He had acted, yes. But without ever apologizing for taking the twins in while Chip and Candie went on their second honeymoon. Without explaining that he knew Liz had planned the same sort of scheme to show him the joys of parenthood. Without a word about the fact that he knew she was pregnant—and that *she* knew that he knew she was pregnant.

And all without a word of love, or commitment—or ever getting down on one knee and just *asking* the woman to marry him.

"I blew it, I blew it, I blew it!" he exclaimed when another line of cars moved down the street, and Liz's limo was still not in sight. "Not only is my mother going to kill me for not inviting her to the wedding, but I never even invited the *bride*." He turned to Chip. "You did say the limo would be there at six, didn't you?"

Chip nodded. "At the condo at six, here at six-thirty, with the chapel at Treasure Island reserved for seven-thirty. Get married, have a little wedding dinner, and watch the pirates blow the British navy all to hell. Now would you relax? You're giving me the creeps. I mean, you look great in that tux, but I'm beginning to think a straitjacket might have been a better choice." He pushed himself away from the wall, rolling his eyes. "Thank you, Lord, here comes the bride!"

Doug turned in the direction Chip was pointing and tried to take a step forward. His legs wouldn't work! And he couldn't breathe. What if Candie were alone in the limousine? What if Liz had only thought she wanted romance and flowers, and what she really had wanted was a calm, controlled discussion of what had gone on these past five days, laid out in order, commented on, dissected, and then laid to rest with mutual apologies? What if she didn't really want to marry him? What if she did, but she was stuck in the bathroom again, sick to her stomach?

Stop it! his inner voice ordered, after a silence of several days. *Men! We go to war, we conquer worlds, we build empires, we climb mountains, cross deserts—and damn near every one of us falls apart at the seams the moment we fall in love. You can do this, Doug. Liz loves you. Remember?*

"She loves me, she loves me," Doug chanted under his breath as the limo pulled up to the curb and he reached out to open the door.

"Oh, don't you look handsome!" Candie exclaimed a moment later as she all but tumbled out of the back seat and gave Doug a big kiss. "I'm sorry we're late, but the baby-sitter called with a question about where I keep the extra disposable diapers, and—"

"Excuse me, Candie," Doug said, picking up the chattering woman at the waist and literally handing her to Chip before climbing into the back seat and shutting the door.

Liz was sitting there, the soft folds of the skirt of the gown he had picked for her spread out on the seat, the full, short veil pinned to the back of her head. She didn't look at him, but kept her eyes on her lap, where she was plucking at the ribbons on her wrist corsage with the fingers of her right hand.

"Hi," he said when she didn't say anything.

She still didn't look at him. "Hi, yourself," she whispered, her voice almost breaking.

He sat back in the seat beside her, staring straight ahead.

And said nothing.

While she said nothing.

Until she said: "I was going to have the twins stay with us so that you could fall in love with them and want a baby of our own."

"I know."

"And you had the twins stay with us so that I could fall in love with them and want a baby of our own."

"It's the curse of great minds, Liz. They think alike."

Silence fell inside the limo.

"I do want us to have babies, Liz," Doug said at last, turning on the seat and taking her hands in his as he tipped his head so that he could look into her tear-bright eyes. "I want us to have lots of babies. But not as much as I want to spend the rest of my life with you, loving you, being loved by you. I—I just think you should know that."

He watched as she blinked, and a single tear dropped onto the back of his hand. "I love you so much, Doug," Liz said, looking at him, her heart exposed, a trace of reticence still evident in the tone of her voice. "But I should have told you, and probably should warn you that—"

"About your pregnancy?" he interrupted, tipping up her chin with his crooked index finger. "Darling, you don't have to say anything. I already know all about our own miracle."

She let out her breath on a sigh. "You do? You know *all* about it? Did you talk with Dr. Wilbert? I didn't think you knew it all, because even I...

And now you're doing all of this—'' she gave a small wave of her hand, indicating the limo, her gown, the whole range of romantic silliness he had chased with such fervor all of the afternoon.

"I'm doing this—we're doing this—because we love each other, Liz. The pregnancy is just our wedding present to each other. If you'll have me?"

And then Liz smiled at him, and it seemed as if the sun had come out inside the limo. "If I'll *have* you? Oh, Doug—did you ever doubt it?"

"Didn't you doubt me?" he asked, easing his hand into his tuxedo pocket and pulling out a small jeweler's box containing an engagement ring that would soon be joined by its matching wedding ring. "It took us a while, darling, but I think it's time for our journey to begin. Inside that building, at the chapel at Treasure Island, in Hawaii—and all the way to the end of our lives. Liz, I love you with all my heart and promise to tell you so every day we're on that journey. Will you marry me?"

She put a hand to her trembling mouth. And then, being Liz, being the woman he loved with all his heart and soul, she smiled through her tears and said, "Oh, why not. After all, I am dressed for it."

Epilogue

On the Way to Twenty-one...

"You know, the next time you're about to make a small confession to me in the back of a limousine, I think I'm going to take you up on it," Doug said as he stood in his borrowed hospital greens, trying to remember to breathe.

"But, darling," Liz said, reaching up a hand to him from the hospital bed, "I did try to say something. You, however, cut me off by saying you already knew everything. I didn't know *how* you knew everything but, being a good little wife-to-be, I believed you. Besides, we've known for four months that we were having more than one baby."

"Two, Liz. Dr. Filbert said *two*. Three is one more than two. How in hell did the guy miss four and one-half pounds of baby?"

"Doug, you have to stop calling that poor man Dr. Filbert, even if it is a joke. I think he's beginning to feel insulted. And the third little guy finally did show up on ultrasound in the delivery room, after hiding behind the other two all this time."

"Three babies," Doug said, shaking his head. "And us with a nursery ready for two of them.

Time to get the plastic out again, Liz, to order another bassinet, another crib, another high chair—and we can probably return the stroller and get that bigger one. Thank God we were able to buy that four-bedroom house in Chip and Candie's neighborhood. We're going to need all the help we can get, the first couple of months at least.''

''You're upset,'' Liz said, pushing out her bottom lip.

''I am *not* upset,'' he hastened to tell her sincerely, because in truth, he wasn't. He was delighted. Overjoyed. Overwhelmed, definitely, but also over the moon. He was the father of three children—two boys and one girl. All three of them healthy, all three of them snuggled up in the nursery down the hall, being fussed over by a small battalion of nurses who had told him in all sincerity—and he could tell they were being very sincere—that his were three of the prettiest little babies they'd ever seen.

''We have to come up with another boy's name,'' Liz reminded him just before she yawned. Poor baby, she'd had a busy day, he thought. ''We only had 'Eliza' and 'Garrett' picked out. Any suggestions?'' She giggled. ''We could name him 'Fred,' I suppose. Then we'd have an *E* an *F* and a *G*. At the rate we're going, we might be able to cover the whole alphabet.''

''Very funny.'' Doug smiled, then shook his head. ''To tell you the truth, I'd like to name him

'William,' if you don't mind. And William Marlow sounds a lot better than William Wilbert Marlow."

"You want to name our son after Dr. Wilbert?" Liz asked him as a soft knock sounded at the door to her private room. "Why, you softie, you. He was brilliant in the delivery room, wasn't he?"

"No, hon," Doug said, leaning down to kiss his wife's forehead. "*You* were brilliant. And, in case I haven't told you so in the past five minutes, I love you, Elizabeth Marlow. I love you twice—no, *three* times more than before. And I thank you from the bottom of my heart for being you."

"Well, that was lovely," Chip Risley said from somewhere behind Doug. "And Candie heard it, which means that I'll be lectured all the way home about how romantic you are and what an insensitive schmuck I am. Thanks, Doug. Thanks a lot."

"Oh, put a sock in it, Chip, and move over so I can go give Liz a kiss," Candie ordered, also motioning for Doug to get out of the way as she approached the hospital bed and embraced Liz. "Had to go one up on us, did you, Liz? Chip says there has to be something in the water here in Las Vegas, with the two of us having multiples. Of course, you do know this means the C-C's hand-me-downs are going to be one matching outfit short? We just saw the babies in the nursery, and they look magnificent! Two of them with fuzzy blond hair, and the third with hair as dark as

Doug's. You'll be turning heads everywhere you take them!''

Doug was content to stand in the corner of the room, allowing Candie and Chip's bubbly conversation to wash over him as he watched Liz smile and answer questions—and look in his direction every few minutes, to mouth the words: "I love you."

He blinked away tears, not the first he had shed on this most trying, emotional, incredibly fantastic, never-to-be-forgotten day. She loved him. As he loved her. And, together, they would hold their children's hands and guide them, teach them, and show them this great wide world where magic and mystery turned into a most wonderful reality.

* * * * *

DADDY'S GIRL

Kathleen Eagle

For Elizabeth, who is
her daddy's little girl,
her mother's beloved daughter and dear friend

Chapter One

The blasted dipsticks had turned pink. All six of them.

Dana Barron had never dreamed it could happen to her. She had never truly understood how an intelligent woman could permit such a thing to happen. When her friend Sandy Wentz had confided the news of her unplanned pregnancy, Dana had actually said, "How did *that* happen?"

As soon as the words had cleared her throat, she'd realized how stupid they sounded. "The usual way," Sandy had quipped, obviously too depressed to manage the clever, snappy sarcasm she'd always been so capable of producing. Impending motherhood, Dana had then surmised, softened a person. She had apologized profusely. Sandy was newly married, but married, nonetheless. She and Tom had been planning to wait for a couple of years, take one thing at a time, get themselves settled into married life before they started a family. Wise decision, Dana thought. Her friend Sandy had always been as prudent as she, which was why she'd blurted out the first words that had come to her mind when Sandy had broken the news.

How did that happen?

It happened to people who thought they were too smart, too sophisticated, entirely too far above the teeming, breeding masses. It happened to people who thought they had everything under control. It happened to people who knew it all, or thought they did. Dana quite plainly fit the profile to a tee, and she deserved her comeuppance. She believed in justice. Well, justice had surely been done.

But the stupid question of all stupid questions wasn't *to whom* did such a thing happen, but *how?* That was the part that was especially hard for Dana to think about. For Dana, the coy smile she'd seen on Sandy's face, the remembrance of pleasure, the sparkle in the eyes, weren't there when she secretly tried out the words, *the usual way*. She envied Sandy that look. Sandy and her husband had taken a chance *the usual way*. It was a chance taken by two people who loved each other; and because they loved each other, all would be well.

Such was not the case for Dana. She'd wanted to love Gary Broder. She'd tried. He'd seemed like such a safe bet that she'd managed to convince herself she wasn't gambling at all. After all, Dana Barron never took chances. *Never*. She didn't know how.

Maybe that was the problem.

But every problem had its solution. A problem was simply a puzzle, which could always be solved with clear, cool thinking. It was Dana's problem, and she would solve it. She had discussed the matter with Gary—a difficult meeting at best, but it was the right thing to do. He'd behaved badly. Accusations, denial, undignified self-pity. He'd made such an unpleasant spectacle of himself that she'd let him off the hook completely. It was now entirely her problem, which was fine. She would handle it most ably, most sensibly.

Able, sensible handling was, in fact, in the works. Dana had taken a leave of absence from her teaching post at a small community college in Wisconsin and enrolled at the University of Minnesota, her alma mater. She would not have to explain anything or justify anything. She would not suffer stupid questions. It wasn't as if she were hiding or, God forbid, taking to her bed for nine months. Ever the proponent of making the best of things, she would be putting her time to good use by completing her work for her Ph.D., which she'd intended to do anyway. It was simply a matter of moving the timetable up a year or two, which she could easily handle.

Right now it was the first doctor's appointment that had her rattled. Just a little, just a tad. It didn't make much sense, because she knew exactly what the score was.

She knew, but no one else did.

Well, Gary knew, but that was almost the same as no one else. He was now a nonperson, a persona non grata. Out of sight, out of mind, out of her life. So the doctor she would be seeing today would be the first real person with whom she would actually speak about this matter, the first to look at her and know that she'd made a terrible mistake. A doctor wouldn't judge her for it, of course. A doctor would deal with it in a clinical way, because it was a clinical matter. Purely clinical.

But it was changing her body and her routine, and it would soon change the way people perceived her. And this doctor would be the first. The prospect was a little disconcerting, which was part of the reason she'd called a cab. She'd been having so much trouble with her car that she was ready to trade it in. She didn't like driving, anyway. Whenever she could, she used her bicycle. She was always getting lost in her car, taking the wrong turn, getting turned around. She had no sense of direction in a car, but she never got lost on a bike.

Dana waited on the wrought-iron bench outside the small apartment building. It was a warm autumn day, too beautiful to stay cooped up inside. The trees on the boulevard shimmered with early yellows and hints of pink in the mid-morning sun. The sun felt good to her, too, as though it might be injecting her with a little color. Pink, not yellow. In the pink, she told herself. Revitalized enough to propel herself right off the bench when the green and white Suburban Cab turned the corner. She opened the back door just as the car rolled to a stop at the curb.

"You must be in a hurry," the driver said, raising his voice above the saxophone wailing from the cab's front speakers. "Where to?"

She'd written down the address of the medical center, and when she looked up from her notebook, she realized that he was staring at her. She knew him. Oh, yes, she would have recognized the eyes even if she could see nothing else. Dark brown eyes that drew a person in like a sweet-shop window. She could tell that he couldn't place her. He was trying to, but after almost ten years, she was only vaguely familiar. In a moment he would surely shrug it off, put the car in gear and move on.

"Dana," he said with a slow grin. "Hey, what a surprise. Alex, remember? Alex LaRock. We went to school—"

"I remember." She smiled, too. He got bonus points in her book for getting her name on the first try. She glanced at the picture on the cab ID. It looked like the mug shot of a man who had no time for pictures, but his good looks could not be denied. "This is a surprise. How...?"

"Great," he said, hooking his arm over the back of the seat as he turned to her more fully. His bicep wasn't quite as beefy as a football player's, but it still filled out his short-sleeved shirt nicely. "You?"

"Fine, thanks. I'm just..." She showed him the address in her notebook. "I have a doctor's appointment, but it's nothing— I mean, I'm fine, thank you."

"That's good." He waited for a car to pass, then turned on the meter and pulled away from the curb. "So, you live around here?"

"No." He turned the radio down, and she spoke up. "Yes. Yes, I do, temporarily. I just moved here, actually. I haven't been back since..." She slid to the middle of the back seat so that she could see him in the rearview mirror. "Ten years. Can you believe that? Ten years since we graduated."

"Ten years since *you* graduated. I was a couple of years behind you, and I didn't quite make it."

"Really?" Now she remembered. She'd called him "wunderkind" when she'd learned that he was only a sophomore and already a star player for the Minnesota Gophers, but it had turned out that he wasn't that young. He'd been a star player, all right, but not exactly a star student. He'd graduated from a public high school, but he'd put in a post-graduate year at a prep school that had promised to prepare him for college in return for a winning football season. He'd given them that, but he'd still struggled, which was why the Athletic Department at the U had brought in the big guns. The best tutor available. Dana Barron.

She flashed an apologetic smile toward the mirror. "I failed you, then."

He gave her a look that questioned her sincerity, then laughed. "That's what happened, all right.

Lost my tutor, and it was straight downhill from there."

"As I remember, you were doing quite well. Improving, certainly."

His eyes sparkled in the mirror, and she knew he was smiling. "You always were very generous with your praise. You were planning on being a teacher. I'll bet you're a good one."

"I'm not so sure, now that I find out that one of my first students didn't graduate. That accident you had was a setback, but you were so determined." He'd wrecked his motorcycle early that spring. She remembered how awful it had been to see him in that hospital bed, like a massive redwood felled in the snow.

He shrugged. "I couldn't play football. Lost my scholarship."

"Your injury?" She'd helped him get through the spring quarter. He'd hated using crutches, but it was better than the wheelchair, he'd said, and he couldn't afford to miss too many classes. She'd stuck by him until she graduated, when he'd given her the crystal apple she'd kept on her desk ever since. She remembered asking him to let her know how things went, but she'd never heard from him, which hadn't surprised her. Their social circles didn't exactly overlap. "I thought... Well, I remember you were going to have more surgery that summer."

"I did. They couldn't put Humpty Halfback together again, at least not exactly the way he was before he wiped out on his bike. But I'm back in school now. Taking night classes.''

"That's wonderful. I am, too, actually. Taking more classes.''

"At the U?" He stopped for a traffic light.

"I thought it was time I finished my Ph.D.''

He glanced over his shoulder and whistled appreciatively. "You'll be Doctor Dana, huh? Pretty damned impressive.''

"School is what I'm good at, where I'm at my best.'' She was mesmerized by the couple crossing the street in front of them, the man pushing a stroller, the woman gesturing as she regaled him with some story. The baby's latest achievement, no doubt. Wasn't that what mothers talked about mostly? Diapers and drool and how Baby weighed in at the last checkup? "I love school. Everything about it. I can do no wrong at school.''

"My guess is you can't do too much wrong, period.'' The comment drew a quick scowl, but Alex didn't seem to notice it. "So, what do you teach?''

"Literature, mostly. The occasional comp class, of course.''

"English.'' He dragged the word out on a groan. "I had a hell of a time with English. You got me through the requirements, remember? You helped me a lot. It's been a little easier for me the second time around.''

"You don't have football to distract you." The light turned green just as a pretty blonde in tight jeans and a short leather jacket stepped up on the curb. "Not that football was your only distraction."

"That's all in the past. All the wine, women and song." He laughed as he switched off the radio. "Well, maybe not the song. Radio keeps me company."

He'd been listening to a jazz station. She remembered him as a heavy-metal fan. "No more parties?"

"Not too many."

"You've settled down to one woman?"

He shook his head. "Came close twice, but no cigar, or cigar *band*." The reflection of his eyes connected with hers. "How about you?"

"Me?"

"You asked, I get to ask," he insisted, smiling. "Are you married?"

"Yes." *Of course she was married.* She was pregnant. He didn't know that, but she did, and somehow it seemed important for her to start telling anyone who saw her now, anyone who mattered to her at all, that she was married. It would just be easier all around. It amazed her how readily the lie rolled off her tongue, but without elaboration. She couldn't think of anything quickly enough. No name, no circumstances, no time frame, nothing. Simply, "Yes, I am."

"Are you happy?"

"Happy?" The question almost made her laugh. "Why do you ask that?"

"I don't know. It just came out. You deserve to be happy. You were always..." He was looking at her in the mirror. She was staring at the address she'd written in her notebook, but she could feel his attention, and she didn't want to be looking at him when he told her what or how or who she'd always been. "You're happy, right?"

"Yes, of course. I'm—" The car took a sudden turn, and a shadow fell across her lap. She looked up and realized they'd driven under a covered entrance. She swallowed hard. "Is this it?"

"This is it." He pushed a button on the meter, ripped off the receipt and handed her the bill. It embarrassed her when the paper shook in her trembling hand. "You sure you're okay?" he asked.

"I'm fine. I'm going to be just fine." She stuffed the receipt into her purse and paid him, tipping generously. She wanted to shove all the cash she had into his shirt pocket and ask him to hold her hand, which brought a wild image to mind of the two of them doing this thing together. A couple. Two people instead of just one.

She was being silly. There was no reason for her to be jittery over a simple medical examination. It was her pride pricking her, and that was all. She couldn't believe she was saying, "Would you wait for me, Alex? Just keep the meter running."

"I could come back for you." He checked his watch. "Hell, it's almost lunchtime anyway. I can hang around here for a while."

"Oh, no, I don't want you to give up your lunch."

"I won't." He reached under his seat and pulled out a paper sack. "There's probably a bench or a picnic table around here somewhere."

"I really wish you'd turn that back on," she said, indicating the meter.

He brandished a thick textbook beneath her nose. "I really wish you'd get moving and let me get some studying done." His smile faded as he looked at her again, his eyes reflecting what he saw in hers. "You look a little shaky. You want me to go with you?"

"Oh, no. It's just routine." She shook her head quickly and offered a feeble smile. "Sometimes when they draw blood, I get light-headed. When it's over, I just want to be able to go home right away. That's all."

He nodded once. "I'll be here."

"Thank you." She edged toward the door, reaching blindly for the handle. "Thank you."

Alex watched her scurry through the big double doors as though she were moving along just ahead of a cattle prod. He thought about tagging along after her. Whatever this appointment was about, it wasn't routine. The woman was clearly worried

about something, and if she had bad news waiting
for her, she could probably use a friend.

She'd been a good friend to him, and she'd
never given him the chance to return the favor. Not
that he'd tried too hard. A dumb jock he might
have been, but not so dumb that he couldn't see
how different she was. How different *they* were—
from each other. They were every pair of antonyms
in the book—night and day, big and little, poor and
rich, dumb and smart, wild and tame. Sure, he'd
been attracted to her, but was he going to tell her
that back then? Hell, no. Ask her out and let her
politely turn him down? No way.

But he'd thought about it. God knew, he'd
dreamed about it back then, and even once or twice
since. She was so smart, and so quiet, especially
when other people came around. She was the kind
of woman a guy imagined turning himself into a
human wall for. Her serene beauty was a treasure
to be guarded. If she'd needed a defensive line,
he'd have been ready to change positions. He'd
never told her any of this, of course. He'd just
pounded those books, encouraged by her patience,
seeking her approval like a first grader with a bad
case of puppy love. He'd let her see for herself
what a chore it was for him to read, something he
hadn't done in years. Read aloud in class? He'd
learned how to avoid being called upon with a
combination of mischief and charm. But with Dana
it had been just the three of them—her, him, and

his reading problem. He'd stumbled over words right in front of her, and she'd helped him up and gently urged him on, like Snow White befriending Dopey. She'd never made him feel stupid.

He knew he wasn't stupid. He'd known about his learning disability for a long time—the bit of screwed-up wiring in his brain that gave him fits when he tried to read. He'd learned to use a hundred-and-ten tools to compensate, not the least of which was his considerable charm. But knowing he wasn't stupid didn't prevent him from *feeling* stupid. People like Dana, to whom it all came easily, for whom it was all so obvious—those were the people who usually made him feel inadequate. Dana was different. She'd helped him find confidence in places within himself, places other than his bountiful brawn and his winning smile.

And then she'd gone on to bigger and better things. Real teaching, not just tutoring. He was thinking how fine that was as he unwrapped his sandwich. With a brain like hers, she probably could have been a high-paid CEO at some big corporation by now, but she'd gone ahead and become a teacher, just like she'd said she was going to do. It was about the finest turn of events he could think of for Dana Barron—that and a clean bill of health. It was exactly what he'd been studying for, what he hoped for himself.

"So," he asked when she returned, he didn't know how much later. He'd been engrossed in his geometry, and she'd caught him by surprise when she slid into the front seat. "How's everything?"

"Everything's normal." She folded a handful of papers in half and offered him a tight smile. "I'm pregnant."

"You're going to have a baby? That's great, Dana. That's…" The look in her eyes didn't say "great." A sketch of her might be titled *Madonna in Distress*. Still, he gave her a thumbs-up before he started the car. "Congratulations. Is it your first?" She nodded as she stuffed the papers into her tapestry tote bag. "You didn't just find out today, did you?"

"I knew."

"Buckle up." He spared a quick glance for traffic. "I'll bet the ol' man's pleased, huh?"

"The old man?" She pulled the shoulder harness across her small frame.

"Your husband." He signaled for a turn, figuring he could bypass some downtown traffic if he took I-394.

"Oh, yes, my…husband. He's not here. He's…a naval officer. Fighter pilot," she said, as if she were recalling the man piece by piece, bits that she'd been hoarding. "Aircraft carrier. In the, uh, in the Gulf." She looked at him expectantly. "The Persian Gulf."

"I know where that is. If you're gonna be a cab driver, it helps to know your geography." He smiled. "Cruisin' the Gulf, huh? So, what, you got him on the ship-to-shore and gave him the big news?''

"Something like that."

"Bet he was busting with pride, brass buttons flying everywhere. First kid.'' She wanted the man's perspective, he decided, words that might reflect *her* man's perspective. She was really missing the guy today. Had to be. "He'll be back before your time comes, won't he?''

"I don't..." She turned to the side window. "No, actually he won't. That's why I decided this would be the perfect time to go back to school. It's less demanding than teaching.''

He chuckled as he pulled to the right for an exit. "For you, maybe.''

"Yes. I do enjoy—'' She turned to him, eyes wide as though he'd veered off course. "Alex, don't turn here.''

"You're not going home? Guess I should have asked, where to?''

"Anywhere.''

He bypassed the exit. "Anywhere, Minnesota. You got it, lady.''

"Let's go to the park.'' The impulse put a spark in her eye. "The one we used to go to across from the Guthrie Theatre, remember?''

"The one with the cherry in the spoon,'' he said, signaling for a lane change.

"Which you made lewd jokes about.'' He glanced at her, surprised that she remembered, and she smiled. "Neutral ground. I wasn't in the library, and you weren't in the student union."

"And you actually made me study, no matter how nice the day was."

"Just doing my job. I thought I did it pretty well, too."

"You got me through football season with flying colors. I even passed English. 'It was the best of times, it was the worst of times...' Boy, ain't that the truth?" He could tell she was pleased that he remembered a line, at least. Just like a teacher. Truth was, he remembered a lot of it word for word, because that was the way they'd gone over it. And once he'd gotten through the material, it was his for life. "No lie, Dana, Coach used to call you the miracle worker."

"Why? Didn't he realize how much potential you had?"

"Sure, he did. He had me convinced I could play pro ball."

"That didn't take much convincing, did it? When it came to athletic ability, you were always quite confident." She sat back, visibly more relaxed now that the conversation had veered away from her. "I meant academic potential. It was always there, you know."

"Yeah, right."

"There you go, doubting me again. I'd tell you that you were ready for a test, and you'd doubt me. One more time, you'd say." She laughed affectionately, as though she were recalling the antics of a clever child. He chafed at the thought, but he forgave her, figuring she had kids on the brain. "Anyone who didn't see how much potential you had was blind," she insisted. "Even your almighty coach."

"It was the only way I could get you to hang around a little longer." He parked at the curb, then turned to her, flashing his charming smile. "Come on, Dana. Just one more time."

"Oh, look, the mums are still blooming." The "Mini-apple" sculpture glinted in the sun, as did the face of Alex's watch as he reached for the meter. "Don't you dare turn that off, Alex LaRock. Can't I just hire you for the afternoon?"

"Depends on what you've got in mind." He turned the meter off. "You can hire me to drive you around, but not to keep you company. I don't charge for that."

Her whole face brightened, and the intervening years fell away. "I want you to drive me over to our bench, but since the road ends here, I guess you'll have to walk me."

Walk. Damn. Cold suddenly crept into his feet. "I'll wait for you."

"What, you'd rather run?" She got out of the cab, shut the door and leaned back in through the window. "All right, then, I'll run with you, but you have to remember, I'm not..."

He emerged reluctantly, taking his time with his

every move. She'd forgotten how tall he was, how powerfully built, how imposing when he rose to his full height. He looked at her over the top of the car, his eyes claiming her undivided attention as he brushed his lush, dark hair back. "Not what?" he asked.

She shrugged, childlike. "I'm not much of a runner."

One corner of his mouth turned up in a sardonic smile. "Neither am I. We'll walk."

They'd walked several yards before she realized that her gait was smoother than his. She was saying something about the fine autumn weather when the fact that he limped hit her like a dash of cold water. She tripped over her own tongue. Her train of thought went chugging down the paved garden path and left her stammering senselessly.

"I guess I'm not a very pretty walker, either," he said. "But I can get where I'm going, and I wish you wouldn't look at me like that."

"I'm sorry." She glanced away, then back again. "I didn't mean... I mean, I'm not...sorry the way you think, but I didn't realize..."

"I was still on crutches the last time you saw me."

"I know, but I guess I thought..."

"They did what they could. Carved me up a few times, put in a few replacement parts guaranteed to outlast the originals, put me through some therapy and sent me on my way. I can't run worth a damn, but I can walk. If you'd seen the X rays, you'd understand how lucky I am."

She nodded. As many tutoring sessions as they'd had after his accident, and he'd never mentioned even the slightest doubt that he would recover completely. "I'm really—"

"Nothing for you to be sorry about." He slid her a pointed look as they strolled the tree-lined path, side by side. "Okay?"

"I didn't know how bad it was. You didn't tell me."

"I couldn't tell you something I didn't believe myself." He smiled. "You're fine? I'm fine."

"It's hardly noticeable."

He glanced at her waist. "Yours, too."

"Touché." She laughed. "Mine will be. Very noticeable."

"That's the way it's supposed to be. So everybody knows that something special is going on with you and you deserve special treatment."

"Like what?"

"Whatever you want. Whatever you need." He gestured expansively. A blaze of fall colors surrounded them. "Like now. You need some company."

"I'm not sure why." The claim pricked her conscience. She did not relish being a spinner of fabrications, and she cast about for an excuse. "Yes, I am. You know how student housing is. Well, it's not exactly student housing, but it's like student housing. I subleased a furnished apartment, which I was really lucky to find, but it's so small and sterile. I feel like the walls are closing in sometimes," she said truthfully, showing him with her hands. "I don't know what's wrong with me. I've never been claustrophobic before."

"Must be one of the side effects."

"Must be." She shrugged. "Maybe loneliness is, too. That's never bothered me before, either. Being alone."

"Is your husband gone a lot?"

"Oh—" The husband. She'd made him up for the ride. A quick lie for a quick cab ride home. Now she was going to have to live with the man who was no man. She offered a wan smile. "All the time."

"You never go with him when he gets sent to these exotic ports?" She shook her head, and he pulled a quizzical frown. "You picked up and moved here. Seems like—"

"He's on a ship," she reminded him. "And we...haven't been married that long."

"Long enough to get started on a family." They'd reached the massive concrete bench near a fading topiary. "If you were my wife, I'd..."

"You'd what?"

"Take you with me," he said. "Either that or I'd go AWOL."

She laughed. "That's why you're not in the navy, Alex. You're too impulsive."

"And you're not impulsive at all. Maybe that's why you're not my wife, huh?"

"Not impulsive at all?" She sat down on the bench, feeling oddly rejected. "Boring, you mean. I'm not your wife because I'm not your type. I'm too serious and boring." As opposed to giddy and gorgeous, she thought, remembering one girl in particular to whom he'd introduced her. "Seriously boring, that's me."

"I never thought that."

"Then why didn't you ever ask me for a date?" She saw the surprise in his eyes, and she glanced away, astonished herself. "Or something."

"Or something?" He chuckled. "Or what, Dana?"

"Something besides help with English."

"What are you talking about? You were out of my league, and you sure as hell let me know it." He sat down beside her. "Remember that time I kissed you and you gave me the third degree about my intentions? All I intended to do was kiss you. If you didn't like it, all you had to do was say so, but you made it sound like I should have filled out an application first."

"I did like it. It came as quite a surprise, and I didn't know exactly what to make of it. I mean, you were everybody's hero, and there were always so many girls hanging around." She shook her head, thinking back on her righteous indignation with a smile. Oh, yes, she did remember that head-spinning, tantalizing kiss. "But I kept hoping you'd try again."

"Yeah, well, now you know why I never did."

"I was...cold and unapproachable."

"I didn't say that. You were out of my league, pure and simple." He laughed, absently rubbing his palms over the threadbare knees of his jeans. "You were pure, and I was simple."

"You were not simple," she retorted. "Don't you say that about yourself. I've learned a lot since then about how people learn. You're an auditory learner. You're not a reader. You have a slight learning disability that should have been discovered when you were in grade school but never was because you were able to compensate for it pretty well, cover it up, charm your way through and basically get along pretty well on your athletic talents."

"I was pretty good in math." He turned, pleased to tell her, "Still am."

"You were good at a lot of things. A person has to be very smart to compensate as successfully as you did. *Do*," she amended emphatically. "As you do."

"I know that. You think I don't know that?" He grinned. "Wanted to see if I could get you to come to my defense. Like you did that time I flunked that test and you talked the prof into having his TA give it to me orally."

"And you aced it."

"Yeah, well, the TA was…"

"Charmed, I'm sure." She laughed. "You were never simple, Alex LaRock."

"You weren't cold, either."

Her smile faded, and she sighed. "But I *was* unapproachable when it came to…"

"In some ways, yeah. When it came to…" He tossed her a merry wink. "But now you're married, and you're gonna have a baby. And you're happy. You said you were happy. Obviously, somewhere along the line, you solved that little approachability problem."

"Yes, I guess I did." She studied the bandage the technician had put on her finger after she'd drawn blood. "And if lack of impulsiveness is a problem, I must have solved that, too. My decision to come here was pretty impulsive, and I was beginning to think I'd made a big mistake. I just thought…why not go back to school full time? I'd been plugging away at it forever, it seemed, and I only needed about six more months, which was just about right with this…pregnancy and all, so I thought, why not?"

"Pretty impulsive," he observed.

She looked up. "But I don't know anyone here."

"You know me." The warmth of his smile glowed in his eyes. "I've changed some, but basically…"

"I know you." She touched the hand that lay

on his thigh. The fire flickered in his eyes. She could see that her gesture had surprised him. "I'm really glad to see you. I... Thank you."

"Nothing to thank me for. You're a good tipper." He pressed his business card into her hand. "You ever need anything, a ride, or..." He shrugged boyishly. "Well, a ride. That's what I do. I drive people around. Call me, okay?"

"I will."

Chapter Two

Dana drew her panty hose over her rounded belly and let the waistband snap into place. *Support* panty hose, no less, and "into place" was a couple of inches higher than normal. She felt like an old man who habitually hiked his pants halfway up his chest. Her body was changing so fast she could hardly keep up with its additional needs. Larger bras, easygoing shoes, elastic waists, loose tops. She was determined to take care of herself, her body, and certainly the baby, as long as it was in her care.

The baby, not *her* baby. Adoption was the only way to go, she'd decided. A child deserved two parents—mother and father—and that was exactly what this child would have. She hadn't looked into agencies yet, but the decision was firmly in place in her mind, and she was getting comfortable with it. She was strictly schooling herself to think of it as *the* baby.

A knock at her door prompted her to drop a knit dress over her head and pad to the front room in her stocking feet. She'd had no visitors since she'd moved in, didn't plan on having any, didn't *want* any. Her face was an ice carving, the words *not interested* on the tip of her tongue.

But they all melted.

"Alex."

He smiled, his dark eyes sparkling with some ulterior motive. "Did you call for a cab?"

"No, I..."

"Why not? You promised to call me when you needed a ride."

"I... Come in." She stepped back to admit him, explaining, "I haven't gone anywhere. Every place I go is within walking or bicycling distance."

"That's what I was afraid of. You're becoming a shut-in."

"No, I'm not. There's class, grocery store, class." With a small fist she demonstrated her Ping-Pong comings and goings. "I get out every day."

"I propose a little variety." He reached inside his brown leather bomber jacket and produced an envelope; the look in his eyes indicated that he considered it pure gold. "Vikings tickets. I took a guy to the airport, and he gave me these as a tip." When she didn't jump for joy right away, he pulled a frown. "You remember the Vikings."

"The football team?"

"The football team." He waved the envelope under her nose, as though the smell might ring some bells. Her composed smile was not the response he was looking for. "Look, I know it's not the ballet, but there's no accounting for the taste of some passengers. A tip's a tip."

"The Vikings." She stared at him. "I'm from Wisconsin, you know."

"Packers fan, huh? So was this guy. He was really ticked about having to cut his trip short." With a self-satisfied smile Alex tried waving the envelope one more time. "Guess who we're playing."

"Really? The Packers?" Her pulse rate was still perfectly stable, but she regarded his treasure more appreciatively, just to please him. "My father would kill for those tickets."

Alex grinned. "Him and about a million other guys."

"I'm not a fan, exactly. I still don't know much about football."

"What about your husband? Wouldn't he kill for these tickets?"

Her shoulders stiffened. She'd almost managed to forget about the blasted husband. She was going to have to start a file on him, just to keep his profile straight. "He's not much of a football fan, either."

"Good, because I don't wanna catch any long bombs off a fighter pilot."

"I won fifty dollars in a Super Bowl pool once," Dana said, acknowledging his pun with a tight smile.

"Hey, there you go. You know how to pick a winner."

"Luck of the draw, same way I got you as a tutee. And you were the closest I ever got to the game of football. Would you like something to drink?''

"No, thanks." He followed her into the kitchen. "I kept saying it was going to be my turn to teach you, but that would have meant getting you to go to a game."

"You did," she said as she poured herself a glass of orange juice. "You got me to go to a game."

"I did?"

His look of surprise reminded her that she'd never gotten around to telling him. She'd had a hundred questions, like what do you talk about in a huddle, and why do you slap each other's bottoms, and why does everybody have to pile on the poor guy when he's down, but she'd never asked them. She'd never admitted to having gone to a game.

But now she did. "I wanted to see what all the fuss was about. It was about you. Even I could tell that you were quite remarkable." She shrugged. "Me and about a million other girls."

"You went to see me play?" She nodded. "How come you never told me?"

"Just stubborn, I guess. You knew the crowd was there."

"I didn't know you were ever part of it." He folded his arms and challenged her with a suggestive smile. "What did I do? How could you tell that I was quite remarkable?"

"The idea is to take the ball and run with it, right? Well, first I got your number from the program, and then I watched you. You kept getting the ball and running over those lines. It was very exciting."

"Sounds like it." He eyed her speculatively while she downed a mammoth vitamin pill with her juice. "I don't suppose you remember what game it was, who we were playing."

"Oh, no."

"But it was exciting to watch me take the ball and run with it."

She shrugged. "You seemed to be working very hard to pass English just so you could continue to play football. I thought it was important for me to understand what motivated you. Since I was tutoring you, I just thought I should know."

"You thought I was trying to pass English so I could play football?" The speculative look persisted. "I love football. I love playing it, or I used to. I love watching other people play it. It's only a game, but it was something I was good at. And football was good to me. Opened a lot of doors for me." He smiled. "It got me a tutor."

"And plenty of other admirers, as well."

"On the field. Nowadays I've gotta open those doors myself." He brandished the tickets. "Okay, so I'm still trying to use football to open doors."

"What door?" She indicated the front entrance with a nod. "This one? I—"

"And I still need a tutor."

"All you have to do is ask," she told him as she rinsed out her glass.

"I did, didn't I?" He scowled, thought back, tried to remember whether he'd omitted something. "Okay, how about going with me to a football game? I'll tutor you in the fine points of gridiron strategy. And then maybe you'll return the favor. I've got a stupid paper to write."

"You'll answer all my stupid questions if I help you with your stupid paper?" She rolled her eyes as though thinking it over. "Sounds like the perfect swap. I'll get my shoes."

"Wanna go get something to eat first? What do you crave?"

"Pizza with Canadian bacon, pineapple and sauerkraut, and mint chocolate-chip ice cream."

His whole face puckered. "Can't we at least have the ice cream on the side?"

Alex took her to the Green Mill, which he declared to be his favorite pizza place. He agreed to try her combination of ingredients, but he ended up removing the sauerkraut after the first bite. She ate the stuff with obvious relish. They talked about his class schedule and her dissertation, and then, out of the blue, he asked her when the baby was due.

"Early spring, huh?" He thought about it for a moment. "New life in the spring. You got names picked out?'' She shook her head, her mouth full of pizza. "Boy or girl, it doesn't matter, right? A healthy baby is all that's important.''

She swallowed, nodding this time. "That's right.''

"Yeah, that's right. A boy or a girl, either one would be fine.''

"You're looking forward to being a father,'' she surmised. "Some day.''

"Soon as I find a mother.'' She laughed, and so did he, palms lifted in testimony. "For the kid. I've grown up. I swear.'' He reached for his beer. "Soon as I find myself a wife who wants to be a mother.''

"Is that a requirement?''

"Does it have to be? Should I have a list of requirements?'' He looked at her quizzically. "Did you?''

"How hard are you looking?''

"I'm not.'' She laughed, and he hastened to add, "Don't you think that would ruin it?''

"Probably. Spontaneity seems to work very well for you. But some people need to...'' Some people need to be more careful, she thought, her stomach suddenly roiling. Some people ought to know better by now. According to tradition, the sickness was supposed to be a morning thing. Hers was unpredictable and generally inopportune. "Excuse me for a moment,'' she said, and she bolted from the table.

She saw nothing of her surroundings except the arrows pointing to Rest Rooms, but on her way back, having turned herself inside out to overthrow the nausea, she had a new perspective. She noticed the long table crowded with small children, the balloons tied to their chairs, the half-eaten, fully-forgotten plates of pizza, and small voices singing "Happy Birthday." A little girl in a ruffled smock knelt on her chair, trying to achieve superiority over the six flames bobbing on her cake. Her puffed cheeks looked like twin pink gum bubbles. She tipped her head first to one side, then the other, looking for the proper angle while her friends coaxed, "Blow! Blow!" She must have felt the intensity of Dana's stare, for she turned suddenly and stared back, her cheeks deflating. *She knows,* Dana thought. *Children connect with children, and she can see a child in my eyes, and she knows.*

The little girl smiled, a big, bright-eyed birthday smile. "Want some cake?" she said.

Dana's own smile felt as artless as the little girl's. "I wanted to see if you could blow out all those candles."

"I'm six!" She puffed up and blew, extinguishing all but one flame, which she attacked with a bit of breath she'd held in reserve. While her party applauded, she looked up at Dana again. "See?"

Dana clapped, too. "You really must be six, if you can do that. Happy Birthday."

"What's going on?" Alex asked, draining the

last of his beer as she returned to the table. "Are they holding a blood drive back there? You look like you gave an extra pint." He watched her slide into the booth. "You okay?"

She smiled. She still felt a little shaky, but relieved. "I guess I've had enough sauerkraut."

"You ready for ice cream now?" She shook her head, a little embarrassed by the failure of her boast, but there was nothing but sympathy in his eyes. "You ready to go home?"

Not really, she realized, and the thought surprised her. But he thought he had a sick woman on his hands, a wet blanket, a drag on his evening. "If you wouldn't mind. You'll still have time to get to the game."

"There's always another game. I want to be sure you're okay." He pulled her plate with the remains of her pizza to his side of the table, as though he were trying to save her from her own gluttony. "Is there something you can take?"

"When you're pregnant, you really don't want to take anything unless you have to. Besides, it's sort of like seasickness. If you don't take preventive measures ahead of time, you just have to ride it out." And she had done that. She felt better. The concern in his eyes was so seductive to her now, she couldn't let him take her home and leave her there. She wanted this togetherness, this friend, the entire evening he'd so thoughtfully planned.

"Maybe I'll just sit for a few minutes. Would that be...?"

"Sure. We can sit till they kick us out. You want me to get you something? Your stomach's empty now. You need—" he shrugged, glancing greedily at the next table, as though he were prepared to make a quick claim "—something."

"Milk and crackers."

"Plain crackers?" He sprang to his feet, grateful for an order he could easily fill. "Comin' right up."

Moments later he returned with a glass of milk and a basket full of two-cracker packets. "How's it goin'?"

"I'm getting my sea legs, which is a real relief. My father would be horrified if he heard I'd wasted Packers tickets."

"Daddy's girl," he called her with a smile, an epithet he'd teased her with long ago. "In Daddy's hand they'd be Packers tickets. In mine, they're Vikings tickets. I'll go see if the birthday kid back there likes football."

"I'm feeling much better." She laid a hand on his arm, preventing him from leaving her again. "I really had my heart set on seeing Wisconsin demolish Minnesota."

"*Demolish?*" He laughed. "And here I had you pegged for a gentle creature."

"Demolish," she repeated, injecting the word

with a defiant note. "Destroy, despoil and denude."

"My God, woman, you sure know how to pick your fighting words. You've got my blood pumping like hell's fury."

"Have I?" She actually managed a coy smile. "You're easily riled, Mr. LaRock."

"Who said anything about riled?" he muttered as he followed her out the door and into the parking lot.

The game was a rout. Alex took time out from his cheering and grousing to explain the finer points of Vikings strategy, which didn't seem to be working. Dana was more charmed than enlightened by his instruction, less interested in what he said than the way he said it. He would condemn the officials to eternal privation, then temper his tone with the next breath and explain why his team was about to kick the ball to hers.

She nodded dutifully, her eyes darting about the huge Metrodome searching for really interesting activity, like the audience bobbing up and down in their seats in a spontaneous "wave," cartoons flashed on the scoreboard, a woman accidentally spilling beer out of a huge paper cup onto the people behind her. But Alex's enthusiasm for the game was contagious. Dana found herself claiming the other side of the seesaw, riding the ups and downs of his team's fortunes, mischievously delighting in the fact that she was getting more than her share of ups from a team she now pronounced to be hers. By the time the game was over, they were cheerfully grabbing each other by the arm, playfully shoving shoulders and laughingly hurling "fighting words" at each other.

"All right, so the boys couldn't quite get it together tonight. We'll get you cheese heads next time around, though." Alex deftly nosed the cab into bumper-to-bumper traffic, wagging his finger at his passenger. "Listen to me. I was raised on a dairy farm. Daddy's girl, on the other hand—" he turned to find that her chin now rested on her shoulder, her eyes were closed, and her left hand lay relaxed, palm up, on the seat next to him "—is fast asleep. And she sure sleeps pretty."

He smiled as he arced the wheel, joining the cab to the segmented worm of cars inching its way down Washington Avenue. "Dana, Dana, Dana. Dana Barron. I don't even know what your last name is now, Dana. Guess I don't wanna know. I like Dana Barron just fine, the name and the woman. Always did, even though she never could admit—" He chuckled. "Yeah, but neither could I. And now she's back, and everything's different, but I still like Dana Barron just fine. Maybe we should stick to first names only, huh? Like a self-help group. A lonely hearts' society of two."

He glanced aside quickly, then paused to give her a sympathetic look. An appreciative perusal. Soft, quiet angel, he thought. "Daddy's girl's still lonely. That much hasn't changed. Why in hell did you pick somebody who goes off and leaves his wife when she needs him most? Hmm? You don't think you need anybody, do you?'' He stared at the brake light in the back window of the car ahead. ''Yeah, well, neither did I. I didn't want anyone to know. Didn't want anyone feeling sorry for me.'' He glanced at her, knowing he would never tell her, but imagining she would understand if he did. ''We're tough, aren't we, Dana? We're chin-up, stand-alone tough.'' He sighed. ''Yep, you sure sleep pretty, Dana Barron.''

''For a cheese head?''

He turned and found himself looking into her sleepy but appreciably merry eyes. ''For a damn possum. I thought you'd fallen asleep on me.''

''Gosh, no, that would be rude.'' She closed her eyes again and smiled ''Besides, you'll know when I've fallen asleep. I don't sleep pretty.''

''That's hard to believe.''

''I am exhausted, though. Pleasantly so. Whatever you said just sort of floated right past.''

''I'll bet. You're a teacher, aren't you? Teachers hear everything.'' He signaled for a right turn and switched lanes.

''My name is still Barron, and I'm glad you like me.'' She laid her hand on his forearm. He felt warm under the sleeve of his jacket where she touched him, and he wasn't sure whether it was his own heat or hers. ''I like you, too, Alex. I always have. And you're absolutely right. I was loath to admit it.''

"*Loath?*" He laughed as he pulled one of his cards from the pocket in the visor above his head. "You sure can pick 'em, Dana Barron. Now put this someplace where you won't lose it and call me when you need a ride. Or a friend.''

She hadn't lost the first card he'd given her. She'd put it with her doctor's number, her adviser's, the number for pizza delivery—all the important contacts she had in this town, this home away from home. Her apartment in Milwaukee was much nicer than this one. It was comfortably appointed with chic contemporary furnishings, plenty of glass and polish, plenty of plush carpeting and pastel chintz upholstery, plenty of clean lines. Her little sublet apartment was clean and functional, but sparely furnished. As spare as the emotions she permitted herself these days.

She picked up the phone on impulse, even though it wasn't "that time of the month," she reminded herself with a chuckle. She could tell when he answered that she'd gotten him on his cellular phone.

"Hello, Dad."

"Dana." She could hear the surprise in his voice, and she imagined him glancing at his watch. "Is it the first Saturday already?''

"No, Dad, I'm a little early. I just thought I'd check in and say hello. Where are you?"

"Phoenix."

"Ah, the miracle of call forwarding."

"How's everything going? Will you be home for Christmas?"

"Will you?"

"Who knows? Maybe we can meet somewhere, hmm?"

Not this year, she thought ruefully. Sometimes he had a couple of days, sometimes no more than a couple of hours. This year it didn't matter. "I've decided to do some research that may take me to London. I'll probably be tied up a lot. But, then, so will you."

"That doesn't mean we can't touch base."

"That's what I'm doing now. Touching base." Home base, she thought. Thin, flat, colorless home base. "Everything's going well, Dad. I'm doing fine."

"You always do fine. I don't ever have to worry about that, do I?"

"No, you don't." She glanced down at the street below her window. Two young women were pedaling by on bicycles. One had a baby in a seat behind her. "Have you heard from Mother?"

"Of course not. I'll have to rely on you for an update on your mother. She'll be flying south for the winter pretty soon, but I'll be headed east, so

I doubt if our paths will cross. They haven't in some time, which is fortunate for both of us."

"Yes," Dana said absently, trying to remember the last time they'd been together in her presence. "For both of you."

"So everything's tip-top, right?"

"Yes, Dad." The day she'd graduated from college. That was it; that was the last time she'd seen her parents together. They'd been polite to each other, but cool. Disgustingly civil. "But, as I said, you may not be able to reach me directly, because, well, like you, I'm going to be very busy this winter. But I will get my messages."

"That's my girl," he said, words she'd once lived for. "Like father, like daughter. Wherever we go, whatever we do, we're right out there in front. We're making it all happen. Am I right?"

"Yes, Dad, we're right out front." She laid her hand on her stomach and wondered how soon it would be true. Irony was such a delightful literary device. She just wished the joke weren't on her.

"And we're close. We keep in touch."

"That we do."

"Do I hear a note of doubt in your voice, Dana? Whatever it is, let's talk about it. This was your idea, to do this thing right now, get it out of the way, and I supported your decision, but I did say— and you'll remember I offered to bankroll the whole project—but I said maybe you'd want to consider another institution, one with a little more cachet. So now you've done the deed, and maybe you're a little disappointed in the actual—''

Done the deed? Dana almost laughed. "I'm fine with it, Dad. Minnesota offers everything I need right now. I wouldn't be here if it didn't.''

"Well, then, it's up to you to make it happen, Dana. All systems are go.''

"They seem to be,'' she said, absently rubbing her belly. One system had definitely proved to be in working order—not that she'd intended to test it.

"'Seems...! Nay... I know not *seems.*''' He laughed. "The old man knows his Shakespeare, too. Like father, like daughter. Listen, I'm on the run. Keep in touch, okay? Love you.''

"Love you, too.''

Who loves you? she thought as she hung up. It was a claim without ownership, words haunted by the chilly echo of what was missing. Beginning the sentence with *I* was too risky. She'd learned this from a man whose wife had left him, left them both, years ago. Don't put yourself on the line when the odds are against you. Hold back. Keep your own counsel. Be conservative. Watch and wait. It wasn't something he'd said, but he'd taught her in all the words that were left unspoken.

Again she laid her hand over the waistband of her slacks, then slid it slowly, lightly over the front seam. So small. Such a tiny tempest in her personal teapot. *Love you,* she thought. *Only trying to do what's best for you.* Her throat suddenly burned with irrational anger.

Like father, like daughter.

She nearly ripped the phone off the wall, her hand trembling as she fumbled for the business card she'd filed with those other important numbers. The few human contacts she had in her self-imposed exile. She had to dial it twice after reaching a "We're sorry" message the first time. She'd hit the wrong buttons. She was a great one for hitting all the wrong buttons.

"Alex?"

"Dana?" He sounded half asleep. "Dana, hi."

"Hi." Now she didn't know what to say. It was a relief to hear his voice, and that was all she knew, except that suddenly something was all aflutter in her stomach.

"What's up?"

"Um. I just wanted to, uh…call…and…"

"Are you okay?" He was awake now. His voice sounded firm, solid, blessedly interested in her answer. "Need a ride? I can be there in ten minutes. Sooner if I—"

"No, no, I don't need to go anywhere. I just thought… Well, you said something about needing a tutor, and I didn't know whether you were serious, but I wanted to be sure you knew that… I mean, I'm more than willing to help if…" She sighed as she toyed with the phone cord. "But, then, I didn't know if it would sound right to offer, as if I thought I were some great—''

''Miracle worker?'' He laughed. It was a beautiful, rich, friendly sound, a soothing balm, and it made her feel better. She smiled at the empty white wall. ''I'm not looking for miracles, but a little scholarly advice would be welcome,'' he told her.

''Advice on the stupid paper?''

''Yeah. I don't know what I'm doing in a psychology class. Hell, I'm a cab driver. I know more about living, breathing people than some guy who only talks to them by appointment. But I needed it for, uh…''

''For what? I never asked you about your major.''

''Phys-ed. Sports medicine. Math minor and, uh…education. That's why I need psychology.''

She smiled as she sank into the saggy cushion of the slip-covered sofa in her temporary abode. ''So you're going into teaching, too.''

''Not college,'' he said quickly. ''I want high school. Junior high, maybe. I want to work with them when they're just trying to get a toehold, you know?''

''Oh, yes, that's wonderful. You'll be a terrific teacher. And a coach, right?''

''Don't laugh.''

''Why would I laugh?''

''You know how much trouble I have with reading. I don't know if I should be teaching kids when I can't...you know, read very well.''

She heard the familiar ache in his voice, the self-consciousness he covered so well, his own soft, vulnerable underbelly. ''You don't have to teach reading. You're so good at— Oh, Alex, you'll be so good.''

''As a coach,'' he said, reading her over the wires with the same proficiency she had with the written word. ''That's what I'll be good at. The rest would just get me in.''

''If you say so.''

''What do you say? Do you think I can...?'' His voice dropped, as though he were afraid of being overheard. ''I mean, you've worked with me, Dana. You know stuff about me that I haven't let too many other people in on. What do you say?''

''I say you'll be a good teacher.'' No hesitation, no qualification. She could see him now, in her mind's eye, working with a child who'd struggled, just as he had. ''You'll be able to show kids how to learn.''

''You think so?'' He sounded at once dubious and hopeful. ''The thing is, I've had a few disadvantages, a few setbacks, but I think I know what it takes to get past all that. I think maybe that's worth something.''

''I think it's worth a lot. And I just want you to know that I'm more than willing to...'' It sounded so immodest, she thought. But it had been his suggestion. "I mean, it would be no imposition. Any time."

"Thanks. I'll probably take you up on that."

"Please do. Any time." *Like now.* "You mean, like, right now?"

"Now would be perfect." She laughed. What a mind reader he was. The evening shadows had lengthened across the apartment, and it was time to turn on a light and face the night music. Distant sounds, melancholy music. "Now would be excellent, Alex."

"Should I come over?"

She nodded, wondering if he could somehow read not only her mind, but her slightest move from the other side of town. "Please do."

next. "I mean, it wouldn't be an imposition, say, one. . ."

"Thanks. I'll probably take you up on it."

"Please do. . ." So warm, so green, I'd like right now. . .

Chapter Three

It drove Alex nuts, watching Dana read his psychology paper. She insisted on reading the whole damn thing before she said anything, getting the "complete picture." She had a habit of snapping her middle fingernail against her thumbnail or running her fingers through her hair and letting it fall back against her cheek like spun silk. He could almost feel it sifting through his fingers. Pretty, slender hands, long fingers—hers, not his. Her hands were magic. Whenever she touched him, he just wanted to wrap himself around her like an alley cat begging to be stroked by those beautiful fingers. God! It drove him nuts to watch her turn those lucky pages.

It had all been perfectly innocent, but they were seeing each other more and more often as the weeks rolled by. They would get together to study, take in a movie once in a while, go out for a bite to eat. All completely innocent, but not completely easy. No, it wasn't easy for Alex to be Dana's friend.

He didn't mess around with married women, and he was pretty old-fashioned about just how good a friend it was okay for a guy to be. He kept telling himself that their friendship predated her marriage, and she didn't seem to know anybody else in town. She'd always had a hard time making friends. She was fine when it was just the two of them. But a few more people would come along, he would introduce her, and she would fade right into the woodwork.

But now she was married, and she was about to have some flyboy's baby, and it was up to ol' Top Gun to be her friend and companion. Alex was getting himself in too deep. Way too deep. He looked forward to going to the library, just the way he did ten years ago, because she would be there to help him get through the mazes on the pages of the damn books he had to fight with. She was one of the reasons he'd decided to become a teacher. She'd shown him ways to tackle the problem of the printed page. She'd eased his panic. He wanted to do that for other people, and he'd been willing to work hard to meet the requirements, to make the grade.

Lately he'd been more than willing. He'd been driven. He was desperately eager to work with her, to learn from her, to *be with* her, when actually he knew damn well he could do it on his own now. He could, and he *should*. But, damn his eyes, he wasn't going to. After all, she needed him, too. She needed a friend, and he was going to be that friend. For all she'd done for him, it was the least he could do. But it wasn't easy to be Dana's friend when deep down in his gut he wanted a whole lot more than friendship.

It was almost Christmas, and Dana had done her usual expert prodding, getting him more interested in the nitty-gritty details of his psych project, not just helping him get it done, but getting him into it more deeply, making it more interesting. He wasn't sure whether it was the subject matter itself—athletes and aggressive behavior, on and off the playing field—or his discussions with Dana, but he'd changed his mind about psychology. It wasn't half bad. He hoped Dana would say the same for the paper.

"I'm telling you, this is the *final* final draft," he warned her. "I am not doing any more—"

"It doesn't need any more work." She looked up, finally, and smiled, blessedly. "It's excellent."

"Really?"

"Excellent," she repeated as she handed the paper back to him.

"Damn." He leaned back on the sofa, relaxing now, thumbing through his work with newfound fondness. It was finished. It was good. "If it is, it's thanks to you."

"I didn't do the work. You did. All I did was crack the whip."

"You pointed me in the right direction, helped me sort things out." He shrugged. "My spelling's still an embarrassment to me."

"Do you know how few good spellers there are

in this world? I'm not going to let you sell yourself short anymore, Alex. If you wanted to switch to an English major, you could handle it."

"Yeah, right." He tapped her knee with the back of his hand. "Hey, I've got a sociology course next quarter that could be interesting. Something about marriage and the family."

"Interesting choice." She folded her arms, gathering in her loose white blouse so that her little pouch of a belly was more noticeable.

"There was room for me in the class," he said with a shrug. He didn't know what was wrong with him. He was dying to measure her girth in man-size hands, to see if he could hold her whole belly in his two expert ballhandler's hands. He glanced away. "Gotta do another paper. Could probably use a little technical assistance."

"We can probably work out a deal. I'm going to need a partner for a project I have coming up. Someone with a cool head, patience, maybe some small measure of—" her tone changed on the next word, became hushed and shy "—regard for me. Someone who can run a stopwatch."

He smiled. He liked that stopwatch part. "Hey, I'm your man."

She wished that were true. More every day. Every time she saw him, basked in his warm, caring smile, she wished he were her man, the father of her baby. *The* baby. Not really her baby, not for long. But Alex was just the kind of father she wanted her...*the* baby to have.

"What do you want me to do?"

"Take a class with me," she proposed, and he returned a quizzical look. "About...having a baby. Actual childbirth."

"Lamaze?" Surprise registered on her face, and he chuckled. He laid his arm across the back of the sofa, behind her, but not touching. Familiar but not possessive. "You think I haven't heard of Lamaze? I have friends who've used it. They told me all about it."

"You're a step ahead of me, then."

"I thought you women talked about this stuff all the time, blow by blow. Like war stories or something."

"I haven't been in the trenches myself yet. No tales to tell." She picked up the Lamaze book she'd checked out of the library, studied the yellow-and-white cover. "This might fit right in with your sociology course."

"It just might." Now he touched her. He laid his hand on the shoulder close to him. Lightly, tentatively, like the change in his tone. "The thing is, maybe you should ask another woman to do this with you. I mean, if you were my wife..."

She stared hard at the cover of the book. His hand felt warm. Her next breath was hung up in her chest. *If you were my wife...*

His fingers stirred against the fabric of her

blouse. "I wouldn't want you doing Lamaze with some guy who wasn't..." She looked up at him, and he smiled sheepishly. "Some guy who wasn't me."

"But you wouldn't want me to do it alone, would you?"

"You wouldn't have to. You'd have me." He glanced down at his own hand. "If...if I were your husband."

"But he won't be here, you see. What he wants or doesn't want is not an issue. It's what *I* want." She felt as though she were shrinking physically, becoming small, becoming a child herself. She needed more than a Lamaze partner. She knew that. Suddenly she was all need. One big imprecise need with no way to satisfy it. "Can't I have what I want? Is it too much to—"

He took firm hold of her shoulder. "Of course, it's not too much. It's...I'd be...very..."

"I don't mean to impose, but I need a friend, Alex." She sighed. She was behaving badly, becoming a sad case, and she realized that she was plopping that sadness in his lap and trusting him not to hurt her more. "I don't want to do this alone, and I don't want to do it with...just anyone. Even if you're not my husband, can't I have you anyway?"

"Dana Barron, you're gonna break my heart. You know that, don't you?" He squeezed her shoulder, rocked her a little. "Of course, you can have me. It's no imposition. I'll be watching my back for dive-bombers, but I'll be glad to take the class with you.''

"Thank you.'' She wanted to kiss him, but she knew she'd already made him uncomfortable enough, so she offered him a bright-eyed smile. "We can think of it as a possible research project for your paper.''

"We can think of it as definite preparation for having a baby. You're having a baby, Dana.'' He glanced at the proof and smiled. "You're getting a cute little belly on you.''

"I hardly think it's...'' She smoothed her blouse over the small mound. "Cute?''

"One friend to another?'' She nodded, and he pointed with his chin. "That is one cute little belly.''

Cute was the wrong word. He tried to imagine what was beneath the white blouse and the black slacks and the black panties—he'd decided they were made of stretchy black lace. He wondered how such a small body accommodated the expansion so quickly. He'd heard about stretch marks, and he wondered what they looked like.

He wondered so hard he had to move away, however reluctantly, subtly adjusting his jeans as he stood. "Time for me to play a little Santa Claus. You're probably getting ready to head out for the holidays.'' He pulled a big shopping bag out of the closet where he'd stashed it when she wasn't looking. He set it on the sofa where he'd been sitting, reached in, then glanced at her, checking his assumption. "You *are* going back to Wisconsin for the holidays, aren't you?" Her eyes said no.

He couldn't believe she actually planned to spend the holidays in this apartment. He didn't want to say anything, but there wasn't a touch of Christmas to be found. It looked like *his* apartment, except that he at least had put up a yarn-and-coat-hanger wreath and a couple of faded construction-paper-and-glitter things that his brothers' kids had made for him. It was the thought that counted, not the sparkle. Besides, he was a man. He didn't "do" Christmas decorations. He was planning to go to the farm, at least for the day.

"The drive would do me in," she was explaining in a small voice, "and I don't even want to think about flying these days. I'm going to have Christmas in July this year."

She looked lost, suddenly swallowed up by the sofa's field of big, gaudy flowers. "That'll be fun, with the new baby and your sailor back in home port."

She nodded. "I'll have my dissertation done, too."

"Yeah. That'll be something to celebrate." Something he didn't want to think too much about. Not that sailor sliding into home port part. "But right now, the whole world is in the holiday spirit. All around you, people are making merry. So,

Merry Christmas.'' He plucked the big red box with the white bow out of its sack and proudly placed it on her knees. ''It's really for the baby, but you might as well open it now.''

She sat up a little straighter, looking totally blown away, as though she'd never been given a Christmas present and didn't understand exactly what she was supposed to do or why.

''So I can play with it,'' he added.

He ended up helping her tear the paper off, because she acted like she was swimming upstream, trying to peel the tape back so damn carefully it drove him nuts. He was dying for her to see it, but the minute the picture of the train and its whole colorful setup was exposed, he thought, It's all wrong. It's for bigger kids. It's for boys. It looks cheesy. It was a dumb—

''It's adorable,'' she said, so softly he could hardly hear her.

When she looked up at him, the sheen in her eyes startled him. Tears? Surely Daddy's girl had had her share of Christmas presents.

''Let's set it up,'' he suggested as he plunked himself on the floor at her feet. Mostly, he had to get her busy doing something. She wasn't going home for Christmas, and she was getting teary over a little present. He was afraid she was going to have *him* blubbering pretty soon.

''It's battery operated, but I remembered to get batteries. Good thinkin', huh?'' He started taking the pieces out of the box, and she joined him on the floor. "I walked by a toy store in the mall, and they had one of these set up in the doorway. Kids were buzzing around it like little bees in your mom's flower garden." He glanced up from the pieces of track he was fitting together. "Your mom have a flower garden?"

"My mother—" she took a covered bridge from the box "—moved on to greener pastures long ago."

"I'm sorry." He was batting a thousand tonight. "What was it? Cancer?"

She smiled tightly. "An insurance salesman."

"Oh. Sorry about that, too." He hoped they hadn't taken the train. "Did you tell me that before and I just callously spaced it out?"

"I doubt it. Let me see your hands." She reached for them, opened them, held them on her lap. He had a curved piece of yellow plastic track in the callused palm of one large hand, a red caboose in the other. "These are the only calluses your body is at all susceptible to, Alex LaRock. Otherwise, you are about as softhearted..." She looked up, smiling. "How did you get them?"

He swallowed hard, thinking he had other places she ought to check out before she pronounced him soft. And not just *that,* he scolded mentally. He had lots of hard places she could rub her thumbs over the way she was doing the ugly hard skin on his palms.

He smiled. "I still help out on the farm. Hauling bales, fixing fence, general manual labor. It's good for the body, good for the soul."

"Does your mother have a flower garden?"

"Sure. It's hard for her to keep up with the yard now. She's got arthritis pretty bad. But she's got a real green thumb." Good thumbs, he thought. Skilled thumbs. All mothers needed dexterous thumbs. "Would you, uh..." He was lost in her eyes, trying to remember what he wanted to ask her. "Would you like to meet her?"

"I'd love to." She glanced away. "Sometime. You know, when things are less hectic."

"What, hectic? It's Christmas."

"That's what I mean." She slid away from him, climbing back onto the sofa, her voice going thin and raspy. "Oh, Alex."

"What's wrong?" He followed her like a puppy, wanting to get back into her lap.

"Nothing, just..." She gestured helplessly at the train, and that sheen was there in her eyes again, but this time it was welling into serious puddles. She took a quick swipe at her eyes, sniffed, tried to draw away. "Pay no attention. I get weepy sometimes. It's the hormones."

"Hormones, hell." He wasn't letting her go. "Tell me what's wrong." He took her by the shoulders and pulled her close. "Talk to me, Dana. *Look* at me."

She closed her eyes and shook her head, her silky hair swishing over his thumbs.

"I'm here, and I'm listening. You go so far, and then you shut it off, and whatever it is, it's eating you up inside. Dana, you've got important stuff, wonderful stuff, going on inside you. You can't let some worrisome pest be gnawing at your gut." He drew her into his arms and leaned back with her, just holding her, just giving her a place to shed her tears. "Come on, give it to me," he crooned. "Let it gnaw on my gut."

"What gut?" She gave a sobby laugh and patted him just above the belt. "You don't have a gut. I'm the one—"

"This is not a gut. This is..." Her belly fit perfectly in one of his hands. It was small and firm, like a ripe piece of fruit, and he wanted to caress it, to pay it homage with his touch, which, under the circumstances, could only profane it. "God help me," he muttered, mentally adding, *to comfort you, to console you, to hang on to my sanity.* "I'm trying to be a friend to you, Dana. You need a friend, and I'm trying to be that friend. Friends talk to each other. Something's bothering them, they share it. Talk it over. Find a way to work it out."

"You've probably noticed that I don't show my feelings readily or...or easily. It makes me mad when I cry. It seems like such a cheap bid for attention, and I don't need that."

"Sure you do." She didn't seem to notice the attention he was giving her. If she did, surely she would push his hand away. "Everybody needs attention. I need attention." A soothing hand stirring attentively over a tender little belly. Careful, harmless attention. "Right now you need a lot of attention. Special—"

"Attention!" She sat up quickly, drawing away, nearly knocking him off the sofa. "Attention, friend. I have something for you, too." Suddenly she was smiling, dashing from the room, her explanation trailing behind her. "It's just a little something from one teacher to another."

Her gift was a leather attaché case. He tore the paper off with relish and greeted the gift with delight, caressed it like a playoff-game ball. "This is terrific." He pulled the buttons with his thumbs, released the brass fasteners, then paused. "Damn."

"What's wrong?"

He looked at her, concerned. "I gave you something that made you sad, and you—"

"Don't you dare start comparing gifts. That's not what gift giving is about." She retrieved the little purple bridge from the floor. "Besides, this darling train did not make me sad. I can't wait to see how it works."

"You're lyin' to me now, straight out. I guess I'd rather have you keep it to yourself than lie to me."

"I'm not.... It's not the train. You know that."

She glanced away quickly, then returned her attention to his briefcase. "Look, this is where you'll put all those hundreds of papers you're going to have to correct. And here's a place for a calculator." She clutched the little bridge to her breast with one hand as she pointed out her gift's special inside features with the other. "As if you need one, the way you're able to do math in your head."

He smiled. "I'll keep one of those spell checkers in there instead."

"And your pencils and pens. See, I gave you your first red pen, right here." She'd tucked it into one of three slots.

"Damn."

"What's wrong now?"

"I want to kiss you."

She looked surprised, a little scared, a little hopeful. He knew willingness when he saw it in a woman's eyes. Maybe she didn't quite understand.

"I want to kiss you in the worst way, Dana. Not some air kiss, or some little thank-you smooch. I want to kiss you like it's New Year's Eve."

"For auld lang syne." She smiled shyly. "That would be okay between friends, wouldn't it?"

"I want to kiss you like it's New Year's Eve 1999 and tomorrow's Armageddon so it won't matter if I kiss you in the worst way—" he leaned closer, the attaché case forgotten between them, his voice dropping a notch with each word until his

breath touched hers "—possible for a woman
who's married to another man."

"Oh, Alex." She closed her eyes. "Alex, don't
do this to us."

"I'm sorry." God help him, she hadn't moved
away. She's said *don't*, but she was so close.

He straightened slowly, taking away a deep
breath full of her flowery scent. "You're right.
You gotta keep some stuff to yourself." He could
have sworn her shoulders sagged under the weight
of the same disappointment he was feeling. "But
just…whatever you choose to tell me, let it be the
truth, okay? I gave you a toy for the baby, and it
made you sad." She nodded. "You don't wanna
tell me why, that's up to you." He laid a forefinger
on the point of her small chin. "I'm pretty smart
about some things. Don't insult what intelligence
I have."

"And don't you denigrate it in any way, shape
or form."

"Deal." He nodded, closing the attaché case
carefully, as though it contained components of the
kiss they'd nearly shared. "You wanna go to the
farm with me for dinner Christmas Day? It's not a
long drive."

"I really…" She slid to the floor, turning her
attention to the train. "I have so much work to
do."

"*Christmas Day*, Dana. You don't have a damn
thing to do." He followed her lead, putting to-

gether sections of track as though he used the toy every day. "The library is not open."

"Your parents might wonder about..." She added the bridge when he nodded for it. "A man doesn't usually take a woman home for the holidays unless they're—"

"Good friends. And there's nothing to wonder about. My parents know a pregnant woman when they see one." She smiled as she set the engine on the tracks. "Come on, Dana, this is not a big deal. Don't worry, don't analyze, don't weigh the pros and cons. Just say, 'Okay, Alex.'"

"Okay, Alex. Dinner at your place."

"There, see? That wasn't so hard."

"I really didn't want to spend Christmas alone. It's just that—" She rolled the little engine back and forth "—I don't know what I'd do without you, Alex. If I lost your friendship somehow..."

"There's no way. You worry too much. One day." He claimed her hand and waited until he had her full attention, her eyes looking into his. "Promise me you'll take this one day off from worrying. Just say, 'Okay Alex.'"

"Okay, Alex."

Fred and Katherine LaRock obviously doted on their sons and their grandsons, and having the family come home to the farm was what Christmas was all about for them. It was more than "touching base." It was nourishing branches that grew far from the roots, drawing together and enjoying the sense of wholeness. Dana was welcomed into the fold without question, without explanation. She was a friend of Alex's, unable to get home for Christmas this year. She made it clear that talking about her husband was difficult, and after a few initial references, the subject was dropped.

Conversation about how well everyone was doing in school took over readily. Alex's older brother, George, and his wife, Denise, encouraged their boys to chime in with their own school stories as everyone sat down to the table for turkey dinner. Young Paul and Greg clearly worshiped their uncle Alex, not for being a football hero, but for being uncle Alex. He listened to their tales with interest, asked the right questions, roughhoused a little and joked a lot. He was wonderful with children, Dana realized. He would be a fine teacher, and, of course, that wasn't all.

Dana prompted a round of polite chuckles when she announced that, for someone from Wisconsin, she didn't know much about milking cows. "I've never even seen anyone milk a cow," she said. "Is there a knack to it?"

"We don't milk cows by hand," Fred said. "Hell, you'd be at it twenty-four hours."

"Used to, though," Alex said, rushing to Dana's defense. "When I was a kid we didn't have much of a dairy operation. We were more diversified— hogs, corn, feeder cattle. We milked a few cows.

Had an old milking machine that broke down half the time, and my older brother always had more important chores to do.''

"Damn right," George interjected. "Milking was good for Alex. When he played football, people used to ask where he got such good hands."

Fred pointed with his fork. "This boy knows his way around a teat."

"Fred," Katherine scolded, laughing. "For heaven's sake."

Her husband ignored her. "He could coax any cow to let her milk down. Beef cow, buffalo cow, moose cow..."

"Yak cow," George teased.

"Manatee cow, sea cow," ten-year-old Paul supplied.

"Give me a break," Alex pleaded, elbowing his nephew.

"County-fair milking contest," George said, "Alex always took first place."

"Until they started razzin' me to beat hell at school."

"Remember when Alfred Lund taped that sign to your back?" George lettered the message in the air. "Dairy Princess, it said."

Alex nodded, smiling, his face turning bright pink as he carefully furrowed his mashed potatoes with his fork. "Good old Alfred."

"Got himself royally decked, as I remember."

"And Alex got himself royally suspended for three days for fighting," his mother reported.

"Fortunately it wasn't during football season."

"During football season you'd've gotten off with a reprimand," George said. "There was a time when Alex was a teacher's worst nightmare. You wouldn't want him in your class, no way, no how. Him going into teaching is gonna be sweet justice for all his former teachers. In their hearts they're all saying, *may you have a classroom full of students just like you.*"

"No, they're not," Dana said. "They're saying, 'Welcome to the ranks, Alex. You're just the person we need.'"

"My tutor," Alex said, beaming. "She speaks with authority."

"But I've still never seen anyone milk a cow." She gave him a pointed look. "And here I am, visiting a dairy farm in the company of a gifted milker."

"I knew I'd have to pay up for that nice comment." He cleared his throat as he reached for his water glass. "For your after-dinner entertainment, Alex milks a cow."

It was after Dana's bedtime when they finally exchanged the last of the holiday good wishes and headed for home. Her eyes had drifted closed as soon as he'd hit the interstate, but Alex didn't dare assume she was asleep. Anything he said to himself right about then would be incriminating in the

PLAY "LUCKY 7" AND GET
FIVE FREE GIFTS!

HOW TO PLAY:

1. With a coin, carefully scratch off the silver box at the right. Then check the claim chart to see what we have for you—**FREE BOOKS** and a gift—**ALL YOURS! ALL FREE!**

2. Send back this card and you'll receive brand-new Silhouette Intimate Moments® novels. These books have a cover price of $3.99 each, but they are yours to keep absolutely free.

3. There's no catch. You're under no obligation to buy anything. We charge nothing—  ZERO—for your first shipment. And you don't have to make any minimum number of purchases—not even one!

4. The fact is thousands of readers enjoy receiving books by mail from the Silhouette Reader Service™ months before they're available in stores. They like the convenience of home delivery and they love our discount prices!

5. We hope that after receiving your free books you'll want to remain a subscriber. But the choice is yours—to continue or cancel, any time at all! So why not take us up on our invitation, with no risk of any kind. You'll be glad you did!

YOURS FREE!

This beautiful porcelain box is topped with a lovely bouquet of porcelain flowers, perfect for holding rings, pins or other precious trinkets— and is yours ABSOLUTELY FREE when you accept our NO-RISK offer!

NOT ACTUAL SIZE

PLAY THE

LUCKY 7 SLOT MACHINE GAME!

Just scratch off the silver box with a coin. Then check below to see the gifts you get!

YES!

I have scratched off the silver box. Please send me all the gifts for which I qualify. I understand I am under no obligation to purchase any books, as explained on the back and on the opposite page.

245 CIS A7YL
(U-SIL-MD-05/97)

Name

Address   Apt.#

City   State   Zip

7	7	7	WORTH FOUR FREE BOOKS PLUS A FREE TRINKET BOX!
cherries	cherries	cherries	WORTH THREE FREE BOOKS!
clover	clover	clover	WORTH TWO FREE BOOKS!
bell	bell	cherries	WORTH ONE FREE BOOK!

The Silhouette Reader Service™—Here's how it works

Accepting free books places you under no obligation to buy anything. You may keep the books and gift and return the shipping statement marked "cancel." If you do not cancel, about a month later we'll send you 6 additional novels, and bill you just $3.34 each, plus 25¢ delivery per book and applicable sales tax, if any.* That's the complete price—and compared to cover prices of $3.99 each—quite a bargain! You may cancel at any time, but if you choose to continue, every month we'll send you 6 more books, which you may either purchase at the discount price...or return to us and cancel your subscription.
*Terms and prices subject to change without notice. Sales tax applicable in N.Y.

If offer card is missing write to: Silhouette Reader Service, 3010 Walden Ave., P.O. Box 1867, Buffalo, NY 14240-1867

BUSINESS REPLY MAIL
FIRST-CLASS MAIL   PERMIT NO. 717   BUFFALO NY

POSTAGE WILL BE PAID BY ADDRESSEE

SILHOUETTE READER SERVICE
3010 WALDEN AVE
PO BOX 1867
BUFFALO NY 14240-9952

NO POSTAGE
NECESSARY
IF MAILED
IN THE
UNITED STATES

extreme. No matter what she said, she slept pretty.
Pretty as an angel. She'd worn herself out, and
she'd had fun doing it. Whatever haunted her day
in and day out had slid to the back burner, and
she'd allowed herself to enjoy every minute of this
holiday. Not once had he seen that familiar shadow
creep into her eyes.

He'd taken the boys out to the barn with them
for his milking demonstration, but once they'd
helped him herd old Gertrude into the milking par-
lor and hook her up in a stanchion, they'd disappeared into the loft to hunt for cats and mice. Alex
had stationed Dana behind a gate before he'd
seated himself on an old-fashioned three-legged
stool and set the bucket in place. He loved the
fecund smell of warm fresh milk on a cold day—
hated it in the summer, but in the winter you got
that steam, and the warmth of the cow, and the
promise of a hot breakfast waiting when the chores
were done.

"But I can't see what you're doing," Dana had
complained.

"I'm just pulling on her nipples."

"Oh."

"Using nice, long strokes. Smooth, steady
strokes." He smiled to himself. He really did have
good hands. "That's right, girl. Let it down for me.
You'll feel so much better afterward. I promise."

"No wonder you got the blue ribbon."

"You stay right where I put you," he warned

when she tried to creep up on him. "This is one sweet-tempered cow, but she'll kick any female who tries to horn in while she's being—" he smiled again "—tended to."

"I guess I would, too."

He'd boasted that he could hit any target with the milk, and she'd challenged him to target her open mouth. He'd given her a clean shot, and she'd squealed with surprise. The white stuff had dribbled down her chin and onto her puffy blue jacket. He'd laughed because he'd never seen her dribble anything. She even dribbled pretty.

He felt good, just thinking about it. It was peaceful sitting there at a stoplight with all those pretty images of Dana floating across his mind like the snowflakes falling past the windshield, with Dana herself sitting so close, her face turned to him, her eyelashes looking so lush lying against her pale skin, her parted lips so satiny, so kissable. Lord!

The last voice he wanted to hear in the back of his head right about then was his plain-cotton practical mother's. She'd cornered him in the pantry when all he'd wanted was a second piece of her peerless pumpkin pie.

She'd pushed a tall stool at him and directed him to sit, which he had. She was still his mother.

And she could see directly into his heart, just like Superwoman. "You're in this with your heels hanging way over your head, aren't you, son?"

He'd tried to play dumb, innocently licking pumpkin from his fingers. "In what?"

"In love with this woman." She might as well have dipped the words "this woman" in vinegar, as if Dana were some hussy leading her boy on.

"It's not like that, Ma. We were just friends when we were in college. If I was gonna fall in love with her, don't you think I'd've done it then, when she was single?"

"That would have been the right way to do it, yes." She studied him, eyeball-to-eyeball. Playing dumb had never worked with Ma. "Life would be so much easier if people could fall in love at the right time with the right person."

"I told you, it's not—" he looked at the pie longingly and sighed, but not, of course, for pie "—like that."

"You can't look me in the eye and say that," she observed. "Which should tell you something you maybe haven't admitted to yourself yet. I can see it, plain as day."

"Dana's married. I respect that. That's the way you raised me, and that's the way I am." Now he did look her in the eye. "I'm not doing anything wrong."

"You were a challenge to raise. The respect was always there. That wasn't a problem. It was the need to take risks. From tree-climbing to football, horses to motorcycles. You had to prove you could stand closer to the edge than anyone else dared."

But her sympathy came through in the tone of her voice. He heard it, and he fed on it a little. He figured he was allowed. She *was* his mother. "It's a tough spot to be in, you know. The one you're walking into. For your own sake, you ought to turn around and walk away."

"I can't." Shamelessly he looked to her for more sympathy, but this time it was for Dana. "How would you like to be all alone when you had your first baby?" That did it. Her eyes went soft as spring rain. "See? How can I just walk away?"

"It'll hurt when *she* does."

He nodded. "I know."

Chapter Four

The Lamaze instructor suggested attending
classes during the last trimester. Dana had decided
on Lamaze from the outset. She believed in being
prepared. She made a habit of studying up on all
her activities and going into them armed with information. She wanted this child to get off to a
good start, and she'd decided, having done a considerable amount of reading, that natural childbirth
was the way to go. She expected pain, and she
wanted to be ready for it. She intended to rise to
the occasion in good form.

But she needed a birthing partner, or a coach, as
Alex preferred to be called. Shanna Bixby, the instructor, explained that Lamaze discouraged the
use of "sporting event" terms. When she turned
away, Alex looked over at Dana, tapped his chest,
winked and whispered, "Coach."

She nodded. "Coach."

The truth was that she had no partner. She'd
always known that child rearing was best managed
by a partnership, but she'd begun to see the need
for a child*bearing* partnership more clearly every
day. She was not simply a conduit; she was a
woman carrying new life within her, and she
wanted to talk and plan and worry and decide with

someone. Some days she just wanted to lean on someone and let him do all the planning and worrying.

But she didn't have that kind of partnership. She was lucky to have a coach. She was lucky to have Alex, whose understanding of anatomy and exercise physiology put him at the head of the class from the outset. He was fascinated with the discussions of pregnancy and childbirth, nutrition and the hazards of drugs. He filled a notebook with wonderful sketches, commenting that his graphic notes were a good companion to her unillustrated, orderly outlines. "One of my picture's worth a thousand of your words," he reminded Dana.

When it came time for the exercises, Alex was right down on the floor with Dana. The instructor claimed that it was important to isolate individual muscles and learn to use them precisely. While Dana chafed at the idea of becoming "intimately aware" of the component parts of her body, Alex did not. "That's what your coach is here for," he teased. "Body parts are my specialty."

"Not *these* parts." She looked askance at his diagrams.

"*All* parts, but these are particularly fascinating." He smiled. "Clinically speaking."

Preparation for labor was the part that unnerved Alex. He was no stranger to pain, and the idea of seeing Dana through what the instructor described as "the most intense physical pain of a woman's life" truly bothered him. "The pain of childbirth would crush a mere man," Shanna said. "Fortunately, women can take it."

"And be back at the plow the next day," one man joked.

Alex wasn't laughing. He was sure he'd been to hell and back with his motorcycle injuries, but looking at those diagrams, thinking about getting an eight-pound baby through that little passage in Dana's body... He couldn't imagine how it would feel. When he'd been in pain, he'd taken whatever painkillers were offered. He admired her for choosing the natural route for the sake of her baby, and he tacitly resolved to do anything he could to help. They practiced controlled-breathing techniques. "But does this help with the pain?" he asked.

"You have to distract her," the instructor said. "Make her think about you rather than the pain. Make her look into your eyes while you breathe together. Go ahead, try it. Make her—"

"Look into my eyes," Alex teased, aping a variety-show hypnotist as he took Dana's chin in his hand and turned her, made her look at him, smiled when she blushed, all the while managing to keep the rhythm steady.

"Hold her hands," Shanna suggested, and he complied, taking her small hands in his without permitting his eyes to waver from hers or letting her gaze stray from his. He tucked her hands against his chest and kept up the breathing pattern.

"That's right, Alex, don't lose her. You're in control. She's feeling intense pain, and she might lose control. It's up to you to help her get it back."

He tried to keep it light, but he found it impossible. The look in her eyes drained him of cool and consumed every emotion but the one he couldn't name, could never declare. It didn't matter what her air of complete trust did to him. It didn't matter that the seduction was unintentional. It didn't matter how lost he was in those sweet, sensitive, starving eyes. He had to recover himself. He couldn't ask her what she was hungry for, couldn't offer to supply it. He couldn't breathe for her or bear the pain for her or carry the ball for her. All he could do was coach.

"This makes me dizzy," she said, then puffed her lower lip out and blew a wisp of hair out of her face.

"Me too." He tucked the strand behind her ear.

"As you move into active labor, your partner's role becomes more active, too. Partner, you'll rub her stomach, her back, her shoulders, whatever needs rubbing."

"Whatever needs rubbing," Alex promised solemnly. Dana's eyes widened. Then she smiled merrily.

The instructor spoke of applying counterpressure during back labor. "Don't worry about pushing too hard," she said. "The stronger your hands are, the more helpful you'll be. You can't match the pressure of those contractions, so go ahead and rub as hard as you can.''

She lay on her side, and he rubbed the small of her back, as instructed. It felt good. He could tell by the way she relaxed under his hands, the way her muscles gave in to him. His hands brought her comfort, and they could bring her much more, if things were different.

She grabbed his hand suddenly, slid it over her melon-firm belly and held it there. He started to massage the spot she'd chosen for him, thinking that was what she wanted, but she kept him still. She turned her head, looked up at him and smiled, a strangely sad smile. "Do you feel it?" she whispered.

He did. A moving bulge filled his palm. A small hand or foot punching against the barrier of her womb, reaching for him, saying hello. He nodded, returning her smile, but there were tears in her eyes now. Just one of the many moods of his melancholy Madonna that tore at his heart. Granted, he would never know exactly how she felt, what this moodiness was all about, but he saw how it was, took it for what it was and saw her through it with all the tenderness he could muster.

She couldn't know how he felt, either; how hard it was, caring this deeply for another man's woman. He hadn't imagined how hard it would be himself, the bittersweet times like this when he felt like a kid looking though the dimestore window, so close...so damned close. Harder still were the solitary nights spent lying awake thinking about her, wishing he could crawl into bed with her and just hold her. That was how different he wanted things to be. If she were his to have and hold, he could keep those wistful tears at bay.

"Does it hurt?" he asked as he rubbed his thumb over the little bulge, saying hello back.

"Not physically," she said. "It just feels so surprising, to know that there's a little person inside me. We've been having talks lately."

"About poetry and stuff?" He figured the kid was probably already signed up for kindergarten.

"About shoes and ships and—"

"All right, now I'm going to show you another way to apply counterpressure," the instructor was saying. "Everybody up. I want you to sit on the floor, back-to-back. She's going to brace herself against you and ride out the contraction. And, remember, the force of that contraction will push a camel through the eye of a needle. Back labor can make or break you as a birthing partner." Shanna Bixby singled Alex out with a look. "Are you up to the challenge?"

"Who, me? A mere man?" He laughed as he aligned his back with Dana's. "Go ahead, woman. Show me what you've got."

She really did want to show him what she had. Doubts, fears, hopes, dreams, all combining to consume her of late. She wanted to share them with him, to let his strong back help bolster hers the way it had when they'd sat back-to-back and she'd pushed as hard as she could against him until she'd felt that they'd melded, blended, formed an impregnable alloy. Still there as two, but stronger as one. She wanted to show him *all* she had, the best and the worst, the love and the lies—but she was afraid that would be the push that would break his back, that would drive him away.

Despite the demands of his own schedule he rarely missed a class, and he never let a day pass without calling her. He insisted on getting her out of the apartment whenever he thought she'd been closeting herself with her books. He dragged her into a mall one afternoon on the pretense that he had to go shopping for a baby as part of his current class project. "Just to see what the latest stuff is," he explained, "and what it all costs."

"The baby's a girl," she told him as she was drawn to a display of tiny, totally impractical dresses. She took a pink-and-white one off the rack. "I found out today. I didn't think I wanted to know, but when Dr. Carpenter said he had the information, I couldn't leave the office without asking."

"Another Daddy's girl, huh?" He turned the key on a stuffed puppy and smiled when it played a familiar lullaby. "It would be great to have a daughter. We don't have any girls in my family.

The LaRocks must be overloaded with that Y chromosome. But I'd love to have a Daddy's girl." The puppy was still tinkling when he set it back on the shelf. "Did you call the ol' man and tell him he's getting one?"

"I haven't had time." She jammed the little dress back into the "newborns" section. "Besides, you know how the time zones screw everything up."

"When was the last time you talked to him, Dana?" She tried to move past him, but he blocked her way. "No, seriously, does the man ever call? I never hear you talking about him calling. I'd kinda like to talk to him myself, just to—"

"Stop it, Alex." She tried to get around him again, and when he refused her passage, she glanced at another couple browsing close by and spoke in a confidential tone. "Please, don't. I really don't want to discuss my relationship with my...my husband." It was more than just a threat to her fairy tale. She suddenly felt ridiculously protective of the husband who didn't exist. "It doesn't seem right to talk about someone who's...not able to be present or...physically involved in the discussion."

"You're saying you don't want to talk about him behind his back?" She nodded. He shrugged and let her pass. "You sure took the long way around."

It was as good a route as any. "I always do, don't I?"

"Only on some subjects." Seemingly satisfied, he tested out a plastic rattle. "Okay, so now we're looking for pink stuff, right? You've been resisting all this time, but now that you know it's a girl, you can get serious about picking stuff out."

This was a bad idea. She knew it. It made her throat feel prickly when she touched a cuddly bath towel and imagined wrapping it around a wet baby. "I've heard it's bad luck."

"What's bad luck?"

"You know, buying baby things too soon."

"I've never heard that." He offered a dubious glance as he rounded a table full of blankets, putting it between them. "Besides, I've got a feeling the big day isn't that far off. You leave everything till the last minute, you're gonna be in the hospital, and I'm gonna be running around looking for stuff to dress her up and take her home in." He appeared to be sizing up a fluffy pink blanket for the occasion. "Unless he comes..." He caught her warning look and shrugged. "Okay, okay, that's probably bad luck, too. You're hoping he'll get some leave, and saying it might jinx it, right?"

She glanced away, guilt weighing on her like lead.

"When did you get to be so superstitious?" he wondered artlessly.

"It's not that I believe in luck," she claimed, avoiding his eyes. "I just don't push it."

She picked up a baby book and started thumbing through it, absently at first. There were pages for lists. List of gifts. There would be gifts from her, she decided. Anonymous gifts, to be used or discarded as the new mother...the adopting mother...the *mother*...

There was a family tree for both sides of the family. Dana realized that she didn't know anything about Gary's family or his medical history. She'd promised the social worker at the agency she'd tentatively selected that she would find out more, but she hadn't done it. She hadn't done much except watch her belly grow and feel sorry for herself and make up a pack of lies and be generally...

The "milestones" page was a real killer. She hated the way it made the back of her throat start burning again. First tooth, first word, first step. Where was first breath? She would be there for that. If she gave the baby up, she would miss all those other things.

If? It wasn't a question of *if.*

"You want this?" Alex was looking over her shoulder. "Let me buy it for you."

"No," she said, too quickly, too adamantly, as she slammed the book shut. "No, I really don't. I mean, I already have one. I've started writing in it already. You know, first urine sample, first bout with nausea, first sign of—''

''Movement?'' She looked up, and he smiled. ''After you let me feel it that time in class, I started noticing. I can see it more all the time. I wonder, Is she punching or kicking? I think, Is that a hand or a little foot?''

''I wonder, too.'' She put the book back and snatched a stretchy terry-cloth sleeper from another shelf. ''A few basics are all we'll need to start with. Little pajama things like this. I think they outgrow everything very quickly. I think...'' She sighed, shook her head and spoke in a small voice. ''I don't want to think, Alex. I don't know anything about babies.''

''Sure you do. You're a woman.''

''So? I haven't been around many babies. I came equipped with a womb, but that's it. All I know is that they're small. They need small things.'' She tossed the sleeper aside and gestured helplessly. She was losing it. Losing touch with reality, losing the baby, losing Alex, losing whatever sense any of this had made in the beginning. Losing a whole list of things she'd never had in the first place.

Losing control. Springing a leak in the dike. ''What would you pick, Alex? Pick out something for her to...go home in.''

''Ruffles and bows.'' He'd laid hands on a frilly dress before he noticed that she was fumbling with a tissue. He had his arms around her before she could protest. "Hey. It's okay to be scared, honey."

"I'm not scared. I'm just...tired maybe?"

"You're not convincing either one of us with that one."

She shook her head, wiping furiously. "Let's go."

"I'm going to buy this first." He kept her close to his side while he shoved his choices into her arms—sleepers, gowns, receiving blankets, a tiny sweater. "And this. A couple of these."

"Alex..."

"Your best friend is supposed to invite all the girls over for a party so they can all give you stuff like this, but I don't know any girls."

She rolled her eyes. "Right."

"But I am your best friend." He looked to her for confirmation, which she gave with a nod. "So I'll just shower you myself. Probably cheaper in the long run than putting up streamers and feeding a bunch of hens."

"Hens!"

"Chicks?"

She laughed.

"There, now, I made you smile, so the least you can do is humor me," he said as he unloaded the baby clothes next to the cash register. "These mood swings go away after the baby's born. Well, there's the postpartum depression, but then things even out."

"According to Dr. LaRock?"

"Haven't you been paying attention in class? You're the one who's about to become a doctor. I'm just getting the regular old bachelor's degree. And I've already perfected regular old bachelorhood."

"Will this be all?" the clerk asked.

Alex answered with a credit card.

"Alex…"

He forestalled her protest with an upraised hand. "I'm really getting some insight here for my sociology paper on men and women and how the differences kinda complement each other. See, there really is an important role for a man to play during this time. He's gotta keep a cool head. You know, even keel, steady as she goes."

"You're saying I'm unsteady? My behavior's uneven?" She gave a quick sniff as she put a hand on her hip. "That I'm—heaven forbid—uncool?"

"Humor me. I'm just a regular old bachelor." He dried her cheek with his thumb. "A mere man."

A few days later she answered a knock at the door with a bright smile for Alex, who was the only visitor she ever had. She was not expecting the man with the white hair, the round, rubicund face and the unruly eyebrows. "Dad." She watched his gaze slip, then his smile. The eyebrows dipped, too, and all she could think to say was, "How did you find me?"

"It wasn't easy." He looked up, shook his head ostensibly to clear it, then peered into her face as if it occurred to him that she might be an impostor. "I mean...the only address I had...that you gave me was the English-department office, and then...you've got this elaborate call-forwarding system set up. I...I checked with your friends—"

"What friends?"

"People you worked with. People..." He risked another glance at her protruding stomach.

"Come in, Dad."

"I know who your friends are, Dana," he said, launching into his best form of defense, which was a nonstop philippic. "You think I don't know who your friends are? I noticed some people seemed a little baffled by your sudden exit, the way you cut everybody off completely. They allowed that it was temporary, but I got to thinking. It wasn't like you."

He tossed his topcoat over the back of a chair, gripped the finial and turned, clearly aghast. He took the tone she hated most—imperiously quiet, oppressively reasonable. "What is going on here, Dana?"

"I think that's fairly obvious. However, I am hard at work completing my dissertation. That part was not—"

"Dana, you're pregnant, for God's sake!"

"That, as I said, is fairly obvious. I'm thirty years old, Dad. This is not something I have to explain or justify to anyone. I'm perfectly—" Another knock at the door. She'd suddenly become a very popular pregnant person. "Excuse me for just a moment, Dad."

No smile this time, not until she opened the door and saw his face, the warmth his eyes extended to hers, the full and unqualified acceptance. Her heart floated above the gloom her father had brought, and she managed a smile. "Alex."

"You forgot about our date?"

No. Never. She hated having to give up any piece of the time they spent together.

"Alex, this isn't a good time. Someone's here." She pulled the door close against her shoulder, hoping to block his view. "I would have called, but it was a surprise. I wasn't expecting—"

"He's here?" Alex glanced over her head. "I'd really like to meet him, Dana. I've kinda felt like I was treading in another man's, uh... I mean, I wasn't...*we* weren't doing anything wrong, I know, but if I could meet the man face-to-face, shake his hand, tell him how—"

She shook her head, sagging against the door, her head spinning. It was all too complicated, and she didn't have a whole lot of energy to spare. "No, Alex, it isn't... That would be..."

"You okay?" He grabbed the edge of the door just above her head. She wasn't going to get away with shutting him out. "There's no trouble or any-thing, is—"

She felt her father's presence at her back. She saw it in Alex's eyes. The man didn't look much like a fighter pilot. She was trapped between the only two important men in her life, and they were both about to demand the truth about the mystery man, the no-man who'd made a brief-but-lasting impression.

"There might be plenty of trouble if you're the man who's responsible for all this," her father said.

"All what?" Alex applied more pressure to the door, and Dana gave in, backed up and let him come inside. "Listen, Dana and I—"

"Dad, Alex and I...are just—"

"Dad?" Alex looked at her, incredulous, then scowled at her father.

"I haven't told anyone at home," Dana told her father. That would be his first concern. "I intended to take care of it without getting anyone else in-volved. I really didn't want any..."

Alex slipped his arm around Dana's shoulders and drew her to his side. "This is our problem, Mr. Barron. Dana's and mine. We're both respon-sible."

"Alex—"

"And we'll continue to be responsible."

"You're not married, are you? Have you gotten married without—"

"No, Dad, we're not." And she didn't intend to lean on him, either, but he was there, and she was so grateful and so tired that she allowed her hip to rest against his.

"Are you getting married?"

She stared coldly at her father. "I haven't seen you in months, and when I do see you, it's 'touching base.' How long does it usually take us to touch base, Dad? Not long enough to discuss anything as complicated as marriage or children."

He looked wounded. "Well, if you'd given me some hint..."

"A hint isn't enough. When that's all we have time for, I'd rather not get into it." She glanced away from them both and sighed. "I've gotten myself into this situation, and it's my situation, and I don't want any advice, and I particularly don't want any judgments made."

"I wouldn't know what to say," her father claimed. "I don't know what to think. I just can't believe it. This isn't like you, Dana."

"Why not?" She stepped away from Alex and looked straight at her father. "Why isn't it like me? What am I like, anyway? Do you know? Do you have any idea?" She fought the tears that scorched her throat, fought the tremor that threatened her sober, sensible tone, but it was impossible to stem the tide of the tremors that shook her hands, her shoulders, her lower lip, the myth of her stability.

"I know what you think about this. You don't have to tell me. You think—"

"It's something your mother would do."

"Really!" she said furiously, then she thought about it, and she almost laughed. "Really? I guess I wouldn't know."

"But it can be remedied. There is no problem without a solution, Dana. No—"

Alex saw the rage on Dana's face, and he moved quickly to put himself between her and the unwitting antagonist. "I think it would be best if you left now, Mr. Barron. I don't know about your blood pressure, but Dana's is getting dangerously high, and we don't want that." He shoved her father's topcoat into his hands and showed him to the door. "Right? We need to put Dana first right now. Where can we reach you?"

"I have a meeting in Denver tomorrow. Dana knows how to reach me." The older man glanced over his shoulder. "I'm never out of reach, Dana. You know that. That's why I cannot believe—"

"We'll be in touch, then," she said, affecting a mordant smile. "That's how it goes, isn't it?"

"There's no need to be rude." Her father shrugged into his coat. He glanced up at Alex as though he wasn't quite sure how far he could push or who was in charge.

"No, I don't need to be rude, and I don't mean to be," Alex told him calmly. "But I do have a need to look after Dana right now. You can appreciate that, can't you, sir?"

"I..." He glanced from Alex's face to his daughter's. "I expect to hear from you as soon as—"

"You will," Alex said. "You have my word."

"Man to man?" Dana asked quietly after the door had closed on her father. Alex questioned her with a look, and she laughed it off. "'You have my word,'" she mimicked. "He appreciated that, I'm sure. Probably the only part of the whole sorry scene that he could really appreciate. One man offering his word of honor to another. You now have his highest regard."

"But not yours," he surmised as he approached her.

"It probably seems very strange to you," she said, backing away. "Hardly Christmas dinner at the farm."

That wasn't what was foremost on his mind. "You're not hiding a marriage from him, too, are you?" She closed her eyes, a small frown creasing her brow. "There is no husband," he concluded.

"No, there's no husband." She shook her head tightly. "There's no Daddy's girl, either. There never really was. Not me." She spread her hand over her belly. "And not this little one, either. She has no daddy yet, but I'm going to make sure that—"

"Dana." He gathered her slim shoulders in his

big hands. "That part of the story was strictly for my benefit, wasn't it?"

"What part?"

"The flyboy husband on the aircraft carrier. You cooked that one up just for me. Why?"

Again she closed her eyes, not because she didn't want to see, but because she didn't want to cry. Her voice trembled. "I'm pregnant, Alex."

"So what? Why did you have to lie to me about being married?" He gripped her gently. "We're friends, Dana. Aren't we?"

"That's just the point."

"What point?" His hands fell from her as he turned away, truly mystified, deeply hurt. "I mean, I thought we were good friends, *close* friends. Don't you trust your close friends?"

"Yes. I trust you. I treasure you." She gripped the back of the chair that had held her father's topcoat. "I couldn't bear to lose your friendship."

"All this time I thought you were married." He'd put some distance between them now; safe, neutral distance. He needed it as his eyes sought hers. "Do you have any idea how I felt? How I *feel?*"

"I have a pretty good idea what you think."

"I think you lied to me, that's what I think. Flat-out lied, and kept lying, and *kept* lying. And for the life of me, I can't understand—"

She sank into the chair. "No matter what you think of me, Alex, there's one thing I want you to know. I care about this baby. I've made some serious mistakes, done some things that were terribly wrong. As you say, just plain bad.''

"I didn't say—''

"But I'm going to do the right thing *for the baby*. She's going to have good parents. I've been vacillating, lately, not getting around to signing papers, putting off—'' She patted the small wooden table with a flat, resolute hand. "But no more. Two good parents. A caring family like yours. That's what my baby deserves, and that's what she's going to have.''

"Are you in love with this guy?'' She looked up at him, and he almost lost himself in the innocent, curious look in her eyes. "The baby's father. Are you in love with him?''

"I'm in love, all right,'' she said sadly, glancing away. "Hopelessly in love, I'm afraid.''

"So marriage isn't really out of the question.''

"It probably wouldn't be.'' She fixed her gaze on the door, as if she were still expecting someone. "If he knew.''

Damn, she was stubborn. "You haven't told him?''

Damn, he was naive. "Barrons don't do shotgun weddings. They don't work out very well.''

"You owe it to the guy to tell him,'' he insisted.

Two different *hims,* she thought. Her baby's biological father and the man she loved. Two very different *hims.* She smiled wistfully. Lovingly.

"You don't know what you're talking about, Alex."

"That's because all I've got to go on is what you tell me." And the message he was getting was that Barrons didn't do cabdrivers, either. "So you're giving the baby up?"

"It's the right thing to do," she said. "The best thing all around."

"And you're not even going to tell him?"

"Tell…" She looked at him, wanting to tell him, wishing she had the right, wishing he would just know and understand and forgive her. But there he stood, defending the paternal rights of Everyman, even spineless Gary Broder. Again she glanced away. "Oh, him. I did tell him that I was pregnant. Scared the living daylights out of him. Threatened his whole agenda." She laughed mirthlessly. "The poor man just wasn't ready, I'm afraid."

"Nice guy." Not the kind who deserved her love, but there it was. Luckily she'd run into a real sucker shortly thereafter, he thought. "But it sounds like you've got everything all worked out the way you want it."

She swallowed hard, nodded briefly. "I want to do what's best for the baby. That's really all that matters right now."

"I can see that." He shoved his hands into the pockets of his leather jacket. "For what it's worth, I don't like being lied to, Dana."

"For what it's worth..." She looked up at him. She was determined not to cry now. There were tears gathering in her eyes, and she could feel them, but she wasn't going to let them fall. No cheap bids, she thought. Just an honest apology and a brave smile. "I'm sorry, Alex. I...don't suppose I could use the hormones as an excuse."

"Oh, I'm sure you could. Why not?" He handed her another business card. "You call me when the time comes if you want me there."

"You'd still come?"

"What do you think?" He studied her for a moment, wondering how such an intelligent woman could even ask such a question. "Maybe you oughta work on that one, huh? See if you can figure it out for yourself. What kind of man do you think this big, dumb jock is, anyway?"

"I already know the answer to that. You're not—"

"I'm your coach. A guy can always depend on his coach." With a jerk of his chin he indicated the card she was clutching. "Call me when it's kickoff time."

Chapter Five

The city sidewalks had been cleared of the previous night's two-inch snowfall, but more flakes were beginning to flutter to the ground. Still, it was a good day for a walk. Bright gray, a little breezy, fairly warm for a March afternoon in Minnesota.

Every day had been a good day for a walk lately. Dana had been taking regular walks, long and purposeful walks, hoping to get the show on the road. She wasn't sure she would recognize the early signs, but with her ever-increasing inward monitoring, she had become generally self-absorbed. Every twinge of discomfort caused her to stop whatever she was doing and take internal inventory. Was it a contraction or gas? False labor or the real McCoy?

Lately she'd made a bad habit of wearing herself out when she walked, of suddenly finding herself unable to take another step. Her coach would have scolded her for it, but he wasn't there. He'd called a couple of times to see how she was doing, but he'd sounded distant, which was understandable. She should have told him the truth long ago. She and her pride were destined to grow old together, and together they would amount to one quite lonely old woman.

She'd avoided Mama's Café because she'd regularly stopped there with Alex, but there it was, handy, and here she was, worn-out. How long had it been since she'd been here with him? Mere weeks. The longest weeks of her life. She chose the corner table they had always shared, but she could have sat anywhere. The place was hardly busy. She took two copies of *The English Journal* from her shoulder tote, ordered her usual large orange juice, propped her feet up on a chair and tried to ignore the fact that she ached all over. She went after the first journal article with a highlighter. There was good information here. Interesting, useful information.

She was glad she wasn't going to be tested on it.

Still, she whiled away some time with the journals and the highlighter. Somebody was playing country music in the kitchen, and the smell of the fried meat and potatoes somebody was cooking up back there was not appetizing. A few people came in for supper, but not many. The swelling had gone down in Dana's ankles, but the low back pain she'd come in with was not going away. Neither was it getting any worse. She decided to give it a little more time. She didn't want to hit the pavement again with an aching back.

"What time do you close?" she asked the frowsy redhead behind the lunch counter.

The woman laughed. "We can't afford to close. Can I get you anything else?"

"I'd love some toast with peanut butter and another large orange juice." She wondered if that was enough to pay for the space she was taking up. "Do you mind if I stay here for a while?"

"Pregnant women are the exception to the no-loitering sign." The woman delivered the orange juice to the table, then took a closer look at Dana's face. "Are you all right?"

"I'm fine." She wondered how she looked. "Are you Mama?" The woman answered with a quizzical look. "The owner," Dana explained, pointing to the logo on the front of the plastic menu.

"I just work here. Far as I know, there is no Mama. It's just a name. A word that reminds people of food. The kind you can depend on."

"Depend on Mama," Dana said wistfully, pulling her juice closer.

"You betcha." The woman tipped her head, indicating the belly Dana had stuffed under the table. "Pretty soon now, I'd say."

"Very soon."

A man dressed in a stuffy black topcoat and fedora came through the door, greeted the redhead and claimed a table not far from Dana's. He was served coffee and the newspaper. Didn't even have to ask. Dana figured that was what it meant to be a "regular." One of these days she'd probably be a regular at a place like this. She would have her regular time, her regular waitress, her favorite table, and she would complain vociferously if they seated anyone else there. She wouldn't have to see a menu. She would bring her paperwork, and it wouldn't bother her that she had no one to share her meal with, no one to talk to.

"I don't mean to intrude."

The voice startled Dana out of her dispirited reverie.

"I'm sorry," the man said. Without the black coat and hat he looked more approachable. Almost bald, but he had friendly eyes. "Is there anything I can do to help?"

"No, I don't think so." She knew she was feeling sorry for herself, but she hadn't realized she'd let any tears show. She wiped her hand across her cheek and smiled. "I... It's just hormones, you know."

"Maybe you could use some company. I'm a minister. That doesn't give me the right to butt in where I'm not wanted, but I know a troubled person when I see one."

"In my case, all it takes is a pair of eyes. I'm obviously in—" She realized what she'd been about to say, and she laughed. "But we don't use that expression anymore, do we? 'Getting a girl in trouble.' That's politically incorrect now, isn't it?"

"I've stopped trying to keep track of what's politically correct. Everybody's tears look the same to me.''

Impulsively she spread her hands over her stomach, which was draped in a full-cut knit smock. ''I can't do this.''

''That baby isn't about to give you much choice.'' He smiled, a little too patronizingly, she thought. ''But you know what?'' he said. ''You're going to surprise yourself.''

''I already have.'' She didn't need any of this, not now, not from a *mere man,* be he minister or mugger. What did he know? ''Myself and everyone else.''

''What you mean is, you can't do it alone. And you won't be—''

''What I *mean* is...'' Her back hurt was what she meant, and she felt like being mean, but she sighed. The man, the *mere* man, was just trying to be nice. ''I'm sorry. I know what you were getting at, and I know that's your job and everything, and I do believe in God, but what I mean is...'' She sat up and shoved her hands behind her, trying to iron the kinks out. ''I don't think I can do it...the way I planned. I know I'm being selfish. I know that. But I just can't.'' She looked up at the man now. He had a kind face. No hair, nondescript features, but there was kindness in the washed-out blue eyes. ''I love my baby. I want to be her mother.''

''And that's not what you had planned,'' he

said, drawing a chair over from his table and strad-
dling it, folding his arms over the back.

"If I back out now, more people will be disappointed." She closed the journal carefully,
smoothed the cover as though she were making a
bed. "I've made such a terrible mess of everything,
and that's not like me. Really. I'm usually very
responsible. Completely dependable." The pain
was beginning to radiate from her spine around the
distended sides of her stomach. Hot, spearing fingers of pain. She'd really done it to herself this
time, walking too far on concrete.

"Are you all right?"

"I'm fine." She was rubbing her lower back. "I
know the difference between false labor and true
labor. I've read up on it. I've taken classes."

"First baby?"

"Well, yes, but I know..." She waved any other
possibility away with a curt gesture. "My coach
keeps telling me that..." The mention of Alex
brought tears back to her eyes, but she smiled
through them and rubbed harder. "He says I've got
it all down pat. We've practiced and practiced and
practiced, and..." She nodded, lips trembling, still
smiling, looking like an idiot, she was certain.
"And he says I'm ready for the big..."

"Your coach," the minister said. "Are we replacing 'significant other' with 'coach' now?"

"He's my friend." The tears were rolling. She
felt like a crying drunk, babbling on, no way to.

stop it. "He's my very best friend. He promised to be there, even though I messed everything up with him, too."

"Maybe you should call him now."

"Not until it's time. I've put him through enough." She sighed, shifted in her seat, found that she had to lift her knees with her hands to get her feet off the chair. "I guess I really should go home pretty soon."

"I'd be happy to take you home."

"No, thank you." She dredged up a brave smile. "I just needed to get off my feet for a little while. Sometimes a little peanut butter and orange juice is all it takes to perk me up."

"Your burger is up, Reverend Henry. And the little mother's peanut butter on toast."

When Dana didn't invite the minister to join her, he left her to her peanut butter. She didn't feel much like talking. She had to tune in to her discomfort. "Make sure it's the real thing," Shanna had said. "You don't want to check in too early. They'll start trying to meddle with nature."

It wasn't that Dana wanted to be a purist about all this, but she wanted to do it right. Give her daughter the best possible start. She nibbled at her toast. She hadn't been paying much attention to the clock, but this was definitely more than discomfort.

The redheaded waitress offered her a refill on her orange juice. "On the house."

Dana offered a wan smile and shook her head. "I wonder if you would call me a cab."

"I'd call you—" she put her hands on her hips and made a production of sizing up Dana's front end "—more like a VW Beetle." The waitress didn't seem to notice that she was the only one laughing. "Sorry," she said, winding down. "I couldn't resist. Sure, I'll—"

"I could—"

"*This* cab." Dana handed the woman the card, then glanced at the minister, who was about to offer his services again. "It has to be this cab."

"Picky, picky." The redhead chuckled as she headed for the phone. "Pregnant lady's prerogative. Do my best for you, dear."

He knew it had to be Dana. The time was right, the place—they'd stopped in at Mama's after baby class once or twice. He wondered how long she'd been there, whether she'd walked. It was dark, and the weather was getting ugly, the sidewalks slippery. What was she thinking? She could slip and fall and he wouldn't be there to catch her and keep her safe. He'd been waiting for her call, dreading its coming, fearing that it would never come. But it was *her* call. Had to be.

She looked bleached out, like something frail and pretty abandoned to fade in the sun, but he wasn't going to say anything about it. It was her call. He stood awkwardly by the table. "How's it goin'?"

"Fine, just fine."

"You need a ride?"

"I need a friend." She looked up and smiled for him, but he saw the uncertainty in her eyes. "Are you my man?"

"Sure." He straddled the empty chair that was pushed back against the table. "What's up?"

She moistened her lips. "I'm scared."

"You're gonna do fine, Dana." He shrugged. "Easy for me to say, huh? Listen, I'm your coach, and coaches know these things. They know when they've got somebody who's ready, and you're—"

She grabbed his arm and hung on tight, as though he might have thoughts of leaving her. "I'm afraid I'm going to do the wrong thing again. I'm sitting here thinking, I can't go through with this, I can't go through with this, and that's wrong. Wrong for me to think that way." She sounded so sure, but her eyes were wild with doubt. "I don't want to give her up, Alex."

"Who says you have to?"

"Nobody." She shook her head. "Nobody. It's the right thing to do, that's all. She needs a family." A fleeting smile crossed her face. "A family like yours."

He studied her for a moment. "I've been thinking about all the things I wanted to do to this fly-boy of yours, and then I found out he doesn't exist.

I oughta be glad, right? 'Cause now I don't have to be a traitor to my country or commit a capital crime.'' He put his hand over hers, the one that held his arm. "But somebody exists. I mean, there's somebody...."

"There's nobody."

"No, you said..." He shook his head. The guy had run off on her. *Hopelessly in love,* she'd said. He smiled. "Is this a miracle or what?"

"I believe it is. I really do." She tried to return his smile. It was a valiant effort, but it fell short. "Only two things matter to me right now, Alex. What's best for this baby and..." She squeezed his arm as she paused, took a halting breath, collected herself and took another stab at smiling. "The fact that you're here."

"I said I would be." She nodded. He nodded, too. "How far apart are the contractions?" She closed her eyes. "You've gotta give me a hint if you want me to do my job. A starting place, you know?"

There were more tears now, streaming silently down her pale cheeks. "I can't do it."

"Honey, you're going to have a baby." And he was going to help her if she didn't rip his heart out first with those frail tears. "You're going to do it beautifully, the way you do everything else. That's all you have to think about right now. Now just tell me—"

She shook her head vigorously. "I can't give her up, Alex."

"You don't have to."

"As long as she's inside me, she's mine."

"How far apart—" He tipped her chin up. "Dana, look at me. We're going to do this together, and you're going to be straight with me, start to finish. Agreed?"

Blasted tears, she couldn't stop them. She didn't care who was looking, who was staring. She felt their eyes, the silence all around her, but she didn't care, because she saw only Alex. There were only the two of them here, she and Alex. She felt terrible, and the pain was the least of it. He'd just made the most beautiful offer she'd ever heard, and she just wanted to crawl into him through those warm, sweet brown eyes of his and be part of him. But she knew he didn't need that. What he needed was to keep his word—because he was that kind of guy—and be done with it, over and done. And she felt terrible, *terrible.*

"You must think I'm an awful person. Irresponsible to begin with. Dishonest. Stupid, just plain stupid. I should have—"

He stopped her with a kiss, his mouth completely covering hers. With an intake of breath, quick and sharp to match her pain, she drew his breath, drew his being, into her own. He filled her like warm, flowing, soothing solace, like a balm made from love. She welcomed his tongue, his lips, the caressing, the caring, the taste and the scent of him, and his magic elixir carried her through the pain.

Regretfully he withdrew his mouth before the end of time, but the essence of him lingered, and she resolved to hold it, keep it inside her, just like the baby. They were hers—her baby and Alex's kiss—never to be taken from her, as long as she kept them inside her.

Happily, when she opened her eyes, his were still there, rational and reassuring and brimming with approval. "I should have done that a long time ago."

"I wanted you to." Oh, God, more tears. She tried to laugh through them. "In the worst way."

"The worst way? Let me give it another shot." He kissed her again, and she hung on during a respite from pain, a moment of wonder. He came away laughing, hugging her. "How bad was that?"

"That was very bad. Phenomenally bad."

"I love you," he said. "You know that, don't you?"

She shook her head, wanting desperately to be persuaded. "You feel sorry for me because I've gotten myself into such a stupid mess."

"That, too." He held her face in his hands. "Hey. I hate pity. You think I'm gonna go around dishing it out when I can't take it?" She shook her head. "Just tell me one thing. Why did you lie to me, Dana?"

"I didn't want you to think badly of me. That's how it started out. And then..." She gripped his forearms, hanging on to the moment, to the spots of clarity in the fog of increasing pain. "And then I couldn't go back...lose your respect. I had... I mean, you did at least...

"Did you hear me say, 'I love you'?" She nodded. "Do you believe me?" She hesitated, realized that this was the one true thing she could hold on to, smiled and nodded again. "Does it matter?"

"More than you can possibly know, but you don't have to—"

"Don't tell me what I don't have to do. Unlike some people, I know what I can and can't, have to and don't have to, do." Her eyes drifted closed, but she was half smiling. "Look at me, Dana. What have you got to say for yourself?"

"I love you so much, Alex." She looked into his eyes and willed him to know. "So much, so much."

"Thank God." He took her hands in his. She gripped them as though she were crossing a rope bridge as he kissed first one, then the other. "We're gonna have to have a baby. We're gonna get married, too, but first we're gonna have to have a baby. How far apart—"

"I don't know," she gasped. Control of her breathing was getting away from her. "You're in charge of the stopwatch."

"It's out in the cab. I've been carrying it with me."

"Shanna said we shouldn't go to the hospital too soon because they'll want to— Oh, dear."

"You'd better get that woman to a hospital," a woman's voice said, but neither of them saw her or acknowledged her, because there was no one else in their world at the moment. Just two people about to have a baby.

"In, out, in, out…" With her hands gripping his, he checked his watch. "That lasted almost a minute," he whispered excitedly when he could feel her relax somewhat.

"It was mostly in my back," she gasped.

"You're gonna drop this baby right in my lap. I vote we go somewhere where I can rub your back." He glanced over his shoulder. They were being watched closely by three people now—the man at the next table, the waitress, and a curious cook. "I can't coach and drive at the same time."

"I'll drive," the other diner said.

"Oh, thank you," Dana said as Alex helped her to her feet. "He's a minister. He's been very nice. I was—" A gush of water flowed down her legs, but the pain that gripped her wiped out any thought of embarrassment.

"Damn." Alex swept her into his arms and headed for the door. "Call 911 and tell them to send us an escort. The reverend's gonna be driving like a bat outta hell."

"I do anyway," Reverend Henry said as he grabbed Dana's coat off the coatrack with one hand and held the door open with the other. "Got a ticket last week."

"Great." Alex got Dana into the back seat of the cab, trying to wrap her coat around her as he handed over the keys. "How fast can you perform a marriage?"

"With no blood tests and no license, it wouldn't be quite—"

"The words. The promises. I want—"

"Yes," Dana said, dimly aware that her trip to the hospital was finally under way. She leaned back in Alex's arms. "I do, too."

"As long as we're married, nobody's coming between me and my wife and baby. That's just in case Mr. Nobody has a change of heart." He leaned over and took a peek at her face. "You'll take my name? You and the baby? My daughter?"

"Our daughter," she said.

"If you change your mind later, if it's not legal anyway, you can just forget it, but—" She pulled his hands over her belly, and he rubbed her, the way he'd been taught. "It should be your husband doing this, right, Rev?"

"Amen to that."

"So let's make me your husband, because I'm gonna be there every step of the way—breathe, that's right, in, out, in, blow—and when we get to the delivery room—in, out, in, out, blow—I'm gonna be seeing you naked for the first time.''

''Oh, Alex...''

''But it'll be okay, 'cause I'll be your husband.'' He glanced at Reverend Henry in the rearview mirror. ''Like a bat out of hell'' was putting it mildly, but a siren had just taken the lead and another was pulling in behind them. ''It's Alexander James and Dana Carol.''

''Dana Carol, do you take Alexander James...''

''Oh, Alex... Oh, Alex, ooooooh, Alex... Yes, I do, I do!''

Alex did, too. And he also took Margaret Elizabeth, who was born forty-five minutes after her parents arrived at the hospital. She shot right out into her daddy's waiting hands. As instructed, he put the squirming little bundle on her mother's flaccid nest of a stomach and drew Dana's hand to the baby's wet head.

''That was some catch,'' Dana said moments later, thoroughly elated.

Alex was busy overseeing every aspect of the handling of his daughter from his post by his wife's side. ''How many points?''

''Ten on the Apgar scale,'' Dr. Carpenter announced.

''That means we win,'' Dana said. ''You really do have fabulous hands.''

''Oh, honey, just you wait.'' Alex kissed her

joyously, his promise couched in a splendid smile. "You don't know the half of it yet, but you will."

"Will you be nursing her, Mrs...." The nurse was looking for a chart.

"LaRock," Dana replied as she took her daughter in her arms. "Yes, I will. I know I have a lot to learn, but that sounds like a good place to start."

"You might as well start now, then," another nurse advised. "I'll bet Dad wouldn't mind assisting in that department, would you, Dad?"

"What?" Alex grinned. "I get to help with the milking?"

"Just the unveiling," the nurse said. "The ties are in the back."

Dana laughed and leaned forward so that Alex could untie her gown. She watched his eyes as he carefully peeled the cotton fabric away, as though he were unwrapping a gift that might easily get broken. His eyes glistened as he admired her breasts for the first time. "Daddy's a blue-ribbon milker, Margaret Elizabeth," he whispered close to his daughter's ear. "You need any help, you just let me know."

Dana smiled when the rooting little mouth found her nipple instinctively. Tears filled her eyes. She kissed her baby's downy head, then her husband's waiting lips. "She's Daddy's girl, all right."

He nodded. "Her mama's Daddy's girl, too."

*   *   *   *   *

A STRANGER'S SON

Emilie Richards

Chapter One

No one in his right mind would choose to rekindle childhood memories during the worst blizzard in twenty years. But Devin Fitzgerald had often done the unthinkable. He had left Yale Medical School three months into his second year to join a struggling rock band with the unlikely name "Frozen Flame." And he had left Flame at the peak of their extraordinary and undeserved success to strike out on his own. Four years into the runaway success of his solo career, he had made a decision to limit touring so that he would have more time to compose and record. Now he was considering a new career entirely.

But none of those decisions seemed as risky tonight as driving the back roads of picturesque Holmes County, Ohio, in a car without chains and a body clothed in nothing warmer than a lightweight leather jacket.

As Devin tapped his brakes to slow his Jeep Cherokee to a crawl, he hummed a few bars of the melody that had been plaguing him for days. Most of his songs started this way. An interval, a rhythm, a melodic mood that expanded in his head one measure at a time until he had enough to whistle and eventually to pick out, one-fingered, on the piano. This particular melody was more elusive than most, but he suspected the finished composition might be his best. Already it made him think of soft summer nights in America's heartland, of fragrant moonflowers on split-rail fences and the winking of fireflies in knee-high acres of corn.

He had needed to come home.

He had needed to come home, but *not* at midnight in the middle of a blizzard.

Devin tapped his brakes again. The Cherokee resented his interference, and the powerful engine sighed in protest. He was barely moving now, but the snow was so thick that he still couldn't see exactly where he was. He knew he was on the right road. It had been years since he had been to Farnham Falls, but little had changed. Before the snow had thickened, he had recognized an old gray farmhouse that had once been the last landmark before the turnoff. There were other houses just beyond it now, but not many. This was still farm country, a stronghold of the Amish and Mennonites, and rural to the bone. The road he was looking for would appear on his right before too long, and if he was lucky and the Cherokee made the turn, he would be home soon.

Home. Devin almost smiled at the thought. He had been everywhere, lived everywhere, for the past eight years of his life. He was an adaptable man, as comfortable in Sri Lanka or Sicily as Seattle. He hadn't missed Farnham Falls particularly.

There had been little here for a restless youth with a Fender guitar, a thirty-watt amplifier and delusions of grandeur. Every day of his adolescence he had dreamed of leaving. But in the past months he had dreamed only of coming back.

He was alone on the road. He hadn't seen a headlight in thirty minutes, and there were no Amish buggies clip-clopping their way home. Everyone with sense was at home asleep, with an extra quilt thrown over them for good measure. The snow crunched under his tires and licked at his windshield wipers. He hadn't been this alone in years; he hadn't experienced silence in quite this way since he was fourteen and slogging his way through the January snow to his aunt's barn to feed the resident animals. Something very much like peace was descending with the snowflakes. He knew he should be concerned for his own safety. If his car stalled he could be in trouble. He had tried his cellular phone just a little while ago, only to discover that it was crackling with static. He wasn't worried. The snow was glorious, and for the first time in months he was feeling almost whole.

The giant oaks that marked the turn seemed smaller now, but the turn led to the same narrow, unpaved lane he remembered. He fishtailed and slid perilously close to a ditch before he steered the car out of the spin. He had another mile to go, maybe two, and he would be home. His cousin

Sarah had promised that the house still looked much the same as he remembered it. Sarah, her husband and two children had lived there in the years since aunt Helen's death, but now they were out on the West Coast, and the house belonged to Devin. Sarah hadn't understood why he wanted it. "You could live anywhere in the world, Dev," she'd said when he'd offered to buy the house from her. "You hated Farnham Falls. You haven't been back since high school."

"But I don't hate it anymore," he'd explained. And he didn't. Ohio represented a time in his life when he had been filled with dreams and the delicious innocence of youth. He wanted to find that place inside himself again.

If it was still there.

He kept his foot off both the accelerator and the brake and concentrated on the middle of the road. The house would be warm. His manager had found someone to clean and ready it for him, stock the refrigerator with food and the shed with firewood. There was no telephone, no television. He had seen to that himself. He was looking forward to a month of quiet nights and quiet days. A month when he could think without interruption. Once he got to the house, the blizzard would make everything that much sweeter. No one would visit. No one would even know he was there.

Unless he stopped just ahead to help the occupants of the car that was half in, half out of the ditch.

Devin tapped his brakes, and the Cherokee began to slide again. He cursed the other idiot who—like him—hadn't known enough to stay off the roads tonight. He couldn't see the car clearly, since it was shrouded by snow, but it appeared to be small, a compact model that probably looked better when it wasn't nose down, belly exposed. He steered to the right until the Cherokee was under control, then tapped his brakes again. He was twenty yards beyond the other car when he finally came to a halt.

For a fraction of a second he considered not going outside to check on the car's occupants. He didn't want to leave the warmth of the Cherokee or announce his presence in town. He told himself a rapid series of lies even as he began to button his jacket. The car was smothered in snow, so it had been there for some time. Whoever had been driving it had already gone for help. There was nothing to indicate an accident so serious that anyone might be injured. But he had already slammed the car door behind him by the time the last excuse had begun to form. He might be world-weary, cynical even, but in the very depths of his soul he was a Farnham Falls boy, raised to care about the people around him and to offer help when needed. Eight years of rock bands and groupies, of incomprehensible adulation and life lived under a microscope, hadn't erased the values his aunt Helen had instilled in him.

Someone needed help. He had help to give.

Devin had left his headlights on, but they did little to illuminate the accident scene, since the Cherokee was so far ahead and aimed in the wrong direction. Two feet into the storm, the wind nearly knocked him off his feet. He shoved his hands in his pockets and leaned into the wind, but it stabbed at his cheeks and neck and sifted through the worn denim of his jeans. He wasn't wearing socks, and he regretted that now. His loafers sank into each drift, and snow packed his shoes. By the time he was ten yards from the car his feet were on fire, which was only slightly better than the inevitable numbness that would quickly follow.

"Is anybody in there?" He shouted the words, but the wind twirled them back at him. He caught snowflakes on his tongue the moment he opened his mouth and swallowed them in a burst of sensation. He repeated his shout as he closed in on the ditch, but he didn't expect a reply. He wasn't going to find out if anyone was still in the car until he was peering in a window.

What if a passenger was injured? He wondered if he remembered any first aid. He supposed that his months in medical school had been wiped away by now. In the past years he hadn't been called on to do anything more than perform, compose and give interviews. There had always been someone at his side to take on anything resembling an emergency. He told people what to do and they did it, no matter how foolish or complicated his orders. But no one was nearby to take orders now.

Lord, he was glad there wasn't. He was so glad to be on his own that even the thought of freezing to death in the middle of nowhere had appeal. It seemed almost justified. Devin Fitzgerald, formerly of Frozen Flame. He had been frozen inside for so long that he liked the symbolism.

"Is anybody in there?" He was close enough to the car now to see into the windows—if the windows hadn't been cloaked with snow. Another blast of air shoved him forward. The wind was howling, a demented, witchy shriek that would have made his skin crawl if it hadn't been nearly frozen. He leaped over a mound that a snowplow had piled there in the last storm and started inching his way down an incline toward the ditch.

The car was in worse trouble than he'd thought. The back wheels were completely off the ground, and the front of the car was more accordion than hood. The driver had probably spun the steering wheel as the car slid off the road, because the weight had shifted toward the driver's side as the car had come to rest. There was no hope of getting in or out that way. He would have to try the passenger's side.

As he had expected, the ditch bottom was ice under snow, inches of it that might or might not

hold his weight. Devin gritted his teeth and tested
the ice with one foot. He thought it shifted, but
there was nothing to be done about it even if it
wasn't frozen solid. He had to get to the bottom
of the ditch to open the door.

He skidded across the ice and reached up for the
door handle just as the ice cracked beneath him.
He hung on, but the handle couldn't stop him from
sinking nearly a foot. Ice water took the place of
snow in his shoes, and he grunted with shock.

"Is anybody in there?" He had sounded more
concerned the first time, but this time he was just
glad his voice was working. He listened, but the
wind was his only answer.

He scrubbed at the window with his hand, but
there was still a layer of ice beneath the loose
snow. He scratched at it with his fingernails and
pressed his face against the window. It took his
eyes a moment to adjust to the nearly complete
darkness of the car interior.

There *was* somebody there.

"Hey!" He banged on the window with the heel
of his hand, then tried to open the door. But the
handle wouldn't give. "Hey!"

He couldn't tell if the shadowy figure inside the
car was a man or a woman, but he saw movement.
A head turned at the sound of his voice.

"Let me in!" he shouted. "You've got to get
out of there. You're going to freeze!" He wondered how badly the person had been injured. He

saw a head loll back against the seat. "Can you unlock the door?"

There was no signal that indicated the person inside could do anything at all.

Cursing like a roadie with a hangover, Devin let go of the door handle. He could try to find something to break the glass, but that might injure the driver. He tried the back door instead, but it was locked, as well. He scraped that window clean and peered inside again. There was nothing to indicate that the opposite door might be unlocked, but it was worth a try.

He gauged the safety of scrambling across the trunk and decided it was safe enough. The car seemed wedged in place, and his weight wasn't going to disturb it. He hefted himself up and slid across the back window to land on his feet on the driver's side. The back door here was high enough that, despite the car's angle, he could probably slide in if it was unlocked. He reached up and pulled on the handle. Nothing happened.

Frustrated and growing numb, he squatted beside the driver's window and began to scratch the ice away. "Can you turn and unlock the door behind you?" he shouted. He could just make out the straight slope of a nose, short dark hair and the glint of eyes, open eyes that were staring in his direction.

When the driver didn't move, he shouted again.

"I'm going to have to break the glass to get to you, if you can't open it yourself."

"Go away."

For a moment he thought the sound he heard was the wind. But the wind didn't speak in syllables. He was so cold that it took him another moment to put the sounds together. Then he knew what he'd heard. The driver was a woman, and she was conscious enough to speak, even if she wasn't making sense.

"Unlock the damned door!" He slapped his palm against her window. "I'm not going to hurt you. I'm trying to save your life! You're going to freeze to death!"

She turned her head away from him.

She had to be injured to act so irrationally. As he watched helplessly, she fell forward toward the steering wheel and her body jerked. It was so dark that he could see only shadows and movement. He shouted to her again, hoping he could convince her to help. "Listen! It's zero degrees out here, and the temperature's falling. You could freeze before I can get help. Please. Help me help you!"

He thought he was going to have to break the window. He was contemplating which window would be safest when she spoke again. "Go. Please…"

He felt around in the snow for help. He needed a rock, and even then he imagined the glass would take a couple of mighty blows to break. He had already decided on the window behind the driver when he heard her sobbing.

He felt like a criminal. He didn't even know what to say to reassure her, but he tried his best. "Honey, it's okay. It really is. I'm a Farnham Falls boy, born and raised. I wouldn't hurt you for anything. I'm going to get you out of there in a few minutes and get you to a hospital."

She was sobbing harder. He stood to broaden his search for a rock or stick when he heard the sound of a window screeching in protest as it was lowered.

With a prayer of thanksgiving on his lips he squatted again and reached inside her window to unlock the door behind her. Then, before she could say a word, he opened the door.

"The car might shift when I get in," he warned her. "But don't worry. It's not going to turn over. It's wedged too tight. I'm going to get in and unlock the other side. Then I'm going around to get you out the passenger side. But you're going to have to trust me and do what I say, or we're both going to freeze before I get you back to my car."

She was still crying, but he glimpsed something like a nod.

A minute passed before he made it back around to the other side and got the passenger door open. "Okay, now. I'm going to get in and pull you out this way. How badly are you hurt?" He wished that he had asked her that before. The possibility existed that he could make matters worse by moving her, despite the cold.

"I hit...my head." She grunted the answer as if she was in pain.

"Okay. Anything else hurting?"

"Please... Just get me out."

"That's exactly what I'm going to do. Just relax and let me do the worrying."

She groaned and bent forward again. He knew better than to panic, but the temptation was there. He lifted a foot to the open doorway and hauled himself up and into the passenger seat. Then he reached for her.

There was a lot more of her than he had bargained for. He released her immediately and leaned away. He managed to dispense with profanity, despite the call for it. "You're pregnant!"

She groaned again and rested her head against the steering wheel, which rested taut against her swollen abdomen.

A terrible thought occurred to him. "Are you in labor?"

She groaned again, and that was the only answer he needed. He touched her cheek in comfort, but she jerked her face away from his hand. "Just...get me out!"

"Right away. Just don't drop that kid in the snow."

She didn't dispense with profanity, although her vocabulary was sadly limited. Despite himself,

Devin grinned. His own shock was quickly giving way to a sense of omnipotence. He was going to get her out of here, and he was going to save her and the baby. For months he had wondered if there was anything more to Devin Fitzgerald than flash and hype. Now he was about to find out.

He put his arms around her again. "Wedge your feet against the side door," he instructed, "and push while I pull. We're going to get you on this seat first, then I'm going to help you out of the car. I'm going to try to carry you up the embankment to mine."

"You...can't!"

"Oh yes I can." He began to slide her toward him. With gratitude he realized she was taking his suggestion. When she was suspended between the two bucket seats, he slid off his seat and down into the ditch, pulling her steadily as he went. When she was settled on the passenger seat he rested a moment before he spoke.

"Okay, swing your legs around to the floor. I'll put one hand under your knees and one around your back."

"You're going to drop...me." The last word was followed by another groan. He suspected it signaled the onset of another contraction.

"We'll wait until that one's finished," he said, as calmly as he could. "Let me know when it's done. But they're coming pretty fast. We've got to get you to a hospital immediately. And I'm not going to drop you. Not on your life!"

Time seemed suspended as he waited. He wished he could see her face, but the light in the car wasn't working—damaged, he guessed, in the accident. Even if there was a moon tonight, it was blocked by storm clouds. The darkness was as thick as the snow. He had only the impression of a small-boned woman, delicate features and shining dark hair.

"Ready?" he asked, when the struggle seemed to be subsiding.

She nodded.

He slid his arms beneath and around her. His feet were wet and quickly growing numb, but compared to what she was about to endure, he supposed frostbite was nothing. He took a tentative step backward and swung her into the air. With relief he realized that he probably *was* going to be able to carry her. She wasn't as light as a feather, but even with the extra weight she was toting, she was a small woman. If he could get up the embankment without slipping and over the mound of snow to the road, they would make it.

"What's your name?"

"Just…get me out of here!"

"Well, Get-me-out-of-here, hang on tight." He started forward. All he could see of her now was shining hair. Her cheek was against his chest, but he thought she was sobbing. "We're going to get you to the hospital. Was that where you were heading?''

"Yes. No. My doctor..."

He tested his path, one careful step at a time. The embankment was slippery, but not the problem he had feared it would be. "You were trying to get to the hospital but couldn't make it?''

"The storm knocked out...my phone. My doctor lives... I was trying..."

"To get to him," he finished. "Bad luck all the way around. Is he close by? I sure as hell hope he's close by." He gripped her harder as she groaned again. He was very much afraid that she was having another contraction.

"Down this road..."

"Where's your husband? Shouldn't he be with you?''

"Bastard!"

So it was like that. Devin wasn't surprised. Men were famous for abandoning women who got pregnant unexpectedly. Something akin to rage filled him. He would like to find the man who had done this to her, then left her alone to have their baby in the middle of a blizzard. "Look, don't you worry." He gripped her tighter and took another step. "I'll stay with you if you want. I'll see you through this. I'm going to make sure you're fine."

She was sobbing loudly now. If he gripped her any tighter he would bruise her badly. He didn't know how to comfort her. They both needed comfort, so he began to sing. Softly. To the top of her head. He made it up the embankment before he realized what song he'd chosen. Not one of his greatest hits. Not one of Frozen Flame's. It was the lullaby his mother had sung to him every night until her death early in his childhood.

The song that he had been hearing in his head for the past weeks.

He spoke without thinking. "I'll be damned...."

"You *are* damned...Devin...Fitzgerald."

He was poised with one leg over the snow mound when she spoke. He was frozen for a moment. Not from the brutal gusts of wind that could turn a man to ice. But from her words and a terrible revelation.

He swallowed an answer and a question. He stepped over the mound and nearly stumbled, but somehow he managed to keep them both upright. Then he started across the road and down to his car. He was silent, and the only parts of him that seemed to be working were his legs. The rest of him was suspended and waiting.

He made it to the car, balancing her against it as he opened the passenger door. Then he settled her inside.

And in the beam of the overhead light he finally saw her face.

He couldn't remember her name, but she had remembered his. "Get me down this road, then get...out of my life!'' she said between gritted teeth.

He squatted beside the open door, squatted in the snow and the wind and the near darkness. But the car light shone clearly on her face. "Is this my baby?'' he whispered.

"Not...in a...million years!''

But Devin knew the truth, even as she began to cry again. The child this woman was carrying belonged to him, as surely as the woman had belonged to him for one magical spring night the previous year.

He remembered that April night as clearly as if it were yesterday. He wondered if she was remembering it, too.

Chapter Two

A sea of daffodils danced in a light spring breeze outside the town-house window, and somewhere nearby a blue jay squawked displeasure at a tabby cat curled up in the sunshine. April was in full bloom in Ohio, but Robin Lansing didn't have time to notice.

"So you think I should wear the green dress?" Robin held up two dresses for her best friend to examine.

Judy McAllister frowned and shook her head. "The red. Sexier. And wear your hair down."

"I'm not supposed to be sexy. I'm supposed to be professional. I'm representing the paper. I'm trying to get Devin Fitzgerald to give me an interview, not a back rub."

"You'll have a better chance at both in the red dress," Judy said wryly. "First you have to get him to notice you."

"I have as much chance of speaking to him as the man in the moon." Robin held the red dress against her chest and decided Judy was probably right. It was worth a chance.

"Look, the guy—or at least his press agent—sent the paper two tickets to his concert and the party afterward. Apparently he's still got a soft spot for his old hometown. You've got an in. Now you just have to use it."

"I'm glad you're coming with me."

"You'd better get dressed or neither of us will make it to Cleveland on time."

Robin finished dressing while Judy closed up the apartment and fed the cat. At the last minute Robin shook out her hair, which had refused to go into a smooth knot at the top of her head, and let it hang loose below her shoulders.

"You know, that dress ought to come with a printed warning." Judy's blue eyes were sparkling. She was dressed up herself, but no matter what Judy wore, with her curly brown hair and round face she managed to look like Miss Wholesome Ohio, the title she had garnered in their senior year of high school.

Robin smiled at her friend. "I'm glad you came to see me. You're good for my ego."

"It's a short trip from Cincinnati. And besides, I'm just glad to see you coming out of mourning."

Robin's smile didn't even falter. It had been two years now since Jeff, her husband, had died. Life had gone on, as Jeff had insisted it would. She was almost ready to step back on board. "Jeff would have liked this dress."

"You know, if you get an interview with Devin Fitzgerald, it could lead to a job on a larger paper."

"I know." Robin had left a job on a larger paper at the beginning of Jeff's final hospitalization. After his death she hadn't been able to face a busy newsroom every day. She had come to the *Farnham Falls Gazette* instead, to take a job as editor and begin the healing process. The job had been perfect for the two years she had held it, but getting free tickets to Devin Fitzgerald's concert was the only exciting thing that had ever happened. It probably was time to move on.

The two women chatted casually on the drive north, but Robin could feel her excitement building. She was an admirer of Devin Fitzgerald's, not precisely a fan, since her tastes ran more to classical and jazz; but Devin hadn't abandoned melody or poetry in his work, as so many rock artists had. He was part James Taylor, part Mick Jagger. Despite the driving beat of drums and the shiver of electric guitars, there was a purity, a raw emotion, to his songs that never failed to touch her.

He was a handsome man by anybody's standards, with golden-brown hair that nearly touched his shoulders, ice-blue eyes, a square jaw and a high forehead. Robin knew from watching his videos that he was large enough to dominate a stage. With his wide shoulders and long legs he looked like a New Age prophet when he performed. She was anxious to see him in person.

She wondered if she would get close enough tonight to even tell Devin who she was and what paper she was from. The tickets and backstage pass had been a big surprise to everyone at the paper.

Devin Fitzgerald had spent most of his youth and adolescence in Farnham Falls, but his connections over the years since had been tenuous. The aunt who had raised him had died a long time ago, and even his remaining cousin had moved to the West Coast. Devin contributed sets of compact discs or generous checks to any fund-raiser in town, but he hadn't been back in years.

By the time the two women arrived in Cleveland and had parked at the hotel where they would spend the night, Robin was almost feeling young again. She was only twenty-seven, but some of those years had been agonizing. She knew plenty about pain, and she supposed that was part of the reason that Devin's music appealed to her. He knew something about pain himself. While she had been losing a husband, he had been losing a wife to infidelity and divorce. Robin's pain had been silent and unheralded, but Devin's had been dissected in public.

"I've read every article about Devin Fitzgerald that I could find, in case I get a chance to interview him," Robin told Judy as they walked amid a swelling mass of young and old toward the downtown arena where the concert was going to be held. "But there hasn't been much written in the past year about his personal life."

"Maybe it's taken him time to recover, too."

"Do you suppose someone like Devin Fitzgerald is allowed to take that kind of time? The pressures on him must be fierce.''

"He's got more money than God and probably more women than a sultan. I'm having trouble working up sympathy.''

Robin smiled, but she wondered if Judy was right. Fame and fortune didn't protect anyone from the realities of life. As she and Judy found their seats at the front and settled in to watch the opening act, she wondered if Devin Fitzgerald had been changed by misfortune in the same ways that she had. Now she understood how short life could be, and how capricious. She intended to fully live each day that was given to her and to savor with gratitude the good things that came her way. If anything positive had come from Jeff's death, it was that.

Devin had braved the first wave of well-wishers right after the concert, but the second wave had been forced to wait until after he showered. Now he dried himself and slipped on a clean pair of jeans and a freshly ironed white shirt.

The concert had gone well. It was one of only half a dozen he would do that year, and all the tickets had been snapped up the first day they had gone on sale. His manager hadn't understood why he'd insisted on a performance in Ohio, but Devin knew he owed something to the state where he'd been born. He wished that he had time to go back to Farnham Falls, to sneak in on some back road and revisit his childhood there. He had almost convinced his cousin Sarah to sell him the house where he had been raised. Maybe then he could go back, dig his roots deep in the county's dark soil and try to remember who he was.

At the same moment he went in search of his shoes the door to his dressing room opened. "We've got a roomful of people waiting to shake your hand." Harry Bagley, Devin's manager, stuck his head through the opening. "You about ready?"

Devin considered refusing. He was bone weary. He had put more of himself than usual into the concert, performing three encores with his backup band and one by himself with nothing but a spotlight and a guitar. But this was Ohio, and he owed these people. "About. You been hiding my shoes?"

Harry shook his head in exasperation. "You need me to hire somebody to dress you, Dev? Is that what you need?"

Devin collapsed on a plaid couch and rested his head against the back. "I need about six months away from you and everybody else. Then maybe I could find my own shoes."

"You need to get laid."

Devin opened his eyes and stared at Harry. It was an old argument. Harry believed that everything could be cured by money or sex. Since Devin had plenty of one, the root of all his problems must simply be a lack of the other.

Harry held up his hand to stop Devin's inevitable reply. "I'll find the shoes. I'll put them on and tie the damn things if that's what it'll take to get you there."

"Get out. I'll be there in a few minutes."

Harry snorted. "If you're not, I'll be back."

"You come back and you're fired."

"Yeah, yeah." The door slammed behind him.

Devin sat up and began looking for his shoes again.

The party was in full swing by the time he joined it. He was mobbed immediately, which exhausted him immediately. He had used up most of his energy onstage. The suite was brightly lit and noisy, exactly what he didn't want tonight. At the beginning of his career he had craved both. After a performance his adrenaline had flowed so fast and furiously that he'd needed this excitement so that he could come down slowly. But more often now he only wanted peaceful conversation, soft music and the warmth of friends.

One look around the room told him that friends, real friends, were in short supply tonight. His band had already come and gone. The best of the myriad people who traveled with him weren't here. The place was filled with strangers and people he didn't want to know better.

Harry took his elbow and led him across the room to introduce him to a small group of men in business suits. He was still making the rounds ten minutes later, listening politely and commenting when it was called for. Someone had gotten him a drink; someone else had given him a plate of food, which he'd had to set down somewhere in the middle of the room to shake a hand.

He was hungry, his head hurt, and his ears rang from all the noise. As he smiled and conversed he backed slowly toward the door, signaling his bodyguard and driver to go for his car.

A soft, warm body stopped his progress.

"Oh, I'm sorry."

He heard the woman's voice before he saw her. He was apologizing as he turned. "No, it's my fault. I..."

Pale ivory cheeks turned pink at his words. He hadn't seen a woman blush in years. For most of the women he knew, it would have been pointless. This one did it naturally, but then, everything about her seemed natural. She was a dark-eyed beauty with long hair that was as black and shiny as a raven's wing. She wore very little makeup, just enough to enhance the delicate features that Mother Nature had blessed her with. She was tiny. The top of her head barely came up to his chin, but she was no child. In a hip-hugging dress the scarlet of tulips, she was every inch a woman.

"I'm clumsy." He recovered quickly. He had met a million women at parties like this one, and too many times he had been disappointed.

"No, I was in the way." She smiled. "I liked the concert."

Liked, not loved. She liked it. She wasn't gushing with praise. She liked it. "Did you?" he asked. "I'm glad."

"I have a neighbor who claims that when he was a boy he could hear you playing the guitar in your aunt's barn all the way from his house."

He tilted his head to get a better look at her. "Really?"

She held out her hand. "I'm Robin Lansing. From the *Farnham Falls Gazette*. Thank you for sending us tickets."

He absorbed it all. She was from Farnham Falls. She knew an old neighbor, someone who had known him as a child. "Us?"

"Yes. My friend Judy. She's here somewhere."

Someone put a hand on his shoulder to get his attention, but Devin ignored it. "Do you like the party as well as the concert?"

"I don't like it at all." She smiled. Her entire face lit up, and he felt bathed in sunshine. "Not until now, anyway. I'm glad I got to meet you."

"Is that why you came?"

"I came to see if I could get an interview, but I can see that's going to be impossible."

"Why?"

"Because this is a zoo. We'd have to shout at each other."

"You're not nearly pushy enough to do what you do for a living."

"Probably not. But most people seem to want to talk to me, anyway."

He wanted to talk to her. Devin suspected this woman might be the only sane person in the room. He had become an excellent judge of character in the years of his career, particularly since his divorce. This woman believed in old-fashioned virtues like honesty and concern. He knew that after one minute in her company. And she was as lovely and fresh as an Ohio spring. He wanted to know more.

"I'm starving," he said. "And I'm tired. I want something to eat and a friend to talk to. Would you like to be that friend?"

He saw the first tracing of wariness cross her features. "To talk to? Is that code for something else?"

This time he smiled. "Talk's what I'm asking for. *All* I'm asking for. You can tell me all about Farnham Falls. Are you willing?"

"May I take notes?"

"I'll tell you when."

"All right. But I need to let Judy know."

"I'll wait right here."

"We've got two choices," he told her, when she rejoined him and they threaded their way through the arena complex toward the place where his limo would meet them. He took her hand and ignored the security trio who trailed behind them. "We can try to find a restaurant that's open and hope I won't be recognized, or we can go back to my hotel and order from room service in my suite."

"Are you ever not recognized?"

"Nope."

"Then we'll go to your suite."

She was silent as they got into the limo and silent as they drove past a squad of cheering fans who had figured out where he would exit. She was silent in the hotel, too, as security whisked them through gathered crowds. She was silent until they got to his suite and closed the door behind them. "I'm beginning to get a feel for the way you live," she said.

"Daunting, isn't it?"

"Do you get used to it?"

"More or less. Less, tonight. I'm not in the mood to be a god."

"Are you ever?"

"Not really." He gestured toward the comfortable leather sofa, and she sat down. He smiled when she took off her shoes and tucked her feet under her skirt. "What do you want to eat?"

"A hot fudge sundae."

"A woman who knows her own mind."

"After you've had to make a few crucial decisions in your life, the little ones are a piece of cake."

He thought about that as he dialed and gave their order. Then he joined her on the sofa, sprawling an arm's length away. He wanted to ask her what crucial decisions she had made, but it seemed too personal. "Are you from Farnham Falls? Should I remember you?"

"No. I grew up outside of Columbus. I graduated from Ohio State."

"Ohio University for me."

"I know. I'm sorry I know so much about you, really. I'd like to hear it all from you, instead."

He would like to tell her, too. She was right. She was easy to talk to. She was certainly easy to look at. "Start with your childhood, and when we've finished your life we'll do mine. Then I want to hear all the Farnham Falls gossip."

"You must be a remarkably patient man, or a masochist."

"I'm just a man hungry for small-town life." Or for one particularly lovely small-town woman. Devin wasn't sure which, and right now it didn't even matter. He smiled lazily and settled in for the evening.

Robin didn't know how she ended up in Devin's arms slow dancing to an old Frozen Flame ballad. He had put on the compact disc to illustrate a point he'd been making about early nineties rock, and the next thing both of them knew, they were moving to the music together. The hour was late. Very late. In fact, it was nearly dawn, and they had been talking without a pause.

She had told him about herself, and he had filled in the things about himself that she hadn't learned from her research. They had laughed together, each delighting in the other's sense of humor. But as the hours had passed they had gotten more personal. She had told him about Jeff and the diagnosis of leukemia that had come just one month after their marriage. He had told her about his brief marriage to Wendy, a blues diva who sang with great conviction about love and in real life had no convictions about it at all.

She couldn't imagine a woman so cold that she couldn't love Devin Fitzgerald, if given the opportunity. Either he was the worst of charmers, the one-in-a-million phony who could get through Robin's personal radar screen, or he was one of the most genuine men she had ever met. She had watched him relax as their time together passed into hours. He was starved for this kind of conversation and intimacy, and she had realized just minutes into the conversation that she was, too.

She had also watched the expression in his eyes warm, and noticed the subtle shifts of his body so that little by little they drew closer. She knew he was attracted to her. She had tried from the moment he bumped into her not to be attracted to him. But it had been so long since she had felt this excitement in a man's presence. She didn't know if it was Devin the man or Devin the star that she was attracted to, and she didn't really care. She felt alive for the first time in years; alive and warm in places no man had touched since well before Jeff's death. She had begun to wonder if she was still a normal woman with normal urges. Now she knew that she was.

The ballad drifted into another, something she hadn't quite expected. She raised her head to smile at Devin, and he smiled back. Then, with a slow, fluid sweep, he lowered his head and touched her lips with his.

"You're so lovely," he whispered. "This has been very special."

It was just a touch, the briefest of kisses, but she knew it for what it was. He had asked her a question. If she answered yes, she could stay. And if she answered no, their time together had ended. It wasn't a threat. He was absolutely right. They had reached the peak of this kind of intimacy, and now they parted or progressed to another. Since the beginning of time men and women had understood this moment and exactly what it meant.

Robin didn't want to leave. Encircled by Devin's arms, she felt as if she was part of something again. She had known she was lonely; she just hadn't known how lonely. She had loved Jeff with all her heart, but his illness had been diagnosed before they'd had time to truly unite. And afterward she had never wanted to burden him with her feelings or problems. He had been given enough to bear.

As if he could read her mind, Devin spoke his question out loud. "Do you want to stay, or shall I have my driver take you back to your hotel?"

"It's been a long time since I've made love to anyone," she said simply.

"Me too."

She read his eyes and decided he was telling the truth. She believed he was an honorable man, despite constant temptation to be otherwise. "Do you think we'll remember what to do?"

"I think it's entirely possible."

She stretched up on her tiptoes and placed her lips against his. His arms tightened around her, and his hands urged her closer.

She was so quickly immersed in desire that there was no time to rethink her decision. She had no hopes that she would ever see Devin again or that this night would lead to something real and permanent between them. This night was a gift from one lonely soul to another, and she gave it generously, without a single doubt that she was doing the right thing.

Chapter Three

"When were you going to tell me? Or were you going to tell me at all?" Devin turned the key in the ignition, and the Cherokee started right up.

Robin heard the slight pause after his first question, a pause where her name should have been. But Devin didn't remember her name. He might not even have recognized her if she hadn't called him Devin.

She closed her eyes and took a deep breath. Then another. The contractions were coming too fast. She was so afraid that the baby had been injured. She had been wearing a seat belt when the car had gone into a spin, but there had been little room between her and the steering wheel. She had braced herself the moment she'd realized there was nothing she could do except slide into the ditch, but she wasn't sure the baby was still all right. She just wasn't sure.

Tears slid down her cheeks. She didn't want to cry. She wanted to be calm for the baby's sake. But she felt as if she was being torn in two, physically and emotionally. She couldn't believe that Devin Fitzgerald was sitting beside her. She wondered if fate was convulsed in hysterical laughter at her expense.

"Where are we going?"

It took her a moment to register his question. Then she realized what he'd asked. "The hospital's...too far away."

"Where is this doctor?"

"Up the road. Turn right. Another mile or two. Maybe...more." The last word ended in a moan as another contraction began.

He shifted gears, and the car began to crawl along the road. He picked up a car phone attached to the dashboard, then slammed it down again. "Damn!"

She tried to breathe the way she'd been taught. But Judy wasn't here to help her. Judy had been her partner in the childbirth classes, and Judy was still in Cincinnati. The baby was making its appearance two weeks early.

"In through your nose and out through your mouth," Devin said.

"What...do you know about...it?"

"I was a labor coach once. For a friend. Just do what I tell you, damn it. In through your nose and out through your mouth. I'll help you count to ten."

"Shut up!" Robin closed her eyes.

"One! Two!"

She slapped her hands over her ears.

He grabbed her hand. "Stop fighting me! I'm trying to help. You've got to calm down!"

"You don't even...remember my name!"

"Look, you only said it once. At a backstage party with sixty people breathing down my neck! And I was embarrassed to ask you again at the hotel. I was going to peek at your driver's license the next morning while you showered. But you left before I even woke up!"

"Just drive!"

He slapped his hand back on the wheel. "One! Two!"

"Stop! Please stop! It's stopped."

"Tell me your name."

"Please! Just drive."

"I'm going to pull over to the side of the frigging road unless you tell me your name!"

She knew he didn't mean it, but his threat of doing something that childish made her realize how childish *she* was being. "Robin."

"Do you have a last name?"

"Lansing."

"And the baby's last name?"

She clamped her lips shut.

"You were going to have my baby, and you weren't going to tell me. What were you going to do? Wait until it was born and sock me with a paternity suit?"

"You bastard!"

"Yeah, you called me that before."

She opened her eyes and saw how white he was, and how angry. "I tried to talk to you. Your manager promised he'd give you my message. That's…all…I owed…you!''

"What's his name?"

She didn't understand. He turned and looked at her.

"My manager. What's his name?"

He didn't believe her. She was filled with such fury that she didn't even consider her next action. She slammed her fist into his arm as hard as she could, then once more. Then she began to cry.

"Damn it! You're probably in transition." Devin pushed down on the gas pedal. The car began to slide. "We'll talk about this later. Right now we're just going to help this baby get born. Are you with me? Can we do that much right?"

"I'm…not…in transition!" Robin knew exactly what that meant. It was the shortest, most intense—and emotional—part of labor. Right before the baby made its entrance.

"How long have you been in labor?"

She tried to think, but the accident had ruined her grasp of time. "I don't…know."

"Do you know what time it started?" His voice was calm, now. Deadly calm.

She tried to remember. "Seven? Eight?"

"This morning?"

"Tonight."

"Then it's a fast labor."

"The blizzard—" She couldn't finish. She had

expected pain, but not pain like this. She wanted to die.

"What are you doing way out here, anyway?"

"I...house-sitting. My managing editor... Florida... I didn't think there'd be a... And the baby's not due for..."

He mumbled something appropriately profane. "Were you going to wait out the storm?"

She nodded.

"Robin, breathe with me. Please. It will help."

She wanted to scream at him again, but she had no breath to do it. She found herself breathing along with him instead.

"Is it helping?" he asked.

"No!" she gasped.

"Then we're going to pant."

She remembered that technique from her childbirth classes. She was supposed to pant like a dog, then blow out all the air, take a deep breath and start all over again. She had been so gripped by panic that she had forgotten everything she had learned. She began to pant with him. Just when she was certain she was going to die, the pain began to subside.

She took a final deep breath. From the corner of her eye she could tell that Devin was looking at his watch. "We're not going to make it to the doctor, Robin. I'm not even sure we could get there in time if the roads were clear and the sun was shining. Your contractions are too close, and they're lasting too long. You're about to deliver."

"No!"

"My house is just up ahead. I can probably get you there. We're going to have to do this ourselves."

She socked his arm again, but weakly. "No!"

"I can get you through this. Damn it, we don't have any choice!"

She was sobbing for real, now. If only she'd left the house at the first sign of snow. But she'd only had a few twinges, nothing more than mild cramps, and she hadn't really believed she was in labor. Then later, when she was fairly certain she was, the snow had been coming down hard. She had expected the labor to last well into the next morning, when the storm would subside and the roads would be clear. She'd thought she could send a neighbor for her doctor if the phones weren't restored. She would have been fine.

She would never have met up with Devin Fitzgerald again.

"Five more minutes," he said. "Just hang on for five more minutes. Then you can have this baby."

She wanted to argue. She wanted Dr. Wright, with his calm voice, capable hands and five hundred babies to his credit. She opened her mouth to tell Devin so, when a new sensation nearly overwhelmed her.

She wanted to push.

She groaned and clamped her lips together again. The baby was coming.

Devin glanced at her, then leaned forward over the steering wheel, gripping it harder. He was whispering something. She thought it was a prayer. She needed prayers, and, God help her, she needed Devin's assistance.

"Pant," he said. "Pant as hard as you can. We're almost there."

She panted, but the desire to push nearly overwhelmed her. An alien force had taken over her body. Her body no longer belonged to her, although she could still feel everything that was happening to it. She squeezed her eyes closed and panted, forcing out air in a gust when she needed to.

"Almost there." The car fishtailed. She could feel it sliding beneath them, but she was beyond concern. The baby was on its way whether this car landed in a ditch or not. She was going to have the baby whether she wanted to or not.

The car stopped, and she heard a door slam. A gust of wind swept over her, and she felt Devin's arms beneath her again. "Hang on. Just hang on another minute."

The contraction ceased, but she knew the respite would be short. Her eyes were still closed, and snow fell against her eyelids. She couldn't find the strength to open them. She knew she was going to need whatever strength she had to bring her son or daughter into the world.

She didn't know how much time passed. Another contraction began, and Devin gripped her harder. She panted, but she was too frightened and too exhausted to control the pain. She made a valiant effort, but the desire to push overwhelmed her. Her body pushed without her help. The baby was tired of waiting.

The snow ceased, and so did the wind. She heard another door slam, and she opened her eyes. They were in a dark hallway; then they were moving up stairs.

"You're going to have that baby in a bed after all," Devin said.

His voice sounded strange. Far away, and sad. She gazed up at his face and saw tears glistening in his eyes.

She had been so angry at him. She was still angry. But mixed with anger was something else, although she didn't care enough to figure out what it was. All her thoughts turned inward. She and the baby were in this together. The baby and her own agony were all she could think about.

She felt something soft beneath her. She opened her eyes again but found she was in darkness.

"The lights are out, Robin. I'm going to have to wash my hands and find a lamp or some candles. Breathe like you've never breathed before."

The last words drifted away, as if he was leaving

the room. She wanted to call him back. He had gotten her into this predicament, and he could damn well get her out of it. But she couldn't call him. Another contraction began, and she felt her body bearing down. She had promised herself that she wouldn't scream when she gave birth. She had handled everything life had thrown at her without screaming. But the promise died on a wave of sound that could only have come from her.

The darkness was shattered by the glow of a kerosene lamp. Devin set it on a dresser not far from the bed. "My hands. Then I'll be back."

"Don't go!"

"I have to!"

Her voice caught somewhere between a sob and another scream. Her head tossed from side to side as if it didn't belong to her. Now she could see that she was in a bedroom, but she didn't care one bit. She just wanted the baby to be born. In a snow-drift, under tropical seas, on camelback. She didn't care.

"All right, sweetheart. Let's get this thing done."

She looked up and saw Devin's face. "I can't!"

His smile was brave. "You're going to, whether you want to or not. Your choices are limited."

She felt his hands against her hips, sliding her pants to her knees. She wanted to slap away those hands. She remembered them touching her with this kind of intimacy once before, and then the aftermath.

"Just another couple of inches." He slid off her boots, then the pants and panties beneath them. "Good girl. I'm going to slide a couple of clean towels under you. Now let's prop up your legs. I'm going to have to check your progress."

"No!"

"Robin, sweetheart. Of course I have to check. Unless you want to do it yourself."

She called him something she had never called anyone before. His laughter sounded strained. "You're absolutely right. But I still have to check."

Suddenly whether he checked or not seemed immaterial. She felt the urge to push out their child, and she felt it so strongly that she couldn't do anything except grip the sheets beneath her and bear down.

"Dark hair. Lots of it, I think." His voice sounded strained, too, although he was obviously trying to reassure her. "One more push will take care of the head. Everything's completely normal. No arms or legs in view."

"How...would you...know?"

"You did the damned interview. I was training to be a doctor."

"You quit!"

"Not before I sat through half-a-dozen obstetrics lectures and a trio of movies."

"Movies!"

"Rest. Gather your strength for one last push, okay? Then you can relax and let me take over."

"Never."

She felt a hand against her cheek. "You were there, Robin," he said softly. "I didn't do anything you didn't want that night. And I used protection. You know I did."

"It...didn't...work."

"Let's get this baby born, then we'll talk."

"I'm going to...die."

"No, you're not. I've never lost a patient."

"You never...had one."

He laughed, but it was forced.

She tensed suddenly. Her body seemed to explode. She gripped the sheets again.

"Grab your legs. Like this." He helped her get hold of them. "Okay, pull against them as you push. Push hard. Harder. Let's meet this kid once and for all."

She pushed, despite the pain, despite her exhaustion, despite the indignity of having Devin Fitzgerald between her legs. Suddenly the pain stopped. She felt a relief so total that for a moment she thought she had died. Then she heard a baby's weak cry.

"A boy," Devin said. "Perfect, and breathing on his own already."

She felt something warm against her abdomen.

Her legs collapsed to the bed, and she looked down to see her son. "Oh, my God..."

"I've got to find something to tie off the cord and cut it with. Don't move. He needs your warmth."

She heard Devin rummaging around in the dresser, but she felt as if she were floating somewhere far away. Her baby was here. Her son.

"Okay. I've got what I need."

"Is he really...all right?"

"Better than that."

She watched Devin tie off the cord with something that looked like shoelaces, and snip it with what looked like embroidery scissors.

"We're lucky all this stuff is here. My cousin didn't take many of my aunt's things from the house when she moved."

"Your cousin?"

"I bought this house from her. This is the house where I grew up."

She knew exactly where they were, then. The house had been pointed out to her once, before Devin had become the father of her child. She had avoided this road ever since.

Until tonight.

"Okay. I'm going to wrap him up. Then you can hold him. But we're not quite finished with you yet."

She knew she should feel completely humiliated. But all she could think about was the fact that her baby was about to be placed in her arms. Her son was crying. Little tired cries that were growing louder. She wanted to comfort him more than she had ever wanted anything in her life.

Devin nestled the baby in her arms. "If you've got the strength to raise yourself a little, I can tuck another pillow under you to prop you up."

She managed nicely, although she was shaking all over. She cuddled her son as Devin took care of the final details, sliding clean sheets under her at last and covering her with a warm blanket.

"Are you going to nurse him?"

She looked up. Some part of her wanted to tell him it was none of his business, but she couldn't. She had been angry at him for so long. Angry at him for getting her pregnant. Angry at him for ignoring her when she had tried to get in touch with him. But she couldn't dredge up any anger now. Not with her newborn son in her arms; the son he had started on this journey and had just brought into the world.

"Just try and...stop me."

He sat on the bed beside her. "You can start now, if you'd like. It's good for you."

"I'm so weak."

"I'll help."

She started to refuse. But this was her son, and she wanted to comfort him.

Devin unbuttoned her blouse. She looked up at

him as he did. His eyes were on her face. "I have the right to know, Robin."

Robin knew what he meant. Devin believed he had the right to know if this was really his son. She had told him that he was the baby's father, but she had also told him that he wasn't. "Your manager's name is Harry." She felt his hand against her skin and the cloth of her blouse parting. "Harry Bagley."

"He never told me. Not a word."

"I suppose...he hoped I'd just go away."

"And you did."

"I didn't...want anything from you. I...never have. I just thought—"

"I'd want to know?"

She nodded.

He circled her and the baby with his arms, finding the clasp of her bra underneath her and lifting her slightly so that he could undo it. Then he released her and lifted the bra so that she could bring the baby to her breast.

The baby, *their* baby, knew exactly what to do.

"Now, that's a strong instinct," Devin said, watching them.

She began to cry. She didn't know why, exactly; couldn't figure out which of a million reasons had suddenly hit her with enough impact to bring tears.

"Robin." Devin stroked her hair back over her ears. "I'm so sorry I didn't recognize you at first. I can't believe this. Any of this."

She cried harder.

He continued to stroke her hair. He forced a little laugh. "You've got to admit, you looked a little different last spring. Your hair was long. You were thinner."

"Thank you."

"For saying you were thinner?"

"For rescuing me. Us. For helping."

His hand stilled. "I suppose you think I'm the kind of man who wouldn't care enough to help you."

"Exactly."

"I didn't know about the baby, Robin. Harry didn't tell me. Harry's about to be fired."

"No. It's over now. The baby's here. You know...he's yours. That's all I ever wanted."

"And what if that's not enough for me?"

She looked up at him. The baby was still nursing contentedly. She found it hard to be firm with tears running down her cheeks, but she tried. "It will have to be."

"No. This is my son, too. My child."

"We don't need you."

"That's not what this is about. He's my child. I'm his father. *That's* what it's about." He lifted the baby from her arms.

She sat forward, panicked. Then she realized he was only helping her switch the baby to her other breast. She clutched the baby hard when Devin settled him against her again—so hard that he gave a yelping cry of protest before he began to nurse. "You can't have him!"

"Hey, calm down. I'm not going to take him away from you."

"I can support him. I have a decent job here."

"I know you do."

She thought fast. Devin was obviously having an attack of conscience. If he wasn't allowed to do something, the consequences might be disturbing. "Look, start a trust fund...or something." She closed her eyes. "A college fund in case he wants to go somewhere...more expensive than I could manage."

"Do you think this is about guilt? Do you think that will make me feel I'm off the hook?"

"You're not on the hook. I'm releasing you. Swim away."

Devin was silent. She watched her son nursing. *Her* son. But her emotions were so confusing that she couldn't enjoy it in all the ways that she should have been able to.

"You told Harry I was the baby's father?" he asked.

"I told you I did."

"Then if you try to deny it, I have enough proof to demand a paternity test. Harry will testify."

Her eyes narrowed, and she looked up at him. "Just a while ago you were accusing me...of demanding one."

"Do you have any idea how many women each

year claim that I've fathered their babies? Women I've never seen in my life?"

She stared at him.

"I know this is my son." His voice caught. "I'm sorry I doubted you for even a moment. Will you forgive me?"

She didn't nod or shake her head. Her gaze didn't flicker.

"I want to be part of his life."

"No." She had to force herself not to tighten her arms around the baby.

"Yes. He's mine. But I'm not going to take him away from you. I promise that. Just let me visit. Let me be part of his life. Let me watch him grow up. He'll need me, Robin. If you love him, you must know that."

She was trapped, as surely as if she had married this man in a crowded cathedral. They were irrevocably bound together because of the baby nursing at her breast; a son who would need his father.

"You're a stranger." Tears filled her eyes. "It was a one-night stand."

He didn't protest. "We needed each other that night. And now, whether you know it or not, we need each other again. You need my help and support, and I need your cooperation." He touched the baby's head, stroking it as he had stroked her hair. "And he needs us both."

She couldn't respond. The words caught in her throat.

"Do you have a name for him?"

She shook her head.

"He's a North Pole baby. Shall we call him Nicholas? Nicholas Fitzgerald?"

She looked away. She couldn't tell Devin that before the birth she had nearly settled on the name Nicholas for a boy, and that she had only waited until he was in her arms to make the final decision.

It seemed like a sign. She closed her eyes. She could not banish Devin from their lives, despite her urgent need to do so.

He was a stranger, but Devin Fitzgerald was Nicholas's father.

Chapter Four

Devin lifted Nicholas high and watched his son break into an ear-to-ear grin. "Mommy's coming back soon," he promised. "She's always right on time."

Nicholas chortled and drooled simultaneously. At six months he still had his mother's dark hair, but he also had his father's pale blue eyes. His face was shaped like Devin's, too. If Devin had harbored any doubts that this baby was his, they had dissolved the first time he'd gotten to examine Nicholas thoroughly. Devin still had some of his own baby pictures. This child belonged to him.

He lowered Nicholas to his lap, and the baby's chin began to wobble. "You miss your mommy, don't you, Nick? You don't like being away from her for so long. Even if you're with me."

Devin rose and shoved Nicholas under his arm like a football. Nick squealed with delight. Devin began a slow whirl. "And it's a rush to the ten-yard line. Steve Young passes the ball and its a—"

"Touchdown?" Robin slammed the door behind her. Her arms were filled with groceries. "More boy stuff, huh?" She smiled, but, as always, her eyes were wary.

Devin stopped whirling. "I'm glad you're back. He was starting to miss you."

"Let me put these away, then I'll take him." She kissed the top of Nicholas's head as she passed by, but she was careful not to touch Devin.

Devin followed her into the kitchen, Nicholas still tucked securely under his arm. "I think he's hungry."

"Did you give him his cereal?"

"What little he'd take. He'll want more after you've nursed him."

"I left you a bottle."

"He doesn't want a bottle. He wants his mommy."

"Everybody and their great-aunt Tillie has told me I should wean him."

"Are you going to?"

"Nope." Robin set the grocery bags on the kitchen table. "Not until he wants me to."

"I'm glad."

She looked up at him as if to say that was nice but she didn't really care. He held her gaze, and she smiled at last. "Well, we're in agreement," she said. "That's good, I guess. One decision of about a million we'll have to agree on in the years to come."

"Robin, I've told you before. I'm not in this to control you. I just want to be part of his life."

She didn't answer. Instead she looked away. "Did he get a good nap?"

"No."

"Really? He always sleeps a couple of hours in the afternoon."

"I hovered over him hoping he'd wake up, and he did after half an hour. He's got me figured out by now."

She rummaged through the bags for a half gallon of ice cream and two boxes of frozen vegetables and slipped them in the freezer.

It was Devin's freezer. Two weeks after Nicholas's birth, Devin had convinced Robin to move into his childhood home. He didn't live here with her, of course. When he was in town visiting Nicholas, Devin stayed nearby at a small bed-and-breakfast with discreet owners who had agreed to keep his presence in the area a secret.

He had wanted to give Robin the house free and clear, but she had refused to accept it. She had refused child support, as well, but he had finally persuaded her that living in his house made sense. She wouldn't have to pay rent for her town house, and she would have more privacy. *They* would have more privacy when he visited, which he did twice a month.

So far they had kept Devin's paternity a secret. Nicholas's birth certificate claimed that someone named "William Fitzgerald" was the baby's father. Since William was actually Devin's first name and Devin his middle name, the certificate didn't lie. There were a host of Fitzgeralds in the area.

And since Devin had bought the house under the name "William Fitzgerald," no one seemed to have made the connection to the most famous Fitzgerald of all.

But both Devin and Robin knew it was just a matter of time until the truth was made public. Someone would see Devin at the airport and trace him to the house in Farnham Falls. Someone would see him in town despite the fact that he came and went under cover of darkness. But Robin and Devin were hoping to keep their secret for as long as possible.

"You must be tired and more than ready to go. I'll take him now." Robin held out her arms.

Devin reluctantly gave her their son. Nicholas wasn't reluctant at all. He began to swat at Robin's breasts with his fists and whimper.

"Just like a man," Devin said.

"I hope you don't mind, but I'd better nurse him now. Can you let yourself out?"

"You know, I wanted to get some pictures of him, and I just plain forgot. You don't mind if I stay until after he's finished?"

She looked up at him. "You were here all afternoon, Devin."

"I was busy. He's a handful."

Devin watched Midwestern manners war with a mother's fears. "I could make dinner while you nurse him," he offered.

"You cook?"

"I'm not completely irrelevant."

"I really think you should go."

"I'd really like to stay."

She closed her eyes. He knew how tired she was. She had managed to work out a way to keep her job and still do a lot of it at home so that she could be with Nicholas at the same time. But the arrangement had taken its toll. She used the days when Devin was visiting Nick to catch up on all her errands. She never seemed to rest.

"Let me cook dinner," he said. "Please?"

"What else do you want?"

"I've always liked the way you come straight to the point."

"I don't like the way you're scurrying around it."

"I want some more time with my son." That was part of the truth, of course, but not all of it. "I don't think that's too much to ask, do you? I'd like to put him to bed tonight."

"I don't know if I have anything in the fridge that you'd know how to make."

"I brought steaks with me, a salad and a bottle of red wine. I can broil. And I can microwave a couple of potatoes."

She opened her eyes. "You planned this?"

"I hoped you'd let me. I still do."

"I don't know if this is such a good idea. We've got things worked out between us now, more or less. I don't like the idea of making changes."

"We're talking about one night, Robin."

She sighed. "All right. I guess it would be nice if you had a chance to tuck Nick in."

He smiled. He supposed, if he was a completely honest man, he would push on and tell her that he would like a chance to tuck her in, too. Right after he'd made excruciatingly sweet love to her. But that was going to have to wait.

He turned away before she could see any trace of that thought in his eyes. "I'll put the rest of the groceries away, then I'll start on dinner. Nick's patience is about all used up."

"Thanks."

He listened to Robin's retreat. He could see it in his mind. The sway of her hips as she walked, the way she pillowed Nick against her soft, soft breasts, the way delicate wisps of hair tickled the back of her neck.

In the past six months, as he had slowly positioned himself in her life, he had memorized every little detail about Robin Lansing.

"You are an insatiable little boy who is always going to get everything he wants, aren't you?" Robin cooed the words as Nicholas nursed contentedly, one hand spread wide against her breast as if to hold her in place.

She rocked him as he nursed. On one of his visits Devin had told her that this rocking chair had rocked generations of Fitzgerald children. She didn't know exactly how that made her feel. She didn't want to be part of the Fitzgerald legacy, but she understood the benefit for Nicholas. She hoped she wouldn't pass on her worst fears to her son—fears that Devin would someday grow tired of this arrangement and sue for custody. Or the opposite; fears that Devin would someday grow tired of this arrangement and abandon the son who had grown to love him.

Devin had given her no reason to be afraid. He had promised repeatedly that he would never take Nicholas from her, and he certainly had shown no signs of tiring of his son. Yet she had experienced so much loss in her life already that she was terrified of losing more. And Nicholas was everything to her now.

Almost everything.

She glanced toward the kitchen. She couldn't see much from this angle, but occasionally she caught a glimpse of Devin striding back and forth. He was large enough to take up a sizable portion of the kitchen, and his long steps took him quickly from one end to the other. In the smallest of rooms he moved with electric energy, just as he did on a concert stage.

She remembered that energy in the most intimate of ways. He made love the way he did everything in his life; with restless intensity and complete concentration.

She remembered.

She shook her head and switched Nicholas to the other breast, trying to put the thought of Devin as a lover out of her mind. He was not here as a lover, but as the father of her son. And despite the arrangement they had worked out one tension-filled step at a time, she was increasingly uneasy.

When Devin had first begun to visit he had been religious about arriving and leaving at the times they had agreed on. Now he seemed to find almost any excuse to stay longer. He adored his son. She knew that was every mother's wish, yet the depth of his love frightened her.

When was he going to realize that he could have more of Nicholas than he was settling for? When was he going to take her to court and demand more?

When was he going to realize that she was so head over heels in love with him that just the sight of him at her front door twice a month made her want to throw herself into his arms and beg him to love her, too?

Robin didn't know when she had fallen in love with Devin Fitzgerald. Perhaps it had been that first and fateful night together. Afterward, despite everything she had told herself at the time, she had foolishly hoped that he would call. She hadn't left Devin a number, but he certainly knew what town she lived in. She would have been easy to locate at the newspaper. But there had been no phone calls, no flowers or notes. She had continually reminded herself that neither of them had made a commitment. They had indulged in the perfect one-night stand, and it should be a glorious memory.

And it might have been, someday, if she hadn't discovered soon after that she was pregnant.

"How do you like your steak?" Devin came to rest exactly where she had been staring.

"Medium."

"Me too. Another thing we have in common."

"Steaks and one greedy little boy. We're on a roll." She tried to smile.

"I seem to remember more than that. Wasn't there one spectacular April night when we talked till dawn? I thought we'd discovered a lot in common."

Her breath caught, and she looked down at Nicholas. "The thing I remember most clearly about that night was the epilogue."

"Not me."

She looked up again, but he had disappeared. Her cheeks warmed. Their night together—"spectacular," had he called it?—had been off conversational limits until now. Neither of them had mentioned it in all the months since Nicholas's birth. It was almost as if their child had been conceived without sex as well as without love.

Nicholas finished nursing at last, and she laid him against her shoulder to burp him, although he could do it quite well without her help.

Devin appeared in the doorway again. "Would you like me to take him so that you can change?"

"I wasn't planning to."

"Why don't you get into something comfortable? You're home. You should relax."

She would have protested, except that it seemed like a good idea. She was still wearing a dress and panty hose. She held out their son, and Devin came over to take him. He leaned over, and his arm lightly grazed her breast as he lifted Nicholas. Her breath caught. She was acutely sensitive to his touch. She remembered his lips in the same place.

Devin's eyes flicked down, and she realized her dress was still unbuttoned and her bra undone. Her cheeks heated again. She stood and turned away, fastening her bra and buttoning her dress as she crossed to the stairs.

His voice was husky. "Robin, are you getting dressed again so that you'll have more to do when you undress completely in a few seconds?"

"I have some modesty left." She didn't turn around.

"Too bad."

She hazarded a glance over her shoulder, but Devin and Nicholas were already back in the kitchen.

Upstairs, she stripped off everything and decided to take a quick shower. The woman staring back at her from the bathroom mirror couldn't really be in love with a world-famous rock star. She looked much too sensible. Take her haircut, for example. She had cut it short to lessen the demands on her time before Nicholas was born. And earrings. She had given up wearing earrings in her pierced ears because Nicholas liked to pull on them. She wore almost no makeup, and she hadn't gone shopping for anything new to wear since before her pregnancy. She looked a little tired, a little harried.

She looked like every other new mother in the world. She didn't look like someone who was insane enough to be in love with Devin Fitzgerald.

In the shower she inspected her body with a practiced eye. She was slender again, although her breasts were certainly larger. She had several fine, silvery stretch marks across her abdomen, but it was flat enough to please her. All in all, she had survived the pregnancy well. But not well enough to appeal to a man with his pick of women the world over.

She had planned to dress with that in mind, but she found herself choosing spruce-green leggings and a matching scoop-necked T-shirt that ended mid-thigh. At the last minute she found some simple gold studs that might escape Nick's notice and threaded them through her ears. She added a gold locket just before she started down the stairs.

"Much better," Devin said when she entered the kitchen. "You look...comfortable."

She told herself she wasn't disappointed that

"comfortable" was the best he could manage. "Do you need help?"

"No. Sit. Have a glass of wine. The urchin's had mashed banana and rice cereal, so don't let him con you into thinking he needs more."

She looked at Nicholas, who was swatting at toys on the tray of his high chair. He was a beautiful little boy, rosy-cheeked and big-eyed. "He's going to be huge."

"I was a big baby. I'll bring you pictures sometime."

"He doesn't look anything like me."

"No, and I'm hoping he doesn't have your temper, either."

"What's that supposed to mean?"

"Aren't you the same lady who slugged me three times when she was in labor?"

She was beginning to tire of blushing. "I guess I never said I was sorry for that."

"You had a lot on your mind. Besides, it's common knowledge that women in labor like to take it out on their partners."

"You weren't exactly my partner."

"Maybe not, but I got you into this."

"No, you were right about that the night Nicholas was born. We did it together. I remember being there."

"Do you?"

Her voice sounded strangely breathy. "Uh-huh."

"Funny thing. So do I. I remember it well. And I remember thinking how wonderful it felt to go to sleep with you in my arms. Then I woke up the next morning and you were gone. No note. No phone number. Nothing. It seemed like a pretty clear message."

She stared at her wineglass without saying anything in return.

"Why did you leave like that?"

She shook her head. She didn't know how to explain what it had felt like to wake up beside him, to realize what she'd done and with whom. Panic had set in. She was no rock-star groupie, and sex had always meant more to her than pleasure. It had meant commitment and love. It had meant Jeff.

"I picked up the telephone more than once over the next weeks to call your paper and wheedle your name and phone number from them," he said.

"Why didn't you?"

"A lot of reasons, I guess. I was just getting over a bad marriage and wasn't ready for new entanglements. I was embarrassed that I didn't know your name. And I was afraid I'd make your guilt worse if I called you."

"Guilt?"

"Wasn't that why you left? You felt like you'd been unfaithful to your husband?"

She let out a long breath. "I think you'd better flip the steaks."

"I've done that. They're ready."

She watched him open the oven door and slide the steaks onto a platter. His words were like cannons going off in her head. She didn't want to believe him.

He was seated and they were eating before he spoke again. "Do you have many thoughts about the future, Robin? Do you think you'll stay here to raise Nicholas?"

She shook her head. "No. It's perfect now, and I love Farnham Falls. But I want better schools for him and more opportunities. I think he'll need music lessons, don't you?"

He smiled, and the expression in his eyes was so warm that it seemed to heat the air between them. "Yeah. But they could be arranged anywhere. And when he comes to visit me—"

"He won't be coming to visit you, Devin." She set down her fork. "You can see him here or wherever we are, but I never said that you could take him anywhere without me."

"No?"

She heard the steel in his voice. Her heart began to beat faster. "No. What can you be thinking? He'll go from being Nicholas Fitzgerald to being the illegitimate son of Devin Fitzgerald. What kind of experience would that be?"

"Is that it, or are you afraid I'll forget to bring him back?"

She balled up her napkin and set it on the table

as she rose. "I think you've overstayed your welcome."

Devin rose, too. Nicholas, sensing the tension, or perhaps just from exhaustion, began to cry.

Devin stroked Nicholas's hair. "I'm his father, not a kidnapper. I love him. I'll always want what's best for him. And I know that means living with you. But when he's older I'll also want to have him with me sometimes. Surely you can understand that."

She *could* understand it. That was the hard part. She could understand it, but it frightened her so much.

Devin sat down. "Sit down. Please. Finish dinner. I'm not trying to take Nick away from you."

She reached for Nicholas instead, to comfort him or herself, she wasn't sure. She brought him back to her seat.

"How did that get started?" Devin asked. "We're fighting about the future. Who knows where we'll be by then, or what we'll feel?"

"I already know what it feels like to lose the person I loved most in the whole wide world. I couldn't live through it again."

"You won't have to."

"You don't understand."

He didn't smile. "Oh, I think I do. All too well."

She supposed Devin was talking about his ex-wife, although according to everything he'd told her, theirs had never been a fairy-tale marriage. "I'm sorry. I guess you do."

"All these doubts and fears are going to eat away at both of us unless we put an end to them now. And in the long run that's going to be bad for Nicholas."

She nodded, ashamed, but still wary.

Devin reached for her hand and covered it with his. She worked overtime not to touch him, but she couldn't seem to make herself pull away. "We need to give him the gift of our friendship," he said. "Can we work on that?"

"We aren't friends, Devin."

"But we could be. If you'd let us."

She couldn't imagine being Devin's friend. Her feelings were too tumultuous, too intense, for friendship.

"Will you try?" he asked.

She nodded again.

"We'll take it slowly. Then one morning you'll wake up and wonder how you ever existed without my...friendship."

"Think so?" She made herself pull away. She lifted her fork. Nicholas was now playing contentedly with her locket.

"I have to think so," Devin said. "I have all our best interests in mind."

Chapter Five

Robin heard squeals coming from the living room of the house even before she opened the front door. She couldn't fault Devin for playing with his own son, particularly when he only saw him for two days, twice a month. But the squeal foretold a frantic baby by bedtime. On the days that Devin visited, Nicholas was always hard to get to sleep. Already he adored his father, and he seemed to know that if he closed his eyes, when he woke up Devin wouldn't be there.

From the foyer she could see that the two men in her life were playing hide-and-seek. The game was still relatively uncomplicated. At eight months Nicholas had not yet graduated to crouching in closets or basement corners. Devin could hide behind the same sofa time and time again, and it was more than all right with Nicholas.

Robin's head ached; her neck was stiff, and she felt as if she hadn't slept in weeks. She had taken a cut in pay to spend so many hours at home with Nicholas, but there really hadn't been a cut in her workload to go along with it. Free time was a concept she might resurrect when Nicholas graduated from high school, but until then, she had resigned herself to never reading a novel, watching a sitcom or going out on a date again.

"You look whupped."

She smiled wanly, too exhausted for once to be wary of what she was communicating to Devin. He looked particularly wonderful this afternoon in dark brown trousers and a woven shirt that was almost exactly the golden brown of his hair. By the standards of his profession he was decidedly conservative. No tattoos or body piercings marred his tanned skin. And she had seen attorneys and accountants with longer hair.

She supposed that someday she might walk into a room inhabited by Devin Fitzgerald and not feel this instant tug at her heart. But she wasn't going to count on it.

"I finished at work," she said. "I thought I'd change my clothes before I started in on my errands. Is Nick doing all right?"

"Nick's fine. You're not. No errands."

"Excuse me?" She was almost too tired to be annoyed, but not quite. Her temper soared.

"I said no errands. You're going to drop in your tracks, Robin. Please. Take the afternoon off. Spend some time with us."

If he hadn't said please, she might have thrown a tantrum right then and there. Realizing how close she had come to one made her realize something else. He was exactly right. She was exhausted. She was not particularly temperamental, yet these days she dissolved into tears at the slightest opportunity. This morning at work she had snapped at a co-worker for nothing more than a misplaced comma. She was headed for trouble.

She was so lost in her thoughts that she hadn't realized how close Devin had drawn to her. She felt his palm against her cheek, and God help her, she leaned into it like a dog aching to be petted.

His arms closed around her. Lightly, as if he wanted to let her know she could step away any-time. "I hate seeing you this way," he said softly. "This is supposed to be a good time in your life, Robin."

"It is." Her protest sounded weak, even to her own ears.

"May Nicholas Fitzgerald and his father have the pleasure of your company at a picnic this af-ternoon? Just the three of us? Then I'll do whatever I can to help you get everything else finished to-night."

"You? You're the mystery man. You can't even be seen at a grocery store."

"I'll wear a wig and sunglasses."

She gave a dry laugh. There wasn't a wig that had been made that would disguise him. "Even if that worked, you wouldn't know what to do at the laundromat."

"Laundromat? What's wrong with the washer and dryer?"

She cursed silently.

"Robin, you should have told me you were having problems. I'll have them fixed or order new appliances."

"Just the washer."

"Why didn't you tell me?"

She shrugged. She wanted to lean against him and feel his arms tighten around her. But that was exactly the reason why she hadn't told him about the washer. She didn't want to need Devin or anything he could give her. She had to do this on her own, or the consequences might be terrible for them all.

"What else isn't working?" he asked.

"Everything else is just fine."

"Then what else do you have to do?"

"Winter's coming. Nicholas needs a snowsuit and warm pajamas. I have to go to the post office to get stamps and mail a package. I have two sweaters at the cleaners'..." She paused. "This is deadly-dull stuff. Stuff you haven't done in years."

"Let's stop talking about what I haven't done. Will the grocery store and dry cleaner deliver?"

"If you pay them an arm and a leg."

"We'll pay it, then. Do you have catalogs for children's clothes?"

"Yes, but—"

"We'll look through them together tonight and make out an order. Will the rest of this stuff keep until tomorrow?"

"I suppose."

"Then let it go."

Devin was trying to take over her life, but despite her best instincts, she couldn't summon the energy to refuse. "What kind of picnic?"

"The kind I plan and execute perfectly. With whatever you happen to have in the refrigerator."

"There's not much. I could—"

He touched her lips with a finger to silence her. "You could change your clothes and lie down for a few moments of peace and quiet while the kid and I get everything ready."

She was supposed to say no. Enough of her mind was still working to know that. But the temptation was too great. An afternoon with Devin and Nicholas. The three of them. Almost like a family.

Dangerous dreams.

His arms tightened subtly. She sagged a little closer. "It's going to be winter again before too long," he said. "It's a sin to waste the best days of autumn shopping for groceries and mailing packages."

"I don't know what to say."

"'Yes' will do for a start."

"The last time I said yes to you, Devin, I ended up in a snow-filled drainage ditch having your baby."

"But look how well it turned out."

She felt his lips against her forehead. By the time she was sure he had kissed her, he had released her, and it was too late to object.

"Scoot," he said. "Junior and I have a picnic to put together."

"I don't know...."

"Yes, you do."

And despite everything she had said, and every argument she hadn't articulated, he was right.

Devin plundered cabinets and the refrigerator, dressed Nicholas for a walk in the woods and called the dry cleaners to have them deliver Robin's sweaters and pick up the dirty laundry that afternoon. He ran a test cycle on the washing machine, discovered the problem—as well as the fact that he couldn't fix it—and called the nearest appliance store. They promised him a new machine by the end of the week.

He had made a tentative grocery list and gotten a promise that they would deliver whatever he ordered in the early evening before he began to worry about Robin. She should have been downstairs by now. He had called up to her once to let her know he and Nicholas were ready. He went to the bottom of the stairs and tried again, but she still didn't appear.

"What do you think, champ? Maybe I ought to go get her?"

Nicholas, who was happily settled in a playpen with a new cloth book Devin had brought for him, just cooed and waved the book in answer. Then he began to gnaw at it.

Devin took the steps two at a time. He hesitated at Robin's door, then knocked softly. There was no answer.

He pushed open the door and stuck his head inside. "Robin?"

She had taken him at his word. She had lain down to rest, and now she was fast asleep.

For a moment he considered leaving her that way. She certainly needed the rest. But he knew she would be mad or embarrassed, or both, if he did. If she had to, she could sleep on a blanket in the meadow where the Fitzgerald men were planning to entertain her.

He crossed the room and sat on the bed beside her. She had changed into jeans, black jeans tight enough to stimulate his imagination—as well as a more visible portion of his anatomy. She had topped them with a royal blue tank top, and she had a buffalo plaid flannel shirt clutched in her hand, apparently to wear over it.

He wondered if Robin had any idea how hard he was finding all of this. He spent four days a month with Nicholas. During those four days he was lucky to spend two hours with Robin. He lived on dreams of her. He remembered the night they had made love. Everything had been so easy, so perfect. They had fit together as if they had been created for that one purpose alone. As passion had built he'd lost whatever objectivity he had started with and made love to her without thought of the future or of keeping a part of himself inviolate.

And the next morning he'd found himself in bed alone.

He had done everything wrong from that point on. He had been reluctant to follow up a perfect night with telephone calls, recriminations and pleas. He had known she must have been upset, to leave without saying goodbye. He had promised himself he would look for her again, when the time was right. But the time hadn't been right soon enough.

He reached out to stroke her hair. He liked her hair short, although he suspected he would like it any way she wore it. The top was still long enough to sift through his fingers when he touched it. He liked the way it swirled like fine black silk when she shook her head. He liked the way it fell into her eyes, the way she pushed it over her ears, the way it adorned her cheeks and the back of her neck.

He was a lovesick fool.

She was sleeping so soundly that his touch didn't wake her. He drew one index finger over her ear and across her cheek to the corner of her lips. He remembered exactly what those lips had felt like as he'd kissed them. She was a generous woman, and for those brief hours they'd had together, she had held back nothing. He wanted to test her lips now, test their softness, their heat, their acceptance of his kiss. He knew better, but he was seized with a longing so fierce that he found he had kissed her before he could talk himself out of it.

Her eyes opened slowly, and, still deep in dreams, he supposed, she smiled at him.

"A kiss for Sleeping Beauty." He sat up slowly. "I couldn't think of any other way to wake you."

"It's time-honored." She smiled sleepily.

"For good reasons." He smiled, too. He was almost afraid to breathe, terrified that something would break the spell.

Something did. A wail started downstairs.

Her eyes widened, and sleep fled. "You left Nicholas alone?"

"It's okay. He's in his playpen. It was just for a minute."

"Oh."

He stood before she could say anything else. "I'll get him. If you're too tired to go on the picnic...?"

"No, I'm coming."

"We're ready when you are." He made it to the door and beyond. She hadn't protested; she hadn't complained. He had kissed her, and she had smiled at him.

He was grinning as he clattered down the stairs to get their son.

"We're going to squash the wildflowers." Robin looked with alarm at the meadow Devin had chosen for their picnic. The afternoon was warm, and bees and butterflies had claimed it as their own. The meadow was only half a mile from the farmhouse through a forest of oak and wild cherry and across a narrow creek with a stepping-stone bridge. She had hiked here once before with Nicholas on her hip, but that day the journey had seemed a hundred miles. Now, with Devin carrying their son, it had only taken minutes.

"What do you suppose happens to wildflowers at the first frost?" Devin held out his hand.

"They burrow underground and wait out the winter?"

"Not exactly. They go squish. Jack Frost steps on them. Think of us as gardeners, spreading seeds for next year's meadow on the soles of our shoes."

She took his hand with some reluctance. This was entirely too cozy to suit the most rational part of her. Her, Devin, Nicholas. A field of nodding wildflowers and a vast, cloudless sky.

He tucked her hand under his arm as if he was afraid she might change her mind. They started down a dirt path. "It would have been a sin not to spend this day outside."

"Did you come here as a boy?"

"When I was a boy this area was fenced for cattle. I suppose I ought to rent it out for pasture. Sarah and her husband did. But I love the idea of it lying here, basking in the sun and producing nothing except chicory and daisy fleabane and black-eyed Susans."

"You know something about everything. You're surprisingly eclectic."

"For a rock musician?"

"I didn't say that."

"No, I did. It's easy, doing what I do, to forget about everything except the day-to-day trappings of fame and fortune."

"I forget sometimes that you have women all over the world sighing as the sound of your voice comes from their stereos."

"You forget sometimes?"

"Not often," she admitted.

"I didn't think so. It's always between us. My other life has yet to intrude, but it's always there in your mind."

She wasn't about to confess that she had bought every one of Devin's CDs and that she played them for Nicholas whenever Devin had been away from them for too long. And articles. Lord, the articles she'd read. She regularly stopped by the library to search out the gossip magazines to find out what Devin was doing when he wasn't with her. And now she had a subscription of her own to *Rolling Stone*, although she hid her growing collection when she knew Devin was going to be in town.

"Isn't your fame always in the back of your mind?" she asked. "Don't you always wonder if people react to you as a person or a rock star?"

"People in general, maybe. You? No."

She thought his words were a compliment and she nearly smiled.

"I *know* you're just reacting to me as rock star." He grinned over his shoulder as she narrowed her eyes. "I'm kidding."

"Well, there's some truth to it."

"Is there?"

"Don't you think this whole thing would be easier if you weren't who you are?"

"Sure. I think we'd be married now and starting on our second baby. You would have called me after our night together to tell me you were pregnant. I would have dragged you to the altar. Now I'd get up in the mornings and plow the back forty or deliver babies for a living. You'd stay home, change diapers and feel resentful that you'd been forced to marry a stranger."

"Not exactly a stranger. Close."

"The point is that any scenario can be easy or hard, depending on what we make of it. Musician. Farmer. Doctor. Lover. Friend. Husband." He shrugged.

"You've made this scenario as easy as you can. I'm...surprised."

"What did you expect?"

"Honestly? Bribes I'd have to refuse, for starters. Calls from your manager telling me you were too busy to come this or that month. Expensive guilty gifts for Nicholas because you'd forgotten to show up. Instead, everything seems effortless. You always appear at the front door right when you're supposed to. Alone. Without camera crews or flunkies.''

"It's not effortless."

He didn't say anything more, but Robin could imagine the rest. She had seen a little of the way Devin lived. She didn't know how he managed to get in and out of airports without detection. Or how he cleared his schedule without alerting a dozen people where he would be and why.

"Thanks for giving us this time without everything else," she said. "No hoopla. No media circus. Just a father with his son."

"You said 'us.'"

She could feel a stammer coming on. She grabbed a breath of sweet autumn air. "I meant 'us.' It's not easy being a single mom. Being a single mom with reporters camped on her front lawn sounds even worse."

"You could send them out for groceries. Make them do the laundry."

She laughed. "Maybe one of them would babysit occasionally."

"I've tried to make things easier on you," he said, serious again. "As easy as you'll let me. But you know one day things will change, don't you?"

"I don't want to think about that now. Not today."

"Whatever happens, Robin, please don't forget

we're in this together. We can solve any problem that arises as long as we don't let it come between us.''

She thought about that as they lapsed into a friendly silence. What exactly was there to come between? Surely he had only meant that they were two people devoted to bringing up a happy, healthy child. He hadn't meant to imply more.

But he had kissed her today. Twice. And now he was holding her hand. When she had awakened from her nap, he had been smiling down at her as if he had just discovered the answer to all of life's questions.

She was walking a dangerous path. Not the rambling cow path through a wildflower meadow. But a path destined to bring her to the edge of the great divide that separated her life from Devin Fitzgerald's.

She was lovely in sunshine, lovely in shadow. Right now, sun-dappled shade painted patterns on Robin's cheeks, cheeks that were definitely too pale. Devin was frustrated that she wouldn't take his money or let him do anything to make her life easier. He supposed her integrity was one of the first things he had fallen in love with, so it was unfair to be judgmental. But for months he had watched her trying to carry all her burdens alone, and he had swallowed anger that she wouldn't let him share them.

"He's actually asleep." Robin lifted her hand from Nicholas's fanny, a fanny she had been patting for ten long minutes as the exhausted baby fought a nap.

"Once he's down, it takes an earthquake to wake him." Devin beckoned from the blanket beside the one where Nicholas snoozed in the shade of an oak. "Come over here. He'll be fine."

She seemed reluctant to stretch out beside him, but she fussed with Nicholas's blanket for a moment, then joined Devin on his, sitting cross-legged on the far corner.

"Why don't you take a nap, too?" He crossed his arms behind his head and pretended he hadn't noticed she was still four feet away.

"And what would you do?"

"I'd sit here and watch you sleep."

"I doubt it. You're not a patient man."

"No? You'd be amazed at how patient I can be." He stared up at the sky and held his breath.

He heard movement, but he didn't look at her. He just kept staring at the clouds.

"All right, Devin. Exactly what are you looking at up there?"

He turned his head just far enough to see that she was lying beside him. Not close beside him, but within general touching distance. He turned back to the sky. "It's Mother Nature's version of the Rorschach test."

"Inkblots?"

"Cloud blots. What do you see?"

She was silent for a while. He wondered if she thought he was being silly. "Sea horses and picket fences."

"Picket fences?"

"There."

He supposed she was pointing, but he refused to look. "You're too far away. We're looking at different clouds. Come closer."

"They're the same clouds."

"But from different perspectives."

She edged a little closer. He could hear her sliding along the blanket. "Uh-uh. Same clouds here, too. But the sea horses are gone. Changed into...dolphins."

He edged toward her. "Don't move. I'm going to try to see them your way." He stopped before he got so close that she scooted away again. "Let's see now. Dolphins? Nope. I see...Charlie Chaplin."

"What?"

"There. The Little Tramp. See his cane and hat?"

"Nope."

"Now that surprises me. He's putting on a show for you."

"What else do you see?"

"Bow ties. Circus tents. Madison Square Garden."

"Come on..."

"Actually, that's where I have to be after I leave tomorrow."

"You're doing a concert there soon, aren't you?"

He turned to look at her. "How did you know?"

Her eyes widened innocently. "I guess I saw it somewhere."

"Would you like to come?"

Her head turned, and her eyes met his. "You know I can't. I can't leave Nicholas, and I sure can't bring him with me."

"We don't have to put a sign on his forehead saying he's my love child."

"Love child?"

He turned away from her and back to the clouds. "Do you like the alternatives better?"

"How about son?"

"The night that Nicholas was created, I was more than a little bit in love with his mother. Love child fits."

He heard her draw a sharp breath.

"I wonder," he continued. "Was she a little bit in love with me, too?"

Robin was silent.

"I think she was," he said.

"We shouldn't have discussions like this one, Devin," she said at last. "What's the point? You were right a while ago when you said we ought to give friendship a try, for Nicholas's sake. But anything else will make this even harder."

"Do you think so?"

"We both know there's...feeling between us. We spent the night together once. We delivered a baby together. We're watching him grow up together."

"'Feeling' covers a lot of ground." He rolled onto his side and propped his head on his hand. "What feeling is there between us, exactly?"

She stared at the clouds. "There's more than one, wouldn't you say?"

"What feelings?"

"Anger, for one. Distrust. Fear."

"Uh-huh." He touched her cheek and forced her to turn her head. "But it's not like you to see only one side of something."

"Then maybe it's your turn." Her eyes were so vulnerable that for a moment he wanted to look away. But he didn't.

"I'm not angry with you," he said softly.

"You're angry that I won't let you do more."

"Frustrated. I want to make your life easy. And trust? I'd trust you with my life. You're honest and fair. Intelligent. And you have a down-to-earth wisdom that impresses me every time I'm with you. As for fear..."

"Devin..."

"You're the only one who's afraid. But your fear is between us. You're right about that."

"I don't know who you are. Are you the man who struts around onstage with women screaming and guitars wailing? Or are you the man who comes to visit Nicholas? The man who brings his son floppy-eared stuffed bunnies and tells him hair-raising stories about his own childhood."

He smiled. "Has Nick been passing those on to you? I told him that was guy stuff."

"Who are you?"

"I'm the man who fathered your son, the man you're looking at with those beautiful brown eyes. I'm exactly that man and no one else."

"You're a millionaire who can buy anything and anybody. You have close friends who use drugs and language I don't want Nicholas to hear. You were married to a woman who looks great in videos but has absolutely no soul. You have more women beating down the stage door every night and offering their bodies, and a manager to keep them away from you the next morning. I don't understand your life, and I'm afraid I don't understand you."

His hand still lay against her cheek. "Are you done yet?"

"More than done."

"I hope that means you know you went too far."

Her eyes were still vulnerable. "You wanted to know what I feel."

"You feel confused. I hear that. Let me clear up some of the confusion. I can buy things, probably anything I really want. But I don't buy people. Not ever. And I don't abandon my friends when they need me, whether I like their choices of recreation or language or not. I work on the campaign for a Drug Free America, and that's enough said about that.''

"You don't have—"

He ignored her. "I married a woman I thought I loved because I was unbearably lonely. She was a good actress—even better in real life than she is in videos, by the way. I knew three weeks into it that I'd made a serious mistake. I learned everything I needed to know about relationships in the next year, and I never make the same mistake twice. And yes, there are women offering themselves to me at regular intervals and more pretending I've accepted their offers than there are nights in the year. But, Robin, I gave up casual sex a long time ago. There was nothing casual about the night you and I spent together. And I've never given up on love.''

"What do you want from me, Devin?"

"I want you to open your eyes. I want you to believe what you see." She didn't answer, and he was glad. Clearly the time had passed when talking was going to do any good. He sighed. He was as afraid of his next move as he had ever been of anything. But he was compelled to make it anyway.

He lowered his lips to hers. "Forget what you hear. Forget what you read. This is who I am.''

Her lips were soft and warm beneath his. He could feel the sun on his back and an ache inside him that was as much emotional as physical. He had kissed her already today, but there was nothing nonchalant in his intent now. He parted her lips and kissed her harder, moving his tongue against hers as his hand slid from her cheek to her shoulder and down her arm.

She made a soft noise—not a protest, but something more elemental and undefined. He felt her hand against his shoulder, then her fingers in his hair. Something more like gratitude than triumph filled him. His hand rested against her side, then slid from her waist upward toward her breast. She was even warmer and softer than he remembered. Welcoming and earthy and lush. His palm rested against her bare skin, and his fingertips slid beneath the top of her bra.

"I've envied my own son," he whispered. Then he kissed her again, slanting his lips over hers with more intimacy.

She moved closer, and both her arms came around him to pull him toward her. He could feel her hands sliding up his back beneath his shirt; soft, smooth hands that were cool against his skin and utterly seductive. His breath was coming in short bursts. He had told her that he was a patient man, but his patience had disappeared with her first sigh of pleasure.

He circled her with his arms and turned onto his

side. There was no space between them now. Her
legs were taut against his, their hips were joined.
He could feel her breasts pressing against his chest,
her hands against his skin. His pleasure was so
intense that he felt as if he were soaring through
the sky, anchored only to her.

He didn't know what would have happened if
she hadn't stopped him. He had lost his head completely by the time she put her hands against his
chest and pushed gently. He might have taken her
there, on a blanket in the sunshine, if she hadn't
stopped him. He had never wanted anything more.

But the moment he felt her resistance, he remembered everything. How much he wanted her,
yes. But even more important, how much of her
he wanted. All of her. Not just her drugging, ecstatic kisses, her supple, beguiling body. But all of
her.

He moved away a little, but he still held her in
the circle of his arms. He was content to watch her
as he forced his body, his heartbeat and breath into
submission. Finally he spoke. "I'm not going to
apologize."

"Aren't you?"

"It would be a sacrilege."

"You're intent on making our lives harder,
aren't you?"

"That's the last thing I want."

Her eyes were troubled, but her lips curled up
in something almost like a smile. "I think I re-

member exactly what happened to turn me into Nicholas's mother.''

"Oh?"

"I've asked myself a hundred times how I could have let that night end the way it did."

"And now you have an answer?"

She didn't speak for a moment. Then she rolled onto her back. Her head was pillowed on his arm. "I'll show you my dolphins and picket fences if you'll show me your circus tents and bow ties."

He settled himself beside her, pulling her a little closer so that her head lay in the hollow of his shoulder. Together they gazed up at the sky.

Chapter Six

"Robin, you're crazy. You know you are." Judy lifted Nicholas skyward and swung him in a circle as his father often did. The baby chortled with delight. "You could have everything you want if you'd just admit some home truths to yourself."

Judy had shown up unexpectedly for the weekend. Robin was delighted to see her, but suspicious about the turn casual conversation had taken so soon after Judy's arrival. In the week since the picnic with Devin she had thought about very little but him. She didn't know how Judy had zeroed in so quickly on her concerns.

Robin waited until the noise had subsided before she answered. "I'm not crazy. My relationship with Devin is an artificial creation. We've been thrown together in a pressure cooker. That's why I... That's why he..."

"You can't even say it, can you?" Judy dropped to a seat at the kitchen table and set Nicholas on the floor with the plastic truck she had brought with her from Cincinnati. "That's why you've what? Fallen in love?"

"That's exactly what I'm not trying to say. I had Devin's baby. He adores Nicholas, and the feeling is mutual. It would be wonderfully convenient for

Devin to fall in love with me so that we could be a family. I think maybe he's capable of that.''

"You're saying he's a manipulator capable of pretending something like love just to get what he wants?"

"No, I'm not."

Judy leaned back in her chair, her arms folded across her chest. "Then what?"

"I think he's capable of convincing himself that there's more between us than there is, just so he can have more than a few days a month with his son. If he has to put up with me, too, so be it."

"I'm sure you're right. I mean, good grief, what could you possibly have to offer a man like that? You're an ugly brainless twit with no redeeming qualities."

Robin scoured the last pan in the kitchen sink before she answered. "I know I have a lot to offer someone. And someday maybe I'll want another man in my life."

"I see. You don't love Devin. I didn't realize."

Robin was silent.

"Gosh, I'm so glad I understand now," Judy said.

"You really are a monster, you know?" Robin faced her friend, drying her hands on a dish towel as she did so.

"Let me tell you what I see," Judy said. "Okay?"

"You will, regardless."

Judy grinned, but the grin faded. "Robin, I know you loved Jeff. Everybody loved Jeff. He was like a brother to me. You and Jeff were pals for years before you became lovers, two peas in a pod. When you found out he was dying, it was like losing a part of yourself."

"It still hurts."

"Of course it does. It always will. But you've recovered in all the ways that matter. And now there's a man in your life who makes you feel different than you ever felt with Jeff."

"That's not—"

Judy held up her hand to stop Robin's response. "I'm sorry, but I have to say this. You and Jeff would have lived happily ever after if he hadn't died. I believe that. But you and Jeff grew into your love, and it took years. Devin Fitzgerald knocked you over the head on your very first night together."

"We made love because we were both hurting. We needed to comfort each other."

"Baloney!"

Robin was silent.

"You're head over heels, Robin. Have been since that night. That's why you didn't try harder to let Devin know about the pregnancy. You were scared to death. And you're terrified now because what you're feeling is brand-new. And it's uncontrollable."

"*You're* uncontrollable."

"I'm honest. More honest than you've been."

Robin bent to push Nicholas's truck back toward him. When she faced Judy again she nodded. "All right. I'm in love with him. Is that what you wanted me to say?"

"It's a start."

"And Devin is trying to fall in love with me. He wants us to be a family. He hasn't told me as much, but I know that's what he wants."

"How do you know he's not in love with you already? That it didn't take any effort on his part?"

"I don't!"

Judy smiled smugly.

"But I'm afraid," Robin continued. "He wants Nicholas. I've never seen a man so besotted with a baby."

"Don't you think that speaks well for him?"

"Of course it does. Who wouldn't want a man like that? But can't you see? How much of what he feels for me is left over from what he feels for his son? What if we live together, even marry, and it doesn't work out? What if he finds that he doesn't love me at all? Do you know how much chance I'd have of keeping Nicholas in a custody battle?"

"Every chance in the world. He's a rock star. You're a good Midwestern girl."

"At the very least I'd lose Devin, wouldn't I? We couldn't even be friends. And I could lose my son. How can I take a chance like that?"

"Robin, you can't let Jeff's death color every decision you make for the rest of your life. Yes, some day you might lose big time again, because this is the real world. But making sure you have nothing to lose isn't the right way to deal with the future. You're afraid of losing Devin eventually? Well, you don't even have him now. Is that better?"

Robin was silent again.

Judy glanced at her watch. "The man in question is going to be here in about thirty minutes, so you'd better go change."

Robin stared at her friend. "What?"

"You heard me. Devin's going to be here in half an hour."

"How do you know?"

"Because he called me last week and asked if I'd come visit you this weekend and stay with Nicholas tonight."

"That's why you're here?"

"The two of you are going to get away together for the evening. And he knew you wouldn't go unless you had someone completely trustworthy watching Nicholas."

Robin opened her mouth to speak, but nothing came out.

"He's coming to see you. Not Nick. Doesn't that say something to you? And don't be mad. He knew if he asked you, you'd refuse."

"He was right about that."

"Go with him, Robin. Take some time alone with Devin for a change. If the moment's right, tell him what you've told me and listen to his answers." Judy shrugged. "Of course, maybe it won't even come up. Maybe he's not falling in love with you. Maybe you're imagining the whole thing."

But Robin wasn't listening. She was staring out the window, at the yard where Devin had played as a boy, at the old red barn where he and his first rock-and-roll band had rehearsed. She was living in his house. She was the mother of his child. He had obviously stolen the heart of her best friend. In a number of ways she already belonged to Devin Fitzgerald, and she could no longer shut her eyes to what was happening. Slowly, inexorably, he was pulling her into the circle of his life and his arms.

She could have said no. It hadn't been too late. She could have stood at the front door, explained that this was not one of the times they had agreed Devin could see Nicholas and stubbornly sent him on his way.

Instead she was in his Cherokee wearing the new white skirt and sweater that she hadn't been able to resist when she'd gone shopping for Nicholas that week. Perhaps she had known there would be an evening like this one, because no mother with a working brain dressed in white. Nicholas could destroy the outfit with one well-placed burp or a leaking diaper.

But she was wearing it tonight.

"I was prepared for almost anything," Devin said. "Murder. Mayhem. The silent treatment."

"This was disgustingly manipulative."

"I would have preferred asking you for a date, like one grownup to another. But I knew I'd fail."

"When was the last time you failed at anything?"

"When was the last time you went out without Nicholas?"

"What if he misses me? What if he starts to cry and Judy doesn't know what's wrong?"

"You need more faith in your friend and your son. He's only nursing occasionally now, and you took care of that before we left. She can do everything else for him that you could do."

"Are you at least going to tell me where we're going?"

He glanced at her and grinned. Her heart did a back flip. "I don't think so."

She smiled, too. She seemed to be congenitally unable to resist his grins. "I really should be mad."

"But you're finding it hard. Even the best mother needs to get away from her kid occasionally."

"You're right. Anywhere. With anyone who offers."

"With the man in her life."

She didn't know what to say to that. Something had changed in their relationship, and she didn't remember giving her permission. Yet it seemed too late now to change things back. She felt a glimmer of panic. She needed Devin in her life, but what if this new increased awareness of each other led to a permanent rift between them? What if friendship died, too?

He seemed to read her mind. "You can handle this, sweetheart. We can handle it together."

"I'm afraid we won't."

"I know you are. Let's just take this one step at a time. Okay? And this is the next step. You and me. Without the little guy, for once. But no pressure. One small step. Okay?"

She watched the autumn foliage flash by. Before long their son would be a year old. How long could she continue to fight Devin or her own powerful feelings for him? Did she owe it to Nicholas to reach for the brass ring? To give Devin a real chance in her life? To marry him and give Nicholas the full-time father he deserved?

"One step," she said.

"That's it. That's all I'm asking for." He reached for her hand. "At least for tonight."

Devin watched Robin wander around the suite that he had rented for their evening together. He was perfectly capable of braving fans almost anywhere, but he knew that Robin would feel exposed and anxious the moment he was recognized. So he had found the nicest inn in central Ohio, a small one tucked away in the woods, and he had rented a suite for the night. They could talk, dine in....

He didn't want to think about the rest of it. He had not brought Robin here to seduce her. Not because he didn't want to. He wanted her with a sexual hunger he hadn't felt since adolescence. But he knew better than to rush her into his bed again. He'd done that once, and he was still trying to work out the consequences.

"We can have dinner whenever you like," he said. "Just let me know."

"You know, when most men invite a woman for a date, it's dinner someplace with crowds of people and a movie theater elbow-to-elbow with strangers."

"We could have done that. But I couldn't guarantee the results."

"Do you ever miss doing things the usual way?"

"Do I miss fighting crowds, talking over the din of a noisy restaurant, sharing you with rows of popcorn-munching strangers...?"

"So I suppose you're saying that there are compensations for the rigors of wealth and privilege." She smiled. "This is so lovely. So peaceful."

"So private."

She looked less pleased about that. "Yes." She

turned to look out the window, where birds fluttered and fed at a rustic feeder.

"Would you like to go for a walk? There are trails through the woods."

"Maybe when the stars come out."

"I brought wine and champagne. Which will it be?"

"Champagne sounds like a celebration."

Her back was turned to him, but he heard just the faintest sparkle of distrust in her words. "I thought getting you out of the house was cause for one," he said. "But I hadn't thought any further ahead, if you're worried."

"The last time I was alone in a hotel with you—"

"We conceived a child. I know. Are you sorry we did?"

"Of course not."

"Well, then?"

"That doesn't mean I'm planning to do it again."

"Neither am I. And I'm not planning to take you to bed tonight. So, that said, would you like some champagne anyway?"

"That said, I'd love some. But just out of curiosity..." She turned and met his eyes. "Why aren't you planning to take me to bed?"

He lowered his gaze to her lips. "Let's see. What are the possibilities? I'm not interested in you sexually? That's going to be hard for you to believe since three hours into our relationship I proved that wasn't true. So maybe it's just that I'm not interested in sex tonight?'' He smiled a little. ''But stand too close and you'll find out that's not true, either. So I guess it's that I care way too much about you to risk scaring you away. Maybe I'm just trying to prove that I can deny myself all the things I really want until you're ready to give them to me.''

''All the things you want?''

''It's too early in the evening for this conversation.''

''Humor me anyway.''

''Robin, you know what I want. You've known for some time. I want you and Nicholas with me permanently. I want you in my bed. I want Nicholas in his bed in the next room. I want us to watch him grow up together, and maybe watch more children, too. I want us to grow old together.''

She didn't say anything. She just stood there, breathtakingly lovely in a fuzzy white sweater and a pleated skirt that stopped well above her knees and made her legs look like they were a mile long. He remembered how those legs had felt entwined with his. She had no idea what looking at her did to him or to all his resolve.

''Did you ever jump rope as a kid?'' she asked at last.

''No. Not a guy thing.''

''There's this rhyme we used to jump to. First

comes love, then comes marriage, then comes Robin with a baby carriage. Somehow you and I have gotten everything backward, Devin. We started by having a baby together. Now look where we are."

He stepped a little closer. "Where are we?"

She shook her head.

"I've talked about marriage, but not about love?"

"Don't talk about it. Please."

"You don't want to hear my thoughts on the subject?"

"Not now."

"I'd like to hear yours."

"I believe in it. And the thought of being in love again scares me to death."

He admired her honesty as well as her ability to stay away from the real subject he wanted to discuss. Did she love him? Was she afraid of something that had already happened or just of something that might?

"I'm going to pop the cork on the champagne," he said. "Then we're going to sit over there by the fireplace and talk. Not about Nicholas, for a change. Just about ourselves. Our hopes and dreams. And the little stuff we don't ever have time to talk about. When you're hungry, we'll order dinner. And when you're tired, we'll go home."

She released a long breath, as if she had been holding it and waiting for something. But for what?

He didn't know. For a moment he wished he was as self-centered and aggressive as the world assumed all rock musicians were. She was confused, but she was also as attracted to him as he was to her. If he pushed her...

"Make yourself comfortable." He turned away before she could see the temptation in his eyes, and went to get the champagne.

She was amazed how many questions she had stored up to ask Devin. By the second glass of champagne, they were both more relaxed. Conversation flowed along with the bubbly. Robin found herself telling him all sorts of things. About high-school boyfriends, the way that Duke, her childhood cocker spaniel, had kidnapped her Raggedy Ann doll to sleep with every night, the trip to Wyoming she and Nicholas would make at Christmas to visit her parents, who had settled there two years before.

"They want us to come and live with them," she said.

"Have you considered it?"

"They're three hours from an airport. I think it would be harder for you to come and visit Nicholas."

"It might be."

"I don't want that."

He smiled. His fingers dangled just over her shoulder. He dangled them a little lower and made contact with her sweater. "I have a house in the Rockies, near Colorado Springs. Did you know that?"

The casual touch seemed to change everything again. She didn't look at him. "I think I might have heard that somewhere." Actually, she knew all about the house. She had even seen a photograph in an old *Architectural Digest*. It was breathtakingly contemporary, cedar and glass, with enough square footage to house everyone Devin had ever met. Somehow she hadn't been able to imagine the Devin she knew living there, and that had frightened her.

"I've been staying there when I can."

"Do you think of it as home?"

"No, I think of home as Farnham Falls."

"Oh."

"Do you ever wonder why I bought the farmhouse from Sarah?"

She nodded. She had wondered about that frequently.

"The night Nicholas was born, I was going back there to live for a while. I needed a place where no one would disturb me, a place where I could work on something completely new. I had planned to hole up there for a month or so and see what I could do with my idea."

"Well, things didn't quite work out the way you intended, did they?" She glanced back up at him. He was smiling.

"I think of Nicholas as a new project. A better one than I was planning."

"What were you planning?"

"Well, it's more than a plan at this point. I'm working on a musical. Hopefully for Broadway."

"Really?" She was amazed. She knew he was extraordinarily talented. She just hadn't realized how far that talent extended.

"Really. It's my story, and the songs are mine, but I've teamed up with someone else who's writing the lyrics. It's good, Robin. I don't know if it's good enough, but it's good. There's already interest. Quite a bit of it."

"But that's great. Is that why you've cut back on performing?"

"I want to stop performing eventually, or at least nearly stop. I really love the writing best, and I don't like what performing does to my life."

"But why Farnham Falls? You could have chosen a lot more exotic locales to hole up and work, Devin."

"The show's called 'Heartland.' It's about the way the heartland was before all the family farms began to disappear. For a rock opera, it's disgustingly nostalgic and sentimental." He grinned. "The main musical motif is a lullaby that my mother used to sing to me."

She had often heard him sing an unusual lullaby to Nicholas. She knew the song he must mean.

He had sung it to her when he was carrying her to the car the night he'd rescued her.

Her throat closed, and she swallowed. She was touched that she and Nicholas had somehow shared in this. "So that's why you were coming home."

"Part of the reason. I wanted to reconnect with myself, and Farnham Falls seemed like the right place to do that. I needed to be among people who believed all the things I'd been taught to believe as a boy. I needed to remember…good things. And there was a woman living in Farnham Falls, someone I'd met some months before, who I was hoping to see again. One afternoon I was going to wander into the newspaper office where she worked, look around a little, ask a few questions, find out her name. And if she was there, I was hoping she might just consider getting to know me a little better. Maybe have a conversation like this one."

She supposed her heart was in her eyes. "Please… If that's not true…"

"I wouldn't lie to you. I'm never going to lie to you, Robin. Not about anything."

She didn't think Devin would lie to her. But she did think he might lie to himself. Perhaps he had thought of her. She had certainly thought of him as their baby had grown inside her. But she didn't believe Devin's thoughts had been anything more than memories of a wonderful night when a man and a woman had come together to soothe each other's pain.

Perhaps Devin had planned to look for her. But Robin doubted that he'd had anything in mind except a brief renewal of their acquaintance. In the light of day, she would have proved to be exactly what she was. A Midwestern woman working at a small, inconsequential newspaper. Pretty enough, intelligent enough, but not what a man like Devin was used to. She was proud of herself. She had no desire to be anyone else. But she was also realistic.

She felt his hand settle on her shoulder. "You're homesick, or you were," she said. "Sometimes home looks better than it really is. Don't the rooms in the farmhouse seem smaller than they did to you as a boy? That's how life in Farnham Falls would seem to you if you had to live there day after day."

He nodded, but his eyes questioned her. She could see he didn't understand.

"You were burned out," she said. "Maybe you still are. But that doesn't mean that the things that might help you recover and go on are the things you really want and need for the rest of your life."

He stroked her neck with his fingertips. "Doesn't it?"

"No."

"I don't plan to live in Farnham Falls day after day. That doesn't mean I can't take what's important with me when I go."

She stopped pretending that they were talking in the abstract. "Look at me, Devin. I'm not glamorous or exciting. Farnham Falls might be too small for me, but living your life would overwhelm me. I want stability. Roots. I want the people I love around me, not strangers who come and go. That's what I want for Nicholas, too."

"Am I one of the people you love? One of the people you want around you?"

"It doesn't matter. Because we're not at all the same. We aren't going to be able to fit our lives together."

"You're sure of that?"

She couldn't answer. His hand was cupping her cheek. Her eyes were gazing into the depths of his. Everything she'd said was true. She thought she believed it deep in her heart. But she couldn't answer, because the answer seemed too final.

"You're not sure," he said. "Somewhere inside you there's a voice telling you that with a little compromise, a little discussion, we can work out anything. We aren't so far apart. And there are a thousand places in between where we could be happy together."

It was time to pull away. This was too intimate, exactly what they had to avoid. But Robin couldn't move. She was caught by the look in his eyes, by a deep loneliness that he didn't often let her see, and by something else. Hope? She didn't know. Did it really matter so much to Devin that they find the compromise that would let them live their lives together?

She saw that he was going to kiss her. Loneliness and hope had warred, and the result was this. She saw that she could pull away from him now, that she could stop this before it started again. He had not brought her here to seduce her. At least, not consciously.

She willed herself to move away. This would complicate a relationship already so complex it might never be resolved.

Instead, her hands lifted to his hair, and she sighed. Relief filled her when he kissed her, because now there was no room for doubt or protest. Instead she was suffused with desire. The part of her that still believed all things were possible kindled into flame.

"Just tell me to stop," he whispered against her lips.

"Don't. Don't stop." She was afraid he might. He hesitated, giving them both seconds to reconsider. But she realized she didn't want those seconds. She didn't know what the future held for them. She didn't want to know. She just knew that she needed Devin now. She didn't believe the things he'd said, but she wanted to. She needed to believe, because with his lips on hers, she couldn't bear to let him go. Not ever. Not even if it was best for them all.

"I love you," he said. "Don't ever tell yourself I don't. And don't tell me it's not enough. We can make it enough." He kissed her again. Harder and more intimately. She felt his tongue stroking hers, his hand sliding up her midriff.

Her bra gave way under his capable fingers, and she felt his palm against her breast. Pleasure shot through her, pleasure more intense than anything she'd ever experienced. It had been more than a year and a half since they'd made love the first time, but she remembered every sensation from that night. And this was better.

Because she loved him, too.

Her sweater was snowflake white against the rug at their feet. His blue wool shirt joined it.

She had forgotten how sweet this was, how perfect to have skin against skin, her breasts pressing and molding themselves to the hard contours of his chest. She had forgotten the feel of his lips at her breasts, the erotic enticement of a man suckling where her son still fed. She had forgotten how his muscles rippled under her fingertips, the smooth, cool expanse of his skin, the silky brown hair on his chest.

Her skirt drifted to the floor with her stockings. She helped him slide down his pants until they were gone, as well. She saw how ready he was to take her; that despite his promise of patience, he had none to promise. He held out his hand, and they walked to the bedroom. Twilight filtered through heavy drapes, but it wasn't enough. She stopped beside the bed to turn on the lamp. She wanted to see him as he made love to her, wanted to remember every move, every expression.

He embraced her, his body lean and hard against hers. He was fully aroused, but he didn't hurry her. He stood with his arms around her and kissed her as if they had the rest of their lives to take their pleasure.

She was the one who pulled back the covers, who slid between them and opened her arms to him. She had made love to him only once. He had been a stranger that night. Now, he was not.

"There is nothing that can come between us unless you let it," he said, as he rose over her.

As he sank into her, she wondered if he was right. In that moment there were only the two of them and their pleasure. And nothing seemed impossible.

Chapter Seven

Devin didn't change a diaper exactly the way Robin did, but he got the job done. She watched him fasten the last tab and pull Nicholas's pajamas up to cover it. Devin wasn't in pajamas himself. He was wearing unsnapped jeans and a flannel shirt he hadn't buttoned when he'd sprung out of bed to see why their son was crying.

Robin knew she should have stayed in bed herself. The luxury of having someone else get up with Nicholas was beyond price. But she *had* gotten up. Not because she didn't trust Devin to handle Nicholas, but because she liked to watch him with his son.

They seemed very much like a real family.

"Go warm up the bed again," Devin told her. "I'll be there in a minute."

"Good luck." She blew Nicholas a kiss and followed Devin's suggestion. Back in her bedroom, she stripped off her robe and snuggled deep under the covers, shivering a little at the feel of the cool fabric against her bare skin. Nowadays the bed seemed huge to her when Devin wasn't in it. And there were long periods of time when he wasn't. Since the night they had become lovers again, he visited more often, and he stayed at the house with her when he did. But his commitments still kept him away for long stretches of time. Each time he left, she and Nicholas waited impatiently for his return.

Devin came back and stripped off his makeshift pajamas. He slid in beside her and opened his arms. "He was already falling back to sleep before I closed the door."

"New tooth." Robin nestled against Devin's shoulder and sighed as he wrapped his arms around her.

"It's hard to believe that he's going to be a year old tomorrow."

"I know. I can't believe the first year of his life has already gone by."

"I feel like I missed too much of it."

"Well, you were Johnny-on-the-spot the night he was born."

"No blizzard in sight for tomorrow. High thirties and sunshine."

"I wish my parents could be here for his party."

He paused before answering. "I'd like to meet them."

Robin sighed. "I'd like that, too. But they don't understand about us, Devin."

"Neither do I."

She could feel sleep slipping away from her. Lately Devin had been the soul of patience, rarely mentioning the future. But she knew their part-time relationship weighed heavily on him. It weighed heavily on her, too. She was the only obstacle to giving her son a full-time father.

She loved Devin Fitzgerald. That wasn't in question and hadn't been for a long time. And she believed Devin when he said that he loved her. But she still didn't know if he loved her the way a woman deserved to be loved—for herself alone. He loved his son's mother. He loved the fact that they were a family. But she didn't know if that kind of commitment would hold up under the bright lights of Devin's life.

Right now she and Nicholas were a safe harbor in the stormy sea of rock and roll. But once they were thrown into it, would they keep their heads above water? Or would they sink together?

Would she lose everything again?

"Are you really unhappy with things the way they are?" she asked, when it was clear to her that he wasn't falling asleep, either.

"I love being with you and Nicholas. But I miss you when I'm not."

"Well, we miss you, too. But you've been able to come more often. That's been wonderful."

"It's not easy, Robin. The more frequently I disappear, the more suspicious it looks. And the harder it is on everybody who depends on me."

She had never thought about that. There were probably a lot of people who depended on Devin for their livelihood. He was a big business.

She had never thought about something else, either. Now she wondered how she could have over-looked it. "Is it dangerous for you to come here? I remember you had a bodyguard in Cleveland."

"I take precautions more to avoid detection than for safety reasons."

"I haven't been fair to you, have I? I've been expecting you to keep this up indefinitely."

"I don't want to keep it up. I'm tired. I want you and Nicholas with me, someplace where we can spend all or almost all our nights together. Someplace where I can be sure you're both safe and happy."

"Where? Manhattan? Beverly Hills? Your rustic little estate in Colorado?" Despite herself, her voice was heavy with distaste.

He rubbed the small of her back. "No. Some-place we choose together. I don't own any property that I care about except this house. We could find a community where we feel at home. A good place to raise our family. If you were just willing to look."

"And if we couldn't? What if we found we couldn't make a life together? It would be too late to turn back then, wouldn't it? We couldn't go back to this."

"I know you're afraid. But sometimes people have to move on. Even if it means taking risks."

She remembered that Judy had said nearly the same thing to her. Making sure she had nothing to lose was no way to deal with the future. But she had so much to lose. Devin and even Nicholas.

"Do you know that you were all relaxed against me, and now you're not?" Devin spread his fingers against her back. His thumb began to make slow circles at the base of her spine. "You're stiff with fear. It isn't going to matter how many times I tell you that we can make this work, is it? You're still afraid you're going to lose something precious."

When she didn't answer he turned her onto her back and began to kiss her. There was more than one way to make her relax. She clung to him and kissed him back. They had made love before falling asleep tonight, but now she was ravenous. She wanted Devin inside her, driving out her fears. She knew the time to make a decision was at hand, but she didn't want to make it now. She wanted to forget that things couldn't always stay this way. She wanted to forget that someday he might not be here to make love to her when she needed him.

"Happy Birthday to you..." Devin started the familiar song, and Robin and Judy took it up quickly.

Nicholas beamed at the sudden burst of music from the people he loved most in the world. He clapped his hands, then his eyes widened as Robin walked toward him with his birthday cake. She and Devin had decided on a sparkler instead of a candle. A candle didn't seem nearly special enough for their son's first birthday party.

Nicholas was entranced until the sparkler went out. Then he frowned and pointed. "Da!"

"Sorry, kiddo, I can't bring it back. But I bet you'll like what was under it." Devin took the cake out of Robin's hands after she had removed the spent sparkler and set it on Nicholas's highchair tray. "Dig in."

"I can't watch." Robin turned away. She'd had the foresight to make two cakes. This one was nothing more than a glorified muffin, but Nicholas didn't know any better.

He slapped his palm into the cake, and it crumbled into a hundred small pieces all over his highchair tray. Nicholas raised his hand to his mouth and began to sample in earnest as Judy snapped photographs.

"Don't you wish the rest of us could get away with that?" Judy said. "Doesn't that look like fun?"

"Yuck!" Robin went to the counter to get the other cake and slice it. "I'll settle for a fork and a napkin."

"When does he get to open his presents?" Devin asked.

"When we've washed the icing out of his hair. Why, can't you wait?" Robin teased.

"I've drawn up plans. With all the blocks we bought him, we can build a dream city."

"You can build. He can destroy."

"Two sides of the same coin."

"Well, I want to see his face when he opens my present," Judy said.

Robin knew that Judy had bought Nicholas a scooter shaped like an elephant. Nicholas wasn't walking yet, although he was on the verge. But now he could hold on to the scooter and make his way around the house on his feet.

The doorbell rang, and Robin wiped her hands. Visitors weren't common this far out in the country, but some of her friends at work knew that today was Nicholas's birthday. She wouldn't be surprised to find one of them at her front door with a gift.

She wondered if she should invite whoever it was inside to meet Devin. Today of all days the need for secrecy seemed almost obscene. They were celebrating their son's first birthday. They had nothing to hide.

She opened the door, and a middle-aged man with a carefree grin moved back a few paces as the aluminum storm door swung toward him.

"You Robin Lansing?" he asked.

"I am." Another man stepped into view from behind the door. She hadn't noticed him, but he'd obviously planned it that way. Before she could say anything, he snapped her photograph.

"We know everything," the first man said, his grin still in place. "We know you had Devin Fitzgerald's baby. We know he's here. You got any plans for the future with him? Or is he just stringing you along?''

She made it back inside somehow and tried to pull the storm door closed. But the grinning man held the handle. ''We hear he's not supporting you. Did you ever think about taking him to court? Or maybe it's not really his kid?''

Robin managed to slam the wooden door and lock it. Then she began to tremble.

''Who was it?'' Judy came into the room. She was licking icing off her fingers. ''More presents?''

''A reporter.'' Robin was surprised that she sounded so normal. She was shaking, but her voice was not.

''Somebody from the *Gaz*—'' Judy looked up. ''Oh.'' Her eyes narrowed. ''So it begins.''

''I don't know how they found out!''

Judy frowned. ''Oh, come on, Robin. It's a miracle no one in the press found out before this. There's been a conspiracy of silence to protect you. Don't you think your neighbors know? Your co-workers? Everyone's been looking the other way. They love you, and Devin's the local hero.''

Robin closed her eyes. There was pounding on the other side of the door, but she ignored it.

''Well, I'm glad,'' Judy said.

''How can you say that?''

''Because I am. Devin's wearing himself out to

keep up this pretense you've insisted on. Now there won't be any more secrets. I wish it hadn't taken a sleazebag reporter to get the show on the road, but I'm glad somebody did."

Robin had expected sympathy. She opened her eyes and stared at her friend.

"What's wrong?" Devin came into the room. "Robin, someone is still at the door."

"'Tis the press," Judy said. "You're going to be in the news, Devin. Not important enough for prime time, probably, but I bet the tabloid shows will pay for this story. And the sleazy supermarket rags." She shrugged.

"Robin?"

Robin turned her gaze to him. "Busted." But she wasn't smiling, and her voice didn't come out as lightly as she'd intended. She felt violated, exposed. But worse—much, much worse—she felt terrified.

"We'll get through this," he promised.

She nodded.

"Do you want me to talk to them?"

"No!"

"Then we have a party to finish. There's a little boy in the kitchen with presents to open. He needs both his parents in there with him."

She heard the words Devin didn't say. Nicholas would always need them both. The time had come for her to face the future. In a matter of hours the world would know everything. They were a family, whether she'd made up her mind to accept it or not.

But she couldn't accept it. She couldn't. Fear was pushing away every other feeling. "I think you'd better plan to leave afterward, Devin. They're going to camp out in the front yard if you don't. And I'm not ready for this."

He didn't say anything for a moment. "What would it take to get you ready for this?" he asked at last. "A signed promise from God that I'm still going to love you when the smoke clears?"

From the corner of her eye Robin saw Judy leave the room. She and Devin were alone except for the reporter and photographer on the other side of the door. "It's just going to take me some time—"

"You've had time. You've had a year. But when it comes down to it, I don't mean as much to you as your fears. You've never gotten over your husband's death. You would rather lose me than take a chance and try to build a life together."

"That's not true. I—"

"It's true. I'll go say goodbye to Nicholas."

"No, please stay for a while. Let him open—"

"I'm leaving." He turned sharply and disappeared into the kitchen. She wanted to follow him, to tell him that he was wrong and plead with him to hold her.

But she couldn't move. On the other side of the

door the reporter continued to pound his fist in rhythm to the agonizing thudding of her heart.

Devin held his squirming son. He didn't care that he would be covered with cake crumbs now, or even, selfishly, that Nicholas wanted to get down. He just held him as tightly as he could without hurting him.

"I've got to go, partner," he whispered into the baby's dark hair. "I hope you have a happy birthday. Build a city for me, will you?"

He'd heard Robin go upstairs and shut the bedroom door. Judy came to stand in the kitchen doorway, her arms crossed over her chest. Devin had liked her from the first moment he'd met her. She was everything that the small-town Midwest believed about itself. Solid. No-nonsense. Wholesome. Compassionate but never sentimental.

"I couldn't help but overhear," she said.

"It's a small house."

"She's scared to death."

"I know."

"She's afraid you don't love her as much as you love the idea of a family."

"I know."

"There's something you don't know."

"What?"

"She was never sure that Jeff loved her the way she needed to be loved, either."

He didn't answer. For a moment it seemed inconsequential to him what Robin had experienced with her husband. He was so hurt that suddenly everything she felt seemed inconsequential. He had a different bottom line than Robin did. It wasn't that he didn't love her. She hadn't loved *him* enough to try to make this work.

"She's never told me this," Judy said. "But I think Robin believes Jeff married her because he knew, at least on some level, just how ill he was and he wanted her comfort and presence in his life while he fought death. They were good friends, and he didn't want to be alone."

"What do you think?"

"I think it's probably true."

Devin tried to tell himself that this was important. But nothing felt important right now except the chubby-cheeked reality squirming in his arms. "I won't be back."

"You can't mean that."

"I mean it."

"What about Nicholas?"

"That'll be up to Robin." He looked up. He was as close to tears as he had come in his adult life. "I can tell you what the press will do with this story, Judy. They'll eat me alive. I'll be the irresponsible rock star who fathered a son, refused to support him, refused to marry his mother, even refused to fight for visitation rights."

"You could tell the truth."

"I could. But how would she look if I did?"

"Are you going to take her to court? Are you going to seek custody? Joint custody? Because you've certainly proved how much you care about Nicholas. You've nearly killed yourself trying to visit him regularly."

"No."

Judy was silent. Devin kissed the soft, icing-sticky hair of his son and set him on the floor at his feet. "When Robin's panic subsides, she'll realize how much Nicholas needs me. Her attorney can contact mine and work out visitation."

"And if she doesn't?"

There were a thousand voices screaming in Devin's head. He wanted to snatch Nicholas and run. He wanted to stand up to the world and tell them how much he loved this child and his mother—and how in the end it hadn't been enough for her. But one voice was louder than all the rest.

"I love Robin too much to do anything to cause her pain," he said. "Even if she doesn't realize how much Nicholas and I need each other, I'll continue to stay away from him."

"Devin..." She shook her head.

"That's the funny thing about this, you know? I couldn't love her more, and she couldn't believe it less."

"Call me. Any time you need to know what's going on with Nicholas."

He nodded.

"I'm sorry."

He tried to smile his thanks, but he couldn't. He knelt and kissed Nicholas's hair and squeezed him tightly once more. Then he stood and left the house without a backward glance. He couldn't look back, because he didn't know what he would do if he saw that Nicholas was crying, too.

Chapter Eight

If he'd really loved her, he would have stayed to work things out. But in the end he hadn't even loved Nicholas enough for that. For the past two months Devin had disappeared from their lives as surely as if he had never rescued her in the blizzard and delivered his own son.

If he'd really loved her.

She had asked him to leave.

Robin sat at the kitchen table with her head in her hands. She had been trying for hours to put together an entertainment-news column for the *Gazette*. In front of her she had two dozen clips about movies and models and what celebrity had been seen with what other celebrity. All of it seemed so foolish.

All except one clipping.

Devin Fitzgerald was holed up in his estate in Colorado working on a musical that was to debut in San Francisco in two years. His faithful fans would be sorry to hear that he wouldn't be touring or recording for a while, but those in the know said that the musical would be worth the wait.

"He's asleep," Judy said.

Robin lifted her head wearily. "Thanks. For coming to see how we're doing. For playing with

Nicholas so I could work. For putting him in for his nap.''

"He misses Devin.''

Robin didn't answer. She knew it was true.

"I thought we could walk through the woods when he wakes up and look for wildflowers. Take advantage of the warm day. And Nick seems happiest if he's on his feet these days.''

"If I can get this finished.'' Robin didn't want to look for wildflowers. She knew what that would remind her of.

And Nicholas was walking now. Devin didn't even know.

"You're working too hard.''

Something snapped inside her. "You're full of criticism today, aren't you?'' Robin sighed before Judy could respond. "Oh, Lord, I'm sorry. I really am. It's not true, and if it were, you could have a field day with me.''

"You're not at your best,'' Judy said. "I'll say that much.''

"This garbage with the press has really gotten me down.''

"Yeah. I'm sure that's all it is.''

Robin dropped her pen to the table. "I'm tired of the questions. I'm tired of the odd looks people give me. I'm thinking about quitting my job here and moving somewhere else so I can start over.''

"Is there a place like that?''

There probably wasn't. It was only March, but

the story about Nicholas had already died down. It hadn't even been that big to start with. Robin had steeled herself to tell reporters that Devin had acted honorably right from the very start, and that the rest of the details were personal and would not be discussed. Devin had refused to comment at all. Eventually more exciting stories had taken the place of theirs.

But Robin was a celebrity of sorts now, the mother of Devin Fitzgerald's son. Someone would always know where she was, who she was. As he grew older, Nicholas would have to field questions.

She thought about the most recent development and decided to share it with Judy. "Devin's attorney has been in touch. He wants the name of mine so that negotiations can begin."

"For custody?"

Robin was puzzled that Judy sounded surprised. "Well, no. He was clear about that. He's not even asking for visitation, Judy. He wants to give us money."

"Oh."

Robin rested her head on her hands. "I don't understand it. Devin adores Nicholas. I'm sure he does. But he hasn't made any attempt to see him since...since he left."

"Did you tell his attorney he could?"

"Of course not! I shouldn't have to. He knows that."

"No, he doesn't."

"Of course, he does. He—"

"Damn it, Robin, don't you see what's going on?" Judy flung her arms out in disgust. "Devin's not going to do anything you'll perceive as a threat. Not ever again. The man's willing to give up his son for your peace of mind. He's not going to ask to visit, and he's sure not going to try to share custody. He knows how scared you are, and he's making the ultimate sacrifice to help you feel secure. If you don't call him and tell him you want him to visit Nicholas, he'll never visit him again. He trusts you to make the right decision, though I don't know why he should."

Robin stared at her friend. When she spoke her voice was barely above a whisper. "How do you know?"

"He told me."

"And you didn't say anything to me?"

"What was there to say? You haven't heard anything that's been said to you for months. The man told you he loved you every which way to Sunday, and you didn't hear that, either."

"He would give up Nicholas?" But even as she asked the question, Robin knew the answer. He would. He had. And deep inside, she had known it for weeks. Devin hadn't stopped visiting his son because the publicity had scared him away.

He had stopped because he loved her.

He loved her that much.

"Call him," Judy said. "Or call his attorney.

Make arrangements for visitation. You owe him that much, don't you?''

She owed him more.

She owed Nicholas more.

Most of all, she owed more to herself.

''What if he hates me?'' She knew her eyes were pleading for reassurance.

But Judy had none to give. ''Maybe he does hate you by now. It's been two months. Maybe he's found another woman. He has more than his share of opportunities.''

Robin knew Judy wasn't being purposely cruel, although it sounded that way. ''All right. I hear you. There are no guarantees.''

''No guarantees. Exactly. You're the only one who can decide whether loving Devin and going to him are worth what you might lose if it doesn't work out.''

The weariness was gone. Suddenly Robin realized how little her exhaustion had had to do with her job and how much it had had to do with Devin. She had been a fool for too long, and being a fool took an extraordinary amount of energy. ''I know where Devin is.'' She held up the clipping for Judy to scan.

''I can stay with Nicholas through the weekend.''

But Robin knew she had denied her son a father for too long. ''No, I'll take Nick with me. I'm not going to keep him away from his father for another minute. We'll leave as soon as I can get a reservation. I'll walk if I have to.''

Judy didn't smile, but this time reassurance gleamed in her eyes. ''I'll help you pack. It will be a pleasure.''

Snow was falling from a dark sky when Robin emerged from the Colorado Springs airport. She hadn't expected snow, but she had come prepared with warm clothes. Nicholas snuggled against her as she negotiated with a taxi driver to take her to Devin's. Judy, without fuss or explanation, had presented her with Devin's address and telephone number.

''I still don't know,'' the driver said. He had the kindly face of a grandfather, but their negotiations had been tough going so far. ''That's pretty far into the mountains. And the roads are getting slippery.''

''Please? I have to get there tonight. There'll be a healthy tip in it for you.''

The driver looked at his watch. ''All right. Get in. But I'm not going to wait once we're there. I've got to be back in town by ten.''

''No problem.''

Robin slid into the seat and fastened Nicholas's car seat beside her. She'd come equipped with everything he needed for a short stay except a crib. Devin had never had any reason to buy anything for their son. She had never allowed him to bring

Nicholas here. And Devin had loved her enough to accept that, despite his own needs.

She had been such a fool.

Nicholas fussed as the cab negotiated streets, passed the Air Force Academy and started into the mountains. He continued to fuss, despite everything she did to try to calm him.

The ride seemed interminable. Between Nicholas's fussing and the gradual slowing of the cab as the roads thickened with snow, time slogged by. She couldn't even entertain herself by looking out the window. There was a sheer dropoff on her side, and the sight of it made her head reel.

What if Devin wasn't home, after all? What if he didn't want to see her?

The taxi slowed to a near halt. "I don't know if we're going to make it, miss," the driver said. "It looks like they've got the road blocked ahead."

"No!" Robin peered out the windshield and saw what the driver meant. There were wooden barriers equipped with reflectors across the road.

"Happens sometimes when the roads get too slick. Too bad. We're not that far."

"How close are we?"

"Three, four minutes. You could walk it in ten."

The taxi slowed to a stop. The road was wide enough to turn around, although Robin certainly didn't want to watch as the driver got that close to the mountain's edge. She quickly considered her

alternatives. She could go back into town and find
a hotel. Then tomorrow she could call Devin directly or call his attorney, explain where she was
and ask him to have Devin call her. Devin could
send someone to get them.

If he still wanted them.

She didn't think she could wait that long to find
out. "Is it just along this road?"

"Straight up the road. I been here before.
There's an iron gate on the left."

"I can't carry my luggage."

"I'll take it back with me, if that's what you
want. I'm going home anyway. I can leave it in
the cab. I'll bring it up first thing in the morning
if the roads are clear."

Robin trusted him. And she had nothing with her
that was valuable, anyway. "Can you wait while I
put the baby in his snowsuit?"

"I can wait."

Minutes later she was heading into the snow,
Nicholas tucked firmly against her hip. The fussing
had stopped the instant they left the taxi. He was
exhausted from the trip, but the snow was a new
pleasure. She didn't know how long he would be
contented, but at least he was snug and warm. The
snowsuit was one Devin had sent him from a cat-
alog, and it was filled with down.

She was wearing ankle-high boots with heels
that dug into the snow and helped speed her on her
way. But when she'd made her decision, she hadn't

considered that ten minutes straight up the road meant exactly that. The road was steep, and the air was thin as well as cold. Nicholas was not a small burden. She was tired almost immediately.

For a moment she considered going back. She turned to look for the cab. Through the snow she could still see lights, but they were rear lights. And as she watched, they grew dimmer.

She had nowhere to go but up. Her choice had been made.

"Okay, St. Nick," she murmured. "I'm game if you are. We're on our way to see Daddy."

"Da!"

She smiled in spite of herself. Then she said a short prayer that Devin and Nicholas would someday forgive her for what she had done. She had never been a coward, but Jeff's death had changed her, and not for the better. Afterward she had told herself that life was short and it was important to live it joyfully. But the real lesson she had learned was fear. Fear of pain, fear of taking chances, fear of falling in love again and losing.

She started to hum. She had gone a hundred yards before she realized what she was humming. It was the lullaby that Devin had often sung to Nicholas, the one he was using in "Heartland."

"Remember that?" she asked Nicholas. He held out his mittened hand to catch snowflakes.

She had a long steep road ahead of her. This wasn't going to be an easy hike. But suddenly

Robin didn't care. She was glad she had left the warmth and safety of the cab. Glad she was out in the middle of a snowstorm. She was going to be fine. She and Nicholas were going to be fine. They were going to find Devin. She was going to take the biggest chance of her life and win.

"We're going to make it, Nick," she said. "You, me and Daddy. We're going to make it!" She whirled around as Nicholas squealed with delight. Then she continued up the road.

"I know you said you didn't want to be bothered." Mrs. Nelson spoke from a crack in Devin's studio doorway that was just wide enough to reveal her worried face.

"That doesn't seem to have stopped you," Devin said. But he smiled as he did. Mrs. Nelson, the housekeeper, had only been at her job for three months, and he knew that she still expected him to behave with complete disregard for her feelings. He had yet to make inroads into her stereotypes about rock musicians.

"A woman named Judy McAllister's on the telephone. She says she has to speak to you now. I looked on your list, and she's—"

"I'll take it. Thank you."

Five minutes later Devin pulled on the last of his winter gear. His feelings were in such turmoil that he had buried them deep inside him. He didn't have time to feel anything.

"I'm going out for a while," he yelled to Mrs. Nelson, as he started toward the front door. No one else was around, even though there were several members of his band staying at the house, as well as the small staff that worked under Mrs. Nelson's supervision.

Mrs. Nelson appeared from the next room and blocked his path. "Mr. Fitzgerald, it's snowing hard out there. Too hard to be driving down the mountain."

Perhaps she was loosening up after all. Devin spared the housekeeper the ghost of a smile. She was a thin woman, easy to sidestep. "My son and his mother are on the way up from the airport. I've got to be sure they're all right."

"Your son?" She broke into a wide, atypical grin. "Your little boy?"

"That's the one." He looked beyond the door, through the glass that constituted the front of his home. Robin would not like this house. It was like living in a fishbowl, even though there were no neighbors in sight.

But maybe it didn't matter. Maybe she was just bringing Nicholas to see him. Maybe she was planning to leave again. Judy had been strangely silent about Robin's state of mind or future plans.

The world outside was the winter wonderland that songwriters extolled and small children adored. Devin was less enthusiastic. Judy had seen a weather report, and that was the reason she had called. Robin's flight had arrived in Colorado Springs. Judy knew that from a call to the airline. But Robin hadn't been in touch with her since arrival. Judy was sure that Robin would have called by now if she'd taken a hotel in town for the night. And since Robin wasn't with Devin, Judy was afraid she and Nicholas might be on the way to his house, snowstorm or not.

Devin started toward his car, a Cherokee like the one he parked and drove in Ohio, like the one in which Nicholas had very nearly been born. Surely Robin wouldn't be foolish enough to rent a car and drive unfamiliar roads during a heavy snowfall. But would she have been able to convince a taxi to bring her here?

He only knew one thing to do. He had to drive down the mountain and look for her, keeping his eyes open all the way. The road was treacherous in a storm, and even the best driver might end up abandoning his car to find help. The snow seemed to fall faster as he settled himself in the driver's seat and jammed his key into the ignition.

Robin was on her way. Nicholas was on his way.

And Devin was on his way to find them.

"Just a little farther," Robin murmured to no one in particular. The only person who might have heard her words was sound asleep against her chest. Nicholas, warm and snug in his down suit, had finally given in to exhaustion.

She had been hiking for more than ten minutes. Twenty minutes, at least, and maybe thirty. She had considered all the possibilities. Either the taxi driver had miscalculated or misrepresented the distance, or she had missed the iron gate.

She wasn't worried, although she was growing tired. She was in no danger of wandering off the road. The snow wasn't thick enough to obscure landmarks, and although the area was remote, she was sure there would be houses up ahead. Even if she didn't find Devin's house, she would find shelter. She and Nicholas were in no danger of freezing to death.

She wasn't worried, but she was sorry the night was turning out this way. She wanted to see Devin right now. She wanted to tell him that she loved him, had loved him from the start. She wanted to tell him that she would brave anything for them to be together. Her days of cowardice were over. She would walk through a fiery furnace for him—for them.

Or a blizzard.

The road made a sharp turn, and she dug in her heels and rounded the corner. She was almost afraid to look up ahead now. She wanted so badly to see Devin's gate that she was afraid she might manufacture one in her mind. She shaded her eyes with her hand and peered into the darkness.

No gate was in view, but a car lay nose down

in a ditch just ahead, a Cherokee just like the one that Devin drove.

Nicholas took that moment to cuddle deeper into her arms. She gripped him tighter and started forward. Ten yards from the car, she gave her first shout.

"Is anybody in there?"

Nicholas stirred in her arms again and opened his eyes. He began to whine. "Sorry, partner," she said, "but we've got to find out."

Nicholas began to whimper in earnest, but she pushed on. "Hey, is anybody in there?" she shouted again. The car wasn't badly mired. It looked as if one good yank from a tow truck would set it on the road again. She doubted that anyone inside had suffered more than a bruise or two. She was almost on top of the car when a man's voice sounded from inside.

"You picked a hell of a time for another reunion, Robin."

She gulped in snow and a huge breath of freezing air. "Devin?"

The driver's door scraped against the side of the bank, but it opened far enough for Devin to squeeze through. He shook his head, as if to clear it, then leaned—or fell—back against the Cherokee. "At least I'm not in the throes of labor."

She had never seen a more welcome sight. He was buried in winter wear, layers of wool and leather, but she couldn't have been happier to see him if he had been naked in front of her in a very warm bedroom. She tried a smile but didn't know if she succeeded. "I'm sorry about the timing, but when I make up my mind to do something, I don't fool around."

"Is that so?"

She wished she could see his face clearly, but the snow was falling too fast for that. She didn't know what he was thinking or feeling. She could only go on faith. "Any chance you could come up here so I don't have to shout?"

"Say whatever you've come to say."

Her courage nearly failed her. There was no welcome in his voice. Nothing but caution.

"I've got Nicholas with me."

Devin was silent—an act of great valor, she supposed, under the circumstances.

"I love you," she said. She cleared her throat and said it louder. "I love you, Devin. And I want us to be a family, to make whatever compromises we have to make together. I want you to help me raise Nick. I want to have more children with you." She hesitated. "And I want to get out of the snow. I've had enough of ditches and blizzards. Do you think we could move someplace warm? Like Tahiti?"

He didn't answer. The sound of her words died, and he just stood silently.

"I'm so very sorry," she said.

For a moment she thought she'd lost it all. Then

he was scrambling up the bank and gathering her and a wide-awake Nicholas into his arms. "I knew you were coming." His voice was husky with emotion. "Judy called. I just didn't know why."

"I'm here because I've been such a fool. Can you possibly forgive me?"

He kissed her hard as Nicholas swatted at him in welcome and babbled happily.

Despite what she'd said, it felt right to be outside in the snow together. But it would always feel right to be together, no matter where they were. Robin cuddled into Devin's arms and held him tightly with her own. Life came with no guarantees, but she could be sure of two things. She and Devin loved each other, and they loved their son. They were already a family. A very lucky family indeed.

*   *   *   *   *

This summer, the legend
continues in Jacobsville

A LONG, TALL
TEXAN SUMMER

Three **BRAND-NEW** short stories

This summer, Silhouette brings readers a special
collection for Diana Palmer's LONG, TALL TEXANS
fans. Diana has rounded up three **BRAND-NEW**
stories of love Texas-style, all set in Jacobsville,
Texas. Featuring the men you've grown to love from
this wonderful town, this collection is a must-have
for all fans!

*They grow 'em tall in the saddle in Texas—and
they've got love and marriage on their minds!*

Don't miss this collection of original Long, Tall Texans
stories…available in June at your favorite retail outlet.

Silhouette®

Take 4 bestselling love stories FREE

Plus get a FREE surprise gift!

Special Limited-time Offer

Mail to Silhouette Reader Service™

3010 Walden Avenue
P.O. Box 1867
Buffalo, N.Y. 14240-1867

YES! Please send me 4 free Silhouette Intimate Moments® novels and my free surprise gift. Then send me 6 brand-new novels every month, which I will receive months before they appear in bookstores. Bill me at the low price of $3.34 each plus 25¢ delivery and applicable sales tax, if any.* That's the complete price and a savings of over 10% off the cover prices—quite a bargain! I understand that accepting the books and gift places me under no obligation ever to buy any books. I can always return a shipment and cancel at any time. Even if I never buy another book from Silhouette, the 4 free books and the surprise gift are mine to keep forever.

245 BPA A3UW

Name	(PLEASE PRINT)	
Address	Apt. No.	
City	State	Zip

And the Winner Is...
You!

...when you pick up these great titles
from our new promotion at your
favorite retail outlet this June!

Diana Palmer
The Case of the Mesmerizing Boss

Betty Neels
The Convenient Wife

Annette Broadrick
Irresistible

Emma Darcy
A Wedding to Remember

Rachel Lee
Lost Warriors

Marie Ferrarella
Father Goose

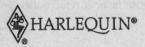

HARLEQUIN®   ♥ *Silhouette*®

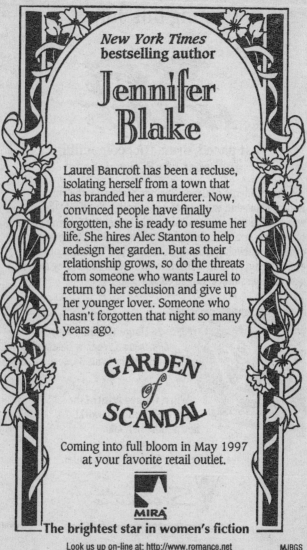